Daring Destiny

Cassandra Moll

Cover design: Caravelle Creates

First edition: March 2025

ISBN: 9798991826013 (paperback)

Author's Note

Dear Reader,

Hi! Thank you for picking up Ronan's and my story! Before you begin, there is something I wanted to let you know.

Although *Daring Destiny* can be read on its own, it is considered book two in the Maple Grove Series. Book one, *Beautifully Broken,* is the story of how our best friends, Claire and Jay, fall in love. It is also where Ronan and I first meet and where *you* will first meet *us*. By starting there, you will get more of our back story and the full details of Jay and Claire's, who are in this book as well.

If you have already read *Beautifully Broken,* then you're all set! You have everything you need to get the most from our book. I will warn you though—You may *think* you know our story, but I could guarantee that you're in for a surprise.

Regardless of where you're starting, if you think you're ready, then dive on in. As always, enjoy the ride.

XO,

Chloe

For those who are afraid to take the leap, whatever it may be.
Take it. *I dare ya.*

"It is not in the *stars* to hold our destiny but in *ourselves*."
-William Shakespeare

Daring Destiny

1
Now

The gravel crunches under my tires as I pull into the driveway of our Airbnb. I feel the long drive in the stiffness of my legs and the ache of my bladder. I've been alone for three hours with nothing but my thoughts and my playlist, two of the most chaotic collections in my life at the moment, and yet it still wasn't long enough. Scanning the lot, I can see from the other cars in the driveway that I'm not the first to arrive. I'm also not the last.

I put the car in park, turning the key to shut off the ignition, as I take in the log cabin in front of me. Long trunks stained the color of deep red cherries fit together to form the exterior, the wrap-around porch framed in twinkle lights and hanging plants of thick greens. To my left, there's a stone fire pit surrounded by wooden Adirondacks the same color as the cabin. The sun is shining, the sky is a clear blue background to the stunning home in front of me, and there are no signs of civilization to be seen for miles. The entire landscape is dreamy—picturesque, romantic, straight out of a movie—the perfect place to spend a weekend with my freaking ex.

Our best friends' bachelor/bachelorette party was supposed to be a quiet weekend away with just the four of us—a benefit of the maid of honor and best man being in a relationship. The problem is, when we planned this trip, Ronan and I *were* in a relationship. But that's all changed recently and therefore, so have my feelings about this whole thing. Now, as I sit in front of our house for the weekend, I'm not flooded with excitement and anticipation of a winter vacation.

Instead, I'm flooded with dread—my heart aching, my palms sweaty—and I still really have to pee.

I open the car door, the January chill hitting me like a much-needed slap in the face. The whole drive here, I flip-flopped back and forth between wallow and worry. I listened to sad songs about heartbreak and happier ones that reminded me of good times long gone, and I stressed about the inevitable. But the time has come to turn all of that off. Now, I need to be the fun and bubbly girl my best friend deserves during one of the most exciting weeks of her life. I need to put on my big girl pants and pull myself together. Big girl pants that will no longer be dry if I don't find myself a bathroom.

All of this would be a lot easier if Jay and Claire, the other half of our group, *knew* about the breakup. But being that it happened over the holidays, just weeks before their big day, Ro and I agreed not to say anything just yet. Lucky me who gets to bottle up this little honeymoon surprise. It's been weeks since I've seen any of them, and I'd like to fall into my best friend's arms and lock the door behind us, leaving Ronan outside alone in the cold. Instead, he and I get to play pretend for the next forty-eight hours... together. Basically, this weekend is going to be a nightmare.

But it'll be fine.

I'm fine.

Everything is going to be fine.

I drag my floral duffle from the back seat and walk onto the wooden porch. A breeze of crisp air floats by as I digest the details that are painted in front of me. There are piles of firewood stacked strategically along the front rail and poinsettias left over from Christmas on either side of the door. There is a rocking chair and an adorable porch swing with a small, outdoor table for your mugs in the morning. The whole thing looks like it's out of a picture book. It even smells log cabiny—like a mixture of wood and possibilities—which causes my heart rate to pick up because there is a very good possibility that I may not survive this weekend.

Claire's laugh echoes from the other side of the bold, vintage door and the knot in my stomach pulls just a little tighter. I freeze as anxiety threatens to consume me. Claire is my best friend in the world, and she deserves all parts of her wedding to be perfect. The idea of spending a weekend with Ronan is far from ideal, but the idea of spending a weekend with Ronan *and* ruining Claire's bachelorette trip, is unimaginable. I take a deep, stabilizing breath, the cool air filling my lungs and simultaneously burning them at the same time. The wind kicks up, almost as a warning, and it's just the jolt I need to snap me back into character as I push open the wooden gates of Hell.

A wall of heat hits me from inside, suffocating me instantly, and I find myself missing the chill from outside. I throw my bag to the floor by the base of the stairs and absorb what I can see of the interior. We planned this trip so long ago, and I've been avoiding it so much the past few weeks, that I haven't even bothered to pull up the listing. I somehow forgot how amazing this place truly is. If I thought the outside was like a scene from a fairy-tale, the inside is even more charming.

The steps to my right curve up to the second floor, connecting to a balcony that sits overhead. Rustic beams flow exposed across the high ceiling, and a country-chic chandelier hangs from the center. Beyond the stairs, I can see just the perimeter of a living space, flames already flickering from the stone fireplace against the wall. The carpet is plush, perfect for cozying up to stay warm, and there's a mismatch of neutral blankets hanging over the arm of the couch.

"Hello?" I call out down the hallway in front of me, where I can make out just the edge of the kitchen. Claire shrieks from around the corner, and within seconds, she's barreling toward me. She rushes past taxidermy animal heads that line the walls, and I inhale loudly at the sight of them, bracing myself for Claire both physically and mentally.

"You're here!" she yells, throwing her arms around me. I tense at first, from both the panic and pressure against my aching bladder, and then settle into the familiar hug. "Jay, Chloe's here!"

Claire releases me, tossing her long, walnut waves behind her. She's dressed in a cream-colored lounge set, looking effortlessly beautiful as usual. Her smile is radiant, that of a damn woman in love, and her golden eyes glisten just a little from the mimosa I can smell on her breath. She's happy, and she's really excited I'm here, which is the exact reminder I need to hold it together.

Jay rounds the corner in jeans and a gray Monroe's Motors hoodie and nods in my direction, the corners of his lips lifting into his usual half-smile. His tattoos are fully covered by the long sleeves, but his muscular six-foot-something frame is hard to hide—especially as he takes my five-foot-nothing body into his arms, bearhug style. I wince under his grip that I swear gets tighter every time I see him, while simultaneously warming from his display of affection. Jay is... an introvert. He's rugged, pensive, and prefers to be alone in almost everything, minus Claire. So, the fact that he even agreed to be here—an unfamiliar place, miles from home—means everything. Another reminder that I cannot mess this up.

"Remember the good old days when you would side-hug me with one arm instead of practically killing me with your massive body?" I squeeze out, just barely lifting my chin above his elbow to breathe. I look at Claire over his bicep as she shakes her head, giggling.

"Yeah, but that was before we were practically family," Jay says. I suddenly lose my breath completely, and it has nothing to do with his arms around me.

Ronan and Jay met at a mutual foster care placement when they were basically kids. Although they didn't live together long, the bond they formed was enough to sustain their friendship through Jay's years in the system. Now, Ronan and his adoptive brother Mikey are more like siblings to Jay than anything else. So, I know what he's trying to say—being with Ronan makes me more family than friend to him too. It's a comment I don't take lightly coming from someone like Jay, who doesn't exactly wear his feelings on his sleeve. My relationship with Ronan meant something to more than just the two of us. Something that we were all too aware of.

I shake the heaviness I feel from both his body and statement as I pat his arm, willing him to release me. I hide my true thoughts in our usual banter. "You're getting soft on me, Jay Jay," I say, straightening my sweater and pulling my hair out from inside the cowl neck.

"Oh my God! Your hair!" Claire says at the same time that Jay whispers a very descriptive, "Woah."

I feel my cheeks turning pink as I chuckle awkwardly. "Do you like it?"

"I love it!" Claire says, reaching over to play with my ends. "But why the change? And why didn't you tell me?" She drops my hair and nudges my shoulder in mock offense.

I run my fingers through my now shoulder-length cut. "Just wanted to surprise you," I say, my voice an octave higher than I intended for it to be.

The truth is, I'm embarrassed to say, but I got a breakup haircut—my straight blonde hair once reaching the middle of my back, now sits layered across my collarbone. But I needed a change. I needed to do something I could control. Something that was only my decision. Even if that something also cut away part of myself. A part that was still so intertwined with Ronan. He loved my long hair. He always said he liked it no matter how I wore it. Cascading behind me, thrown on top of my head, twisted into a braid, wrapped around his—

"Well, I love it," Claire says, interrupting my thoughts and tossing one arm around my shoulders. "And you," she adds, guiding me down the hall. It's only because we're standing side by side instead of face to face that she doesn't see the sadness in my eyes. I lean into her embrace, laying my head on her arm.

I've known Claire for years now, ever since we worked together at Jefferson Middle School, which is where we both took our first jobs right out of college. Claire scored a position as a teacher in her own classroom, and I got stuck as an instructional assistant. Luckily, one of the classrooms I bounced between was hers, and despite the job being short-term, our friendship grew roots.

We spent the next few years supporting each other from different schools as I finally landed a reading support job doing what I love. Now, Claire is out of the classroom, working on her second novel and freelancing on the side, but we still have one thing in common—we tell each other everything. It's the second reason this break-up has been so hard. Not telling Claire feels like a betrayal all its own.

"Okay, I *have* to find a bathroom," I say, pushing off Claire. She points me to a door right before the kitchen. I walk to it, ducking past a stuffed deer head hanging on the wall, and hear Jay grunt in the distance.

"Don't worry, Chlo, I got your bag!" he calls from the entryway, and I'm grateful for the comedic relief. "Jesus, we're here for two nights!"

"Thank you, Jaymie!" I yell back, and I hear him mumble under his breath as he lugs the bag up the steps.

Claire laughs as she walks past me and into the kitchen. "You're going to run out of weird names for him eventually, you know that right?"

"Well, with that attitude... " I say, closing the bathroom door behind me. Mixing up my friends' names is a weird habit of mine. Besides Ronan and Claire, the two steadies that would be impossible to change, I make it my mission to call people different versions of their real names every time I see them. Jay, whose full name is Jamison, is no exception.

Moments later, Claire greets me in the doorway with a bottle of champagne in her hand. "Were you listening?" I ask.

"Ew, no, you weirdo." She turns back to the kitchen, and I follow her the few feet it takes to reach the island.

"So, are you ready?" she asks, pouring maybe an inch of bubbly into a plastic flute. She fills the rest with orange juice, and it's only because she doesn't know the trauma I'm about to endure that I'm able to forgive her for the lack of alcohol she hands me.

Not even in the slightest, I think before taking the cup. "Of course I am!" She grabs her flute from the counter, and we clink them together, the dull thud of the plastic mirroring my true levels of enthusiasm. "The real question is, are *you* ready?" I look over my drink and wiggle my eyebrows at Claire.

She and Jay have been engaged for over a year now, and I say this with all the love in the world—they are the most boring couple ever. It's honestly adorable how they spend their weekends binge-watching *Peaky Blinders* and reading books, but Ro and I always told them they needed to get out more.

Don't get me wrong, Ronan and I spent most nights curled up on the couch watching movies and munching on popcorn, but they take "home-bodies" to a whole new level. It's why when they insisted on not having a "real" bachelor/bachelorette party, *we* insisted that at least the four of us get away. *Genius, Chlo, really.*

"So ready," she says, bobbing her shoulders up and down. "I'm just excited to spend the weekend with you guys away from work and my computer. I feel like I haven't seen you in forever! Between our trip to Jackson's and all of the last-minute wedding things, we've barely even had a second to talk."

"I know," I say, and it's terrible, but what I'm really thinking is, *thank God.* This break-up has been hard enough. If Jay and Claire hadn't gone to see Jay's brother, Jackson, over the holidays, I don't know how I would have been able to keep it a secret. Luckily for him, Ronan had an excuse. He's been back and forth from home in Maple Grove to Grand Oaks a few dozen towns away, dealing with a pizza shop he plans to take over for his uncle. I, on the other hand, didn't have that kind of out.

"Well, plenty of time this weekend," she says as she sips her mimosa.

"Time for what?" Jay asks joining us again.

"To catch up with Chloe and Ronan." She walks around the island to where Jay now stands and lifts on her tiptoes to peck him on the cheek. I offer them both a wide smile, bringing my flute to my lips to hide the fraud behind it.

"Yeah, seriously. Where have you guys been?" Jay asks, and at the same time, the door clicks open.

Claire rushes to the doorframe of the kitchen, like she's unsure who it is, but there are three of us here, and four on the reservation. That means there's only one other person it could possibly be. The once low hum of my anxiety rises to a clanging gong as my body feels his presence before I even lay eyes on him.

Jay follows Claire down the hall, a murmur of voices filling the room, and I'm grateful for these few fleeting seconds to gather myself. I set my cup down and take one deep breath—a poor attempt to calm my nerves.

"I can do this," I whisper to myself, taking a couple of steps in their direction. I've almost reached the doorframe when I leap back toward the cup, grabbing the cheap glass off the counter.

Who am I kidding? I down the rest of my drink, trying to drown the lump in my throat and pray the half-ounce of alcohol rushes straight to my head.

2
Before

Two Summers Ago

"**M**y head. Is pounding," I say, only capable of forcing two words out at a time. My mouth is dry, my body's hungover, and I'm pretty sure my brain has its own heartbeat.

"Well, that's what happens when you polish off the rest of the celebratory champagne... alone," Ronan says, and I don't see a megaphone, but I swear he's using one.

"Just trying to help the environment. You know, prevent waste and all that." I pinch the bridge of my nose and will the drumming behind my eyes to stop.

"Oh, yeah. You're a true hero, Chlo. Saving the world from all of that unrecycled alcohol, three bottles at a time."

I wince at the word *three* and guzzle the water sitting next to the Advil Ro set on the counter. Thank God he brought me home last night because the last thing I remember is popping a cork and missing the kitchen light fixture by maybe an inch.

The housewarming party meant to celebrate Jay and Claire moving into their own home in a cozy neighborhood in Maple Grove, would have been fun enough. There was a small crowd, music, and food, but when the celebration also became about their engagement, the excitement quickly elevated. Everyone started dancing, there were toasts and speeches, and apparently we *(I)* drained *bottles* of champagne.

The whole crowd was shocked when Jay dropped to one knee and pulled out Claire's grandmother's stunning ring. Of course we knew the two would end up together, but Jay, the reserved guy that he is, told no one besides her parents about the proposal. The question itself was a surprise, but what stunned us the most was him being vulnerable in front of all of their family and friends. I always pictured Jay asking Claire to marry him when it was just the two of them, but they'd come a long way, and I guess he wanted everyone to witness it. When he talked about her seeing the best in him, breaking down walls, and helping him build the life he's always wanted, there wasn't a dry eye in the house. It was beautiful—the perfect night for someone like Claire.

The sound of the TV turning on shakes me from my trance. I look around and see Ro's shoes by the door and his wallet and keys on the side table. He already started a pot of coffee, and there's a plate in the drying rack from his breakfast this morning.

"What'd you have?" I ask, pointing to the dish.

"Toasted a bagel," he says. Just the idea of eating makes my stomach churn faster.

It stopped being weird, Ronan sleeping here, after the first couple of times that it happened. He always sleeps on the couch and never makes a move—not even to snuggle if I'm anything but sober. Ronan and I aren't together, but we've hung out dozens of times, some alone and some with friends. He has stayed the night in my apartment, and we've had some long, lingering hugs, but it's never escalated to anything more. Sure, there are heated moments, and he does things like leave medicine out for me when he knows I've been drinking, but he's Jay's best friend. There's no point in worrying about what we are. Or what we could become.

"You go hard, Carlson," he says as I shake from my thoughts.

"Listen," I toss two pills into my mouth before continuing. "My girl gets engaged one time in her life... hopefully... we had to do it big."

"Colossal." He smirks, and I shudder at the memory of drinking right from the bottle.

"Just a little into weddings, then?" he asks, flipping through the channels from his place on my couch. He lands on *8 Mile* and then continues scrolling.

Any other time, I would ream him for skipping right over the iconic rap battle between Papa Doc and B-Rabbit, but my brain might actually combust if I hear even one beat of that bass.

"Not at all actually," I say, refilling my glass before taking a seat opposite him. He throws the blanket that's piled next to his leg so that it covers my lower half. I smile at the fact that he knows my feet are always cold.

"Really?" he asks. He leaves the TV on a rerun of some crime show, *Criminal Minds* or *CSI*—something where hot guys wear guns—but mutes it and turns to me. "No Pinterest board called like, **My Happily Ever After,** with pictures of massive diamond rings and Mason jar centerpieces or some shit?"

I look at him over the rim of my glass. "Okay, first of all, I am extremely impressed that you know what a Pinterest board is." I take another much needed sip of water, hopeful that the painkillers kick in soon. "And second, uh, no. Have you met my family?"

Ronan glances at the TV where a detective is questioning a suspect across a table. "Actually, no... I haven't. But your sister got divorced recently, didn't she?"

"Yeah, the middle one, Casey. Like six months ago," I say. I hold my cup up to the side of my neck, hoping the coolness from the glass will expel the toxins I so willingly poured into my bloodstream. "I blame the curse."

"The curse?" Ronan lifts his eyebrows expectantly but otherwise looks completely unamused.

"The Carlson curse," I deadpan. He blinks several times but says nothing else otherwise. I sigh, readjusting myself on the couch. "Everyone in my family splits up. My parents got divorced—no one saw that coming. My oldest sister, Cara, left her husband three years ago and now Casey. She's the newest victim of the family hex."

Ronan tilts his head before speaking. "It sounds like your family might just have really poor judgment."

"Not true!" I say, my voice way too loud for the state that I'm in. "Not true," I repeat at a much quieter volume. "On paper, everyone is perfectly compatible, but something just always seems to come up. Even my grandpa was married before he met Grandma, and nobody got divorced way back in their day."

"Okay, well, they're still together then, right?"

"They died," I say.

Ronan purses his lips. "Not divorced!"

"My point is, my family is cursed. Everyone gets married, and then out of nowhere, BAM!" I wince at the sound, again forgetting about the truck that ran me over. "Donezo."

Ronan settles back further into the cushion, resting his elbow on the arm of the couch, waiting for me to continue.

"My parents supposedly split because they fell out of love. Cara left her ex because he decided out of nowhere that he didn't want kids. Casey got engaged six months after meeting her husband online and... okay that one actually might make sense."

"Just a little," he scoffs.

"Whatever, it's still true. The curse exists."

Ronan looks at me for what feels like too long, and I notice a small patch of hair that got pressed while he slept. "So, what?" he says, turning back to the screen. "You're just never going to get married then? Because of some curse?" He makes air quotes around the last word, and I squint warily in his direction.

He's not the first person I've explained this to that thinks I'm crazy. Hell, if Claire's honest, I know even she thinks I'm nuts. The bottom line is, curse or not, there is no denying that divorce tends to run in my family. In fact, I don't think I know one couple who is still together or at least happily married. I'm all for people who want to attempt it—Cara and Casey both took the risk—but marriage to me just seems like a hazard. Like a slippery slope towards grave disappointment.

"Eh, I don't know, maybe. I guess I wouldn't say never, but I'm definitely not in any sort of rush."

"That doesn't make sense." He makes a face as if it's the dumbest thing he's ever heard, but his eyes stay locked on the show. "So, you don't want to get married because you might get divor—"

"Will," I say, interrupting him. "From my experience, the chances are good."

He rolls his eyes, then turns towards me. "You don't want to get married because you *might* get divorced, but maybe you will as long as you don't feel like you're rushing."

"Correct."

"You're ridiculous." He sits, seemingly invested in the show, but his tone suddenly reads more like I'm the one under investigation.

"I just mean I don't have plans to run to the altar any time soon, that's all." I'm growing defensive, and Ronan huffs out a breath, which only adds to the weird vibe in the room. *Are we arguing now?*

I'm not naive. I know Ro is at least interested in me. We spend time together willingly, and I don't think I'm that much of a troll, but he's never made any move to take it further. Why does he care about my future plans all of a sudden?

I can't lie and say I never thought of him either—Or that I never considered the possibility that we could be more. Sure, there have been moments where I catch myself staring, or when I think about him while I'm out with some other guy. But that happens to everyone. It's the reason they say two people of the opposite sex can't just be friends. Good qualities stand out. Small gestures get romanticized. You start picturing them in an apron and backwards baseball hat when you daydream at work. It's normal. But we've never discussed it for real, so why is he mad?

"If I meet someone… " I continue, my tone involuntarily coming out hushed. "And we fall in love and are together for, I don't know... years, then maybe we'll talk about wedding bells. I'm telling you though, it never ends well for a Carlson."

Ronan finally breaks his staring contest with the actors on screen and swings his head so he's looking at me. "Curses aren't real, Chloe."

"It sure seems like they are." I say it lightheartedly, knowing how ridiculous I sound tossing around the word "curse," but the weight of this conversation now feels heavier than it should.

"Well, they're not."

"But they might be."

"That's insane."

"Curse three - Carlsons zero."

"Makes no sense to me."

"Why does it matter?" I half yell and half laugh. This conversation is starting to feel like a competition. Like a volleyball game, only nobody's winning. Ronan looks at me, his face a cross between frustrated and confused, but it's hard to tell if it's directed towards me or the commercial of a woman smearing on lipgloss.

"How about you?" I ask when he doesn't respond, my attempt to smooth over the strange tension that lingers.

"What about me?" Ronan asks.

"Do you want to get married?"

He surveys the rest of the commercial like he's wondering what a plumper is. "Absolutely," he says, still facing the screen. Then his eyes drift in thought.

Ronan was placed into the foster care system after both of his parents died in a horrific car accident. He had no living relatives and was only fourteen, so the only option was to place him in state custody. He was adopted a year later by the Carusos. From what I hear, they never treated him any differently than Mikey, but I'm sure he still feels the void of his birth parents. He doesn't talk about them much, but right now, talking about marriage and two people committing "Till death do us part," I can't help but wonder if that's where his head went.

My brain spins with questions—*Is he sad about them? Is he thinking about me? Why am I making this such a big deal?* The last ten minutes have felt like an alternate universe where suddenly my whole future's in question, and I'm just sitting here noticing Ronan has adorable bedhead. It feels like the painkillers have finally kicked in, but now instead of pounding, my mind just races.

"If I fall in love… " His gaze trails to my side of the couch, stopping just short of me, to a spot on the floor. "Then, yeah. I definitely would." His tone is more serious, and I grow instantly warm, as if hearing that word come out of his mouth lit a spark. *Love.*

"I can't wait to be in love," I say more to myself than to him, but Ronan's eyes dart to mine. I get lost for a second in the color of the ocean at night—a sea of gray and deep navy—and wonder, *have his eyes always been that blue?* My chest grows strangely tight, and I look away. I reposition myself on the couch in an attempt to settle the burning I now feel in my stomach that has nothing to do with the hangover. "I just don't want to find the right person, then rush the next step and end up ruining a good thing," I continue, but my voice comes out weighted and thick.

Ronan casually runs his tongue over his bottom lip, but the fire that now blazes in my core is anything but subtle. *What is happening?*

Of course Ronan is good-looking. He's strong and lean and always has this heavy five o'clock shadow that's the perfect combination of grown-out and shaped up. I mean I've seen the man with his shirt off, and I'd be lying if I said I wasn't at least a *little* attracted to him. He's also confident and successful—he opened his own pizza shop at twenty-one years old for Christ's sake—and he has this swagger about him. He walks around like he's sure of himself, but he's far from cocky, and okay... maybe there's slightly more than a *little* attraction.

The best thing about Ronan though, is the way he treats almost everyone he knows like extended family. He would give you the shirt off his back if you needed it, or maybe if you were afraid you'd throw up on yours after doing car bombs all night on the Fourth of July. He'd leave Advil out for you because he knows you'd be too lazy to get it. He'd cover your toes because he knows they run cold. He's kind and considerate and an absolute gentleman.

But Ro is Jay's best friend—practically his brother—so the fact that I'm realizing all of these things is irrelevant. So he's a great guy? Is that enough to risk making things weird with our group? Ro and I have never crossed the line from friends who flirt to more than that. So why all of a sudden does that boundary seem blurred?

"So, what's good to you then?" he asks, and all of the images I just had of Ronan come to a head. I run through them again looking for a different answer. Trying to find a different path through the maze of thoughts in my mind about the guy sitting right next to me.

But I can't.

Because suddenly there's only one solution. Only one way out of the entangled web of ideas in my head. All of these thoughts now have a name. *You,* I think. *A good thing—it's you.*

I brush off my real answer, shoving this new realization back down where it belongs. I won't make this weird. I won't do that to Claire. "Still working on that," I say, shrugging my shoulders, and I swear I see his whole demeanor drop just a little. We stare at each other for the longest few seconds of my life before Ronan turns back towards the TV, his jaw now tighter than it had been before.

I sit in the moment another minute, then realize the only sound I hear is the ringing in my head. In an attempt to unmute the TV, and add noise to the silence, I reach for the remote from his lap. I'm centimeters away when my pinky grazes the length of his zipper because... of course it does. Ro's gaze tightens, his stare hyper-focused, and despite him not even flinching, now all I can think about is what lies underneath.

I realize I'm hesitating, my hand still practically touching his crotch. I clench the remote, and Ro breathes in slowly, trailing my hand as I pull it back to my side of the couch. The look he gives me is heated and thoughtful, like maybe he also just felt the tip of our axis—and my world as I know it—shifting completely.

I pretend to be interested in the credits rolling at the end of the episode, but really I'm stirring, my thoughts reeling like the names on the screen. Why do things feel different today? Why can I now feel that his body sits just a cushion from mine? When did everything completely change? And why do I like that I know his eyes are still on me?

3

Now

I slowly trek down the hall, fidgeting with my bracelet. Suddenly, it seems like the most interesting thing that I own, rather than a faux-gold cuff I got in a family pollyanna. I avoid looking up, giving my face as long as possible before having to plaster on a fake smile for the rest of the weekend.

It's bad enough that I know Ronan's right in front of me, but it doesn't help that I smell him from here—dark, woodsy, almost sweet—lighting up my senses like finding a familiar face in a crowd full of strangers. I bought him that cologne for Christmas last year. *Cashmere Woods.* I remember thinking it was perfect—sexy but warm, bright but cozy, manly but subtle—exactly like him.

"Hey, Chlo." His voice breaks my trance, steady and casual, but sounding more like glass shattering to me—or maybe that was just my heart all over again.

I look up to see him standing in a slate gray henley, a color that only amplifies the blue of his eyes. His deep strawberry hair is longer than the last time I saw him—which is a contrast to my change—and is just starting to curl out from behind his ears. I guess he's been skipping the biweekly haircuts he so religiously had for as long as I've known him. On top of it, his usual stubble has been shaved clean, which only further exposes the dimples underneath.

He looks... good. Sexy, like he just rolled out of bed and into the car, yet is somehow relaxed despite my raging insides. Ronan always has that ease about him. He's calm and unbothered almost all of the time. He's the guy you want around in a crisis. Just maybe not the one in which you and he are co-stars of the emergency.

He steps over the bag he's laid in front of him, and takes both of my hands into his. "I missed you," he says, and my eyebrows shoot up... until I remember he's only pretending.

"I—I missed you too," I stutter, and without having time to see if anyone noticed, Ronan pulls my body flush to his and kisses me hard. I'm a mixture of shock and pure mush as I get swept up in lips I haven't touched in too long, and it takes everything in me not to hum into his mouth. He holds our embrace a second longer, and I try to gauge his thoughts based on our brief moment of contact. But then it's gone.

Ro throws an arm across my shoulders before I'm able to read his expression and pulls me in tight like everything's great. Who knew Ronan Caruso was such a good actor? So good at faking it? That he could play the role of *Totally Fine Ex-Boyfriend* so damn well. Or maybe he isn't acting at all.

The thought hits me like a punch to the gut. It's been three freaking weeks, and he can just pretend like nothing happened? Pretend that we're fine? Like our whole relationship didn't just combust out of nowhere when everything was perfect? Like someone didn't go and mess it all up? A new energy rushes over me, out of motivation or competition, and all of a sudden I'm standing straighter, feeling stronger, thinking bolder. *Two can play this game.*

I lean into Ronan, placing one hand on his chest and sliding the other into the back pocket of his jeans. I can feel the rhythm of his heart pick up beneath my palm as I stroke my thumb over his muscle. I peer up at him, my small frame average-sized next to him, who wasn't quite gifted the Goliath genes that Jay was. He tilts his head to meet my gaze.

Ro stares at me briefly, as if deciding his next move, and I swear I almost see the corners of his lips curl upward. Dropping his arm so it now hangs by my hips, he trails his fingers across the small of my back. I arch in response, pressing my chest to his body, and parting my lips ever so slightly. He holds firm until I slide my hand from his chest to underneath the hem of his shirt, skimming the skin right above his belt loop. The spot where I know he loves to be touched.

His wrist freezes, his jaw tightening as he speaks through gritted teeth. "Why don't you help me take my stuff upstairs... babe."

I paint a smile on my face, squinting and licking my lips, surprised by my ability to play his game. "Sure thing, honey," I answer cheerfully, lifting his bag by the loop at the top.

Ronan's eyes linger on mine, and for a second I catch a glimpse of something foreign. I study him, trying to interpret his look, when he snatches the backpack from my fingers. He takes my hand, guiding me toward the steps.

"Oh, so *now* she can help with the bags," Jay says, exasperated. Claire smacks him jokingly with the back of her hand.

"Leave them alone," she says. "They haven't seen each other all week."

She's not wrong. In Claire's mind, I went back to school after Christmas break, and Ronan went back to his uncle's restaurant to continue renovations. What she doesn't know is that last week was just one of three that we've been apart. Either way, I'm grateful for Claire's intentions, even if it does mean alone time with Ronan.

"We'll see you two in a little," she calls, dragging Jay back toward the kitchen.

I follow a step behind Ro, my hand still in his, and with this view, I can't help but notice how good these jeans look. *Did he always have such a tight ass?* I shake my head, forcing myself to go back to the version of me from five minutes ago—strong, confident, ball in my court—but the truth is, I can't decide if I'm still mad at him for what happened before or slightly aroused by our little charade.

We find the room where Jay put my bag, and I audibly suck in a breath when I see it sitting on a vintage, down comforter of *one* queen-sized bed. I mean, of course we were meant to sleep together this weekend—it's a couple's retreat—it just seems while worrying about everything else, I have forgotten that tiny detail. The one that involves me lying next to my ex for two nights. The ex who I know from experience, sleeps only in extremely snug boxers.

"Don't worry," Ronan says, looking back at me. "I'll sleep on the floor." He tosses his backpack next to my evidently over-stuffed duffle, and the contrast of the two is not lost on me. Yes, I'm a girl, but Ronan has better fashion sense than anyone I know. I mean in shoes alone, I thought he'd bring more than this thing. Does he really care so little about this weekend that he was able to just throw a few things into his old Jansport and call it a day?

With the new reminder that Ro seems to be doing just peachy without me, I respond. "It's fine," I say with more bite than I mean to. "It's not a big deal." *It's a huge deal*, I think, but I am not about to act that way when it's not reciprocated.

He furrows his brow and then turns and sits on the edge of the bed. "So we should probably get our stories straight." He says it more to the soft, cream area rug below his feet than to me, but I'm surprised he said it at all. With the way things were played downstairs, I almost thought Ro somehow forgot that things ended between us.

"We're not telling them this weekend," I say. "We already agreed."

The last time Ronan and I spoke was through text message a few days after the break-up. I don't think either of us really knew what to say, but there was one thing we agreed on.

ME: I don't want to tell Claire and Jay just yet. It's not fair to ruin any part of their big day.

RONAN: You're probably right. We'll wait.

I remember the dull rage that started bubbling deep inside when I saw his response. I even screamed, *"Oh, NOW I'm right!"* so loud, I scared myself and sloshed half of my coffee onto the floor. Add the fact that I now had much less coffee and a stain on my carpet, and I was even more pissed than before.

"I know that," he says defensively. "But things are going to come up. What did we do over New Year's? Why didn't you come with me back to Grand Oaks?" His voice lowers to just above a whisper, his gaze dropping to my hand. "What did we get each other for Christmas?"

I follow his stare, shoving both hands in my pockets the second I realize where it leads. "Okay," I say, walking over to the bed and sitting next to him. I leave an uncomfortable amount of space between us, but there's no way I'm risking another grazing of skin. "I told Claire I was sick over New Year's. She Facetimed me, and I picked up out of habit before I remembered I was sitting in bed with an open jar of peanut butter and a plate sprinkled with chocolate chips."

"Apple nachos?"

"Obviously." We both snicker, and I catch just a peek of our old selves again. "So, I lied and told her I wasn't feeling great and that you just decided to stay in Grand Oaks and keep working."

Ronan nods. "Well I told Jay that Uncle Nico's place was in worse shape than expected, which it is. So, it'd be easy to tell them we thought it would be best if you stayed in Maple Grove, and I got some shit done over at his place."

This is news to me. I want to ask questions. I want to know the details. What needs to be fixed? What have you done already? Are you keeping the old name and menu the same? But I don't. That information no longer belongs to me.

Instead, I say, "Alright, so that just leaves... gifts." I rub my palms over the top of my thighs, feeling about as big as the stitches beneath them.

"Just tell them we didn't do presents this year," he says.

"They won't believe that."

"Then tell them we're planning a trip or something instead. In the summer."

"To where?" I ask.

"Who cares?" he says, growing heated. I pull back just a little, surprised by his tone. "I'm sorry." He inhales deeply. "It's just... say whatever you want. The truth will come out long before it matters anyway." He stands and walks toward the mirror that hangs above the dresser, and I'm left with another punch to the stomach. Obviously being broken up, I knew there would be no more holidays together, no more trips, and no more summers, but hearing it said out loud in his voice, is like ripping the barely-healed wound open all over again.

Looking at himself in the mirror, Ronan runs his hand through his hair and maybe it's the tension in here, or the way I already miss him, but I have the sudden urge to do the same. "So how do we do this?" he asks my reflection.

"Do what?" I say, clearing my throat of the lust that sits in it.

"This," he says, turning around, pointing first to himself and then to me. And now I understand. *How do we convince our two best friends that we're still a couple?*

"I guess there should be rules," I say, standing to join him. "Guidelines."

"I agree." I watch as he almost reluctantly takes me in, his eyes roaming my body from head to toe. His gaze is intense by the time it reaches my face, and my heart-rate quickens from just that look.

Three weeks is long in terms of missing someone. It's twenty-one days for your heart to lose part of itself. That's a lot of time to be sad, grieve, and think about all of the ways that your life is about to change completely. It's five hundred and four hours for your mind to remember. But three weeks is apparently not even close to enough time for your body to forget.

"Kissing?" he asks, dropping his hands to his hips.

"It would probably be weird if we didn't kiss at all," I say, and I mean it. Weird is only one way to describe how it's been not consistently feeling his mouth on mine.

"Alright then. We kiss... " his voice is low as he looks at my lips. He blinks hard, and when he opens his eyes, it's like he's brought back to reality. "If we have to," he continues. "If the situation calls for it. But other than that, I think we avoid it as much as we can." His words are harsh, but his eyes trail back to my mouth, his actions just briefly betraying his speech.

"That's fine," I say. I rub my lips together, my body's subconscious way of responding.

Ronan plays with the hem of his shirt, and I'm all too aware of the dance his biceps do, and the memory of his skin, smooth and warm, underneath. "What else?"

"Touching I guess?" I feel my cheeks flush the moment I say it.

Ronan adjusts his stance, his body now slightly closer to mine. "I mean, they know how we are, Chlo."

What he means, is that we've never struggled with public displays of affection. If anything, Ronan and I have spent the last year making up for the one that we endured without physical contact.

"Right," I say. I don't intend for it to come out a whisper, but it does.

"Holding hands?"

"Sure."

"Rubbing backs?"

"Okay."

"Other things?"

My face must show my feelings—curiosity mixed with hesitation and desire. Ronan takes a step forward as smoothly as if he's on ice, or maybe it just seems like that against my rigid reaction.

"Like this?" He reaches up slowly then brushes my hair behind my ear. "I like it by the way," he adds, moving to my ends, and my breath hitches as his fingertips land by the side of my neck.

"It's different," I mumble.

"Good different," he says.

I catch myself leaning into his touch and counter the pull by standing up straighter. Swallowing hard, I say, "Thanks. That's what I was going for." Our eyes linger on each other for just a second before Ronan exhales, dropping his arm.

I feel him in the spot above my collarbone where he grazed my skin, and I hate my body for still reacting that way. For missing him.

"Ronan I—"

"Don't," he interrupts as he takes a step back. "Let's just... let's not do this, okay?" I open my mouth, but no words come out, an all too familiar feeling.

Neither of us know how to react. We're both angry and hurt, but it's been less than a month. Is it impossible to think our bodies may still pull to each other? Crave one another? I can't speak for Ronan, but I'm a perfect combination of hostile and turned on, and judging by the way he snapped at me one minute but approached me the next, I think he might be feeling the same. Who could blame us? Take a relationship two years in the making and end it in the blink of an eye—in the asking of a single question. Of course there are residual feelings.

"Yo! Get down here!" Jay yells, and we both startle, Ronan running a hand down his face like he's wiping away any visible trace of our conversation.

"I guess we should go," he says, but he makes no motion to leave.

"I guess so." His lips part just enough to make me hesitate, but then he motions toward the door.

I look at him one more time, willing him to speak. To tell me we made a mistake, that we can go back, that not everything has changed.

But he doesn't.

Instead, he simply takes my hand like he has a million times before, completely unaware of the way my skin feels like fire beneath his touch, and guides me toward the stairs.

4

Before

I walk down the wooden steps, fumbling with my zipper that keeps getting caught in my seam. "Claire!" I yell, but she's nowhere in sight.

"They're already in the car," Ronan says, as he walks around the corner. He reaches for my skirt, and as if he's done it a million times before, pinches and pulls and glides the stubborn fabric into place.

I look at him, our bodies alarmingly close thanks to his fashion intervention, our eyes perfectly level with my heels on. Thanks to the summer sun, his hair is still lighter than usual, like the color of a brand-new penny, and he has it gelled back just a little in the front. He looks me up and down, the scent of his product hitting me as his gaze moves towards the floor—a combination of citrus and sea breeze, like sipping fresh lemonade in a cabana at the beach. Normally that kind of thing would be a major red flag—you absolutely can not take longer than me to get ready considering I'm always late—but not right now.

I run my eyes down the rest of him. His army green bomber jacket is layered over a basic, white tee, which is just tight enough to expose the perfect amount of toned muscle beneath it. The toe of his Converse points at me, the hightop leading to the hem of his faded black jeans, which somehow look both rugged and polished. His entire outfit is the complete opposite of mine—a faux-leather skirt and cream graphic tee with giant red lips that says, **Pardon My French**—and yet we somehow seem to complement each other. He is crisp and clean, neutral and subtle. I am bold and loud, almost messy in a good way. I pull my hair around to the front of my body, soft crimps falling down my shoulders, and fluff the top just enough to make it look tousled on purpose.

"You look great, Chlo," Ronan says as I tuck just the front of my shirt into my waistband. Despite my usual easy confidence, it's like he can sense I'm off my game.

Tonight is not a date. In fact, it's quite the opposite. I was supposed to be going out with Claire, Jay with Ronan, and we *(Claire and Jay)* decided last minute that we should all hang together. I can't blame the lovebirds for wanting to spend time with one another—Claire's been busy advertising her first book, and Jay's brother's been in town—but ever since my conversation with Ronan after the housewarming/engagement party, any mention of him makes me sweat. It's the reason I'm just now ready to go. Yes, I'm known for being fashionably late, but I had my outfit all picked out for apps and drinks at my favorite martini bar, not River's Rum for live music... and Ro.

I've spent the last few weeks avoiding any intimate time with him, developing arthritis in my swiping thumb on dating sites. Still though, I can't shake the idea that I might want more. *You're the good thing,* I think for the millionth time—and my best friend's fiance's best friend. God, even the label sounds complicated.

"Ready to go?" he asks, seemingly cool as can be, but I notice the way he rubs his thumb and index finger together like he does when he's nervous.

"Always," I say sarcastically, and we laugh, both of us knowing we were supposed to leave twenty minutes ago.

The bar is buzzing, and the band has already started. There are people at every seat at the counter, but we happen to walk in just as a group of guys abandon the high-top closest to the door. We push their empty, left over beer bottles to the edge of the table, and Claire and I both set our bags in their place to claim our spot.

Fridays and Saturdays are live music nights at River's. They clear out their small dining space to make room for a crowd and put performers of all types on a metal frame they call a stage. Tonight, it's a 90's cover band called **Talk To The Hand**. Most of the audience is bouncing in the front, where the lead singer, a younger guy wearing jean shorts and a neon windbreaker, belts out the chorus of Third Eye Blind's *Semi-Charmed Life.*

"We'll get us a round," Claire calls over the beat of the drums as she nudges Jay toward the bar. Ronan nods, and I give her a thumbs up, both of us hopping onto our stools.

I haven't been here much, since dive bars aren't typically my first choice for a night out, but Ronan and Jay both prefer them, so Claire and I decided to go with their flow. The vibe is interesting, the crowd one of a kind, but sitting here with Ro, I can't help but feel like I'm exactly where I want to be.

"I like the shirt," Ronan says, leaning in to make himself heard over the volume. I notice I'm not disappointed when the edge of his knee brushes mine. I look down at my most recent online purchase and smile at the phrase.

"Thanks!" I shout. "Funky shirts with cool sayings are kind of my... thing." My voice trails off as a rather large, somewhat scary man in a leather vest walks in. He carries a bike helmet under his arm, and the evening breeze follows behind him.

"I know," he says, as Biker Guy walks to the bar. The cool air lingers, and I rub my forearms to warm them back up.

"Know what?" I say, looking back to Ronan.

"That they're your thing."

A heat rises up my neck despite the goosebumps on my arms. "You noticed," I say, not sure if I'm feeling more shy or impressed.

"I notice a lot of things," he says, and my lips separate just as Jay and Claire return to the table. I look across the drinks that Jay sets between us and see that Ronan's eyes haven't moved from mine.

I clear my throat and swallow hard before crafting a smile. Claire and Jay sit, then Claire clinks her glass to mine. "Don't look now," she leans in, "but isn't that Moped Guy?" She speaks in a volume way above a whisper, drawing the attention of the entire table. I whip around to where she's looking, and she slaps me on the arm. "I said don't look now!"

I roll my eyes before responding. "Okay, first, saying don't look now only makes me look sooner. Second, no, that's not him. Thank God."

"Wait, who's Moped Guy?" Ro asks, looking at Jay, who shrugs as if to say he also has no idea what we're talking about.

"Some guy Chloe dated," Claire says. "He wore super tight pants and tried to pass off a moped as a motorcycle."

I close my eyes and shake my head, trying to wash the memory from my mind. "It was *one* date," I clarify, "and tight is so far beyond an understatement." Jay chuckles, and Ronan lifts his eyebrows over his bottle as he sips his beer.

"Speaking of, how was the date from last week?" Claire asks, but before I have the chance to answer, Ronan interrupts.

"Let's go up front," he says, pushing off his stool.

"Ooh, yes!" Claire yells, yanking on my arm. She looks at Jay, and I hop off of the stool before she pulls the whole thing over.

"Nope," he says. "I don't do crowds."

"Oh, come on," Claire whines. She sticks out her bottom lip, and Jay, the broody tough guy that he is, immediately huffs in compliance.

"One song," he says.

"Two," Claire argues. "Please? We're all going."

Jay shakes his head, the corners of his lips curling up just slightly. He reaches over to pat Ronan on the back. "Let's go, brother," he says. Claire claps in celebration.

Ronan takes a long pull of his beer and sets it back on the table, the electric guitar booming through the speakers as the band starts playing Blink-182. "Perfect timing!" Claire yelps, pulling me toward the stage where the singer starts with the first line of the song.

I let her guide me, laughing at her enthusiasm. The boys trail behind us a few feet as Claire and I push our way to the middle of the crowd, our bodies moving to the music as we go. I lose myself in the chorus, jumping up and down to the repetitive beat, looking behind me to see the boys laughing. They yell in each other's ears, clearly making fun of us, but we don't care. Claire and I spend the rest of the song with our arms up or playing air guitar, and by the last chord, I'm hot and out of breath.

"I'm gonna go back and grab my drink," I say to Claire while the crowd cheers around us. She nods, and then forces her fiancé into my spot.

I take my first step, and Jay tries to follow. I hear Claire's, "Nuh-uh! I said two songs," followed by Jay's low growl, as I sift through the audience.

I get back to the table as the door opens again. The gust of air is a welcome reprieve this time, cooling me off from the heat of the crowd. The opening strum of *Wonderwall* starts, and I take a long sip from my straw before I feel someone approach from behind me.

"You know, for such a hardass, my best friend sure went soft." Ronan takes the spot next to me and leans across the table for his beer. As he moves, his jacket strains against the muscles on his back.

"Oh, please, that teddy bear? He practically worships the ground that girl walks on." I laugh, playing with the rim of my glass. "As he should," I add quickly, and Ronan cracks a smile.

"They have a good thing going, those two," he says, looking at our best friends swaying in the crowd.

"Really good," I add, now looking at them too, and I can't help but feel my heart grow warm, thinking of Claire's happiness as she wraps her arms around Jay's neck.

"So, how was the date?" he asks, interrupting my thoughts, and it takes me a second to realize he's finishing the conversation that Claire started earlier.

"Oh, I bailed." I keep it simple, but the full version is, I got dressed and was ready to walk out the door when I decided I was about as excited to go as I would be for a root canal. I canceled at the last minute and did some YouTube Yoga instead. Nama-stayed my ass at home and probably avoided yet another let down.

"Got it," is all he says before an older woman comes busting through the door. She's wearing a cheetah print muumuu and a sash that says, **Over the Hill**. A group of four or five women about the same age come parading in after her, all wearing bright pink t-shirts that say, **Misty is Fifty**.

"You really think you're going to find *'The One,'* " he starts, making air quotes with his fingers, "meeting up with losers from those sites?" He's looking directly at me, right as the first woman, Misty I assume, turns back to her friends still filtering through the door. She spies Ronan, then looks at me and throws a wink in my direction.

"Who says I'm looking for *'The One?'* " I say, my typical response when Claire says the same, only it comes out duller than it does with her.

"Bullshit."

I pull back, caught off guard by his reaction. I shift my feet, not sure how to respond, and because the door's now been held open for so long that I'm borderline freezing.

"I'm just saying," Ronan adds, shrugging out of his jacket. "You said it yourself. You can't wait to be in love." He drapes the sleeves around my shoulders, and I can feel the warmth of where his body once was, enveloping me. "So quit dating your way through Maple Grove, and stop lying to yourself."

I want to speak, but what do I say? He's right—of course, he is. I'm twenty-six years old. I have a good job and my own place. I pay all of my bills on time, and I wash my makeup off before bed almost every night. My life is together! Except, I'm alone.

Yes, I have family, but my parents and my sisters who live nowhere near me don't count as companions. There's Ronan and Jay, but they have each other, and my coworkers are fine, but they're not out-of-work friends. Besides Claire, I don't have anyone close, and now even she's engaged. She's living with the love of her life, while I spend most nights avoiding profiles of shirtless torsos and guys holding fish. I tell myself I'm not worried about finding someone, but it's almost as if, *"The One,"* is becoming more like, *"The One Missing Piece."*

We stand here, our eye contact steadfast, and I think about why none of the guys from these apps seem to stick. The truth is, most of them are looking for a fling, and the few that aren't seem to be looking for an insta-bride, neither of which they'll find in me. I'll go on dates, enjoy a meal, maybe have a few drinks, but I'm nobody's one-night-stand, and I'm definitely not trying to be somebody's wife. Is it too much to ask for a guy to fall in love with me and just let it be that? Spend time together, grow close, and enjoy each other's company, without complicating it with everything else? Why do they seem to want a girl in lingerie or a wedding gown but nothing in between? I pull Ronan's jacket tighter around me, the lyrics of the song invading my thoughts.

Could he be the one to save me from all of that? From the *"losers from those sites"* as he said? From the dating pool I seem to be drowning in? From myself?

I remain silent, wondering whether I should ask him if he feels this too. He looks past me into the distance as I get up the nerve to finally go there. I take one more sip of liquid courage, clear my throat, and part my lips, but as I go to speak, the group of women in pink and cheetah cheer from across the bar. I turn to see Misty licking whip cream off of a shot glass with impressive expertise, and when I look back, Ronan is gone—his back to me as he returns to the crowd.

5

Now

The four of us spend the next few hours essentially just moving from one position to another around the warmth of the fireplace. Us girls are chatting, the boys are playing cards, and it's so nice to just unwind a little after the last couple of weeks that I've had. The majority of the time it feels like the old days. Like two sets of best friends sipping drinks and joking around. But in other moments, when I remember that we're really two couples, one thriving, one broken—my stomach knots, my pulse races, and I'm anything but calm.

Claire and I are sitting, looking at the pictures on her phone of her in her wedding dress, giggling and whispering like two little girls. Jay and Claire both want a smaller ceremony. They plan to have it at a venue with just a few dozen people, but there was one thing her mother insisted on—getting her the gown of her dreams. She did, and it's simple and beautiful, exactly like Claire. It's ivory, not white, which I joke is very appropriate for the way those two act, with long flowing sleeves and a mermaid silhouette that falls right to the floor. There's no beading or lace. The only added detail to the jersey material that fits Claire like a glove, are the three small, pearl buttons that secure the dress right below the base of her spine. The whole back is open in an elegant U-shape—classy, sexy, and just the thing that will drive the groom wild. I'm leaning over Claire to zoom in on the buttons, when Jay interrupts.

"Yo, Dawson, get over here, and let me beat your ass in poker," he calls over to Claire. She swipes out of her photos like just having them open while he's talking to her could ruin the surprise.

"Can't call me that for long," she teases as she moves from the couch to the floor, scooting closer to Jay and the coffee table they've been using for cards.

"Thank God," he says, and he kisses her hard, like they're the only two in the room.

Ronan and I look at each other. My cheeks flush, and he rubs his chin, both of us aware of the distance between us in comparison to them. Jay pulls away, and his gaze shifts to Ronan, whose hand has moved to the back of his neck.

"You guys are being weird," he says. My eyes dart to Ro who somehow manages to play it off naturally.

"No we're not. You guys just can't keep your hands off of each other." He shuffles the cards he's been holding, bending them into a bridge and letting them fall into place.

"And how is that any different from how you guys usually are?"

My blood runs cold, but I roll my eyes playfully. "We're not *always* all over each other." Ro moves the deck to one hand and brushes the thumb and forefinger on his other one against each other.

"I have literally seen you lick Ronan's earlobe," Claire says, looking at me and joining in on the fun.

"That's not—"

"In a movie theater," she adds.

"Yeah, but—"

"When the lights were on."

I close my eyes in defeat, slowly opening them only to see Ronan's jaw is now tight, his face paler than normal. He looks so distressed, and all I want to do is fix it. We may not be together, but I still hate to see him anything but happy. I channel all of my energy, and emotional strength, and help in the only way I can—by proving them wrong.

I slide off the couch, crawling on my knees to where Ronan sits sideways against the table, his legs stretched out in front of him. I pause at his feet, waiting the few seconds it takes for him to realize what I'm asking for. He inhales quickly, then spreads his legs, leaving room for me to climb towards his lap.

I move in closer, only turning my body when I reach the inseam of his jeans. As I settle my weight back to the floor, Ronan sits up straighter, his chest now flush with my back. His muscles tense beneath my touch, his breath quickening on the side of my neck.

This position, though strange right now, is all too familiar. We've sat like this on the couch watching movies, Ro reaching around me to grab a handful of popcorn from the bowl between my legs. We've sat like this on the bed, me writing lesson plans and Ronan leaning against the headboard, rubbing my back or playing on his phone. We've even sat like this as I held Ro's guitar, his arms around my body, guiding my hands so that I played somewhat of a tune. All of those moments were easy and comfortable, but this moment here feels like sitting on one of those couches with the thick, plastic covering.

"Better?" I say mockingly in Claire and Jay's direction. I turn to Ronan so only he can see me, my eyes shooting from his arm to my body. He chews his bottom lip, then slips his arm around me, resting it stiffly on the outside of my knee.

"Yeah, yeah, yeah, whatever," Claire says, thankfully laughing the whole thing off. "So, how do I do this?" she asks Jay, and he starts explaining the rules to Five Card Stud.

I take advantage of the lack of attention on Ronan and me and grab his hand from my leg to give it a reassuring squeeze. I'm not sure if I mean for it to say something like, *"Dodged that bullet,"* or more like, *"We're in this together,"* but either way, I feel his whole body relax beneath my touch.

We sit like this for several hands of poker, to the point where I almost forget that this isn't one of the moments that are easy and comfortable. Claire cheats the whole time, constantly flipping over the cards that face down, and I play knowing Ronan can see what I'm holding. We bet fake money and theoretical wagers—Ronan's business and Claire's firstborn child—and we tease each other until we're all laughing out loud.

The conversation phases out, Ronan seeming to go quiet first, and I collect the cards once more into a pile on the table. I almost have them stacked as I look around for visual confirmation of whether I should deal again, when Jay whispers something in Claire's ear. She giggles in response before winking at me.

"We'll uh... be right back," Jay says, and the two of them scamper up the stairs like a couple of preteens under the bleachers at a high school football game.

"Now who's all over each other?" I call to them as I hear Claire shriek and then the bedroom door slam shut upstairs.

"Can you believe them?" I laugh. "They give us shit, but they're running off mid-game like some horny—" I turn my head, stopping mid-sentence when I see Ronan's eyes are dark, his face serious. My smile fades, and I rotate my body so I'm sideways between his legs. Like muscle memory, my hand glides to his cheek. I pull it away briefly, my mind catching up to my body's response, but for some reason, I bring it right back to his skin.

"Ronan," I whisper, and he hesitates before leaning into my palm and closing his eyes. I drop my forehead to his, and that quickly, he moves his hand to my inner thigh, breathing in sharply and squeezing his legs around mine.

Butterflies awaken deep in my core, and I slide my hand to the back of his head. I play with the hair at the nape of his neck. It's foreign to my fingers which are so familiar with this spot, but I like it. Suddenly his eyes fly back open. They're a mix between hungry and hostile, and I'm not sure if he's pissed off or turned on, but I know that I miss him, and that I feel his hand on my thigh much higher than that.

"Ronan," I say again, tugging gently at his hair. I move my mouth closer to his, but when I'm close enough that I can feel his breath on my lips, he grabs my wrist, pulling his face from mine.

"Chloe, I can't do this," he says, and at the same time, he moves his hand from my leg, the spot where it was, now left barren and raw.

"Um, okay," I say, awkwardly shuffling away from him. For a second, I'm embarrassed I pushed things too far. I stand, adjusting my clothes unnecessarily, and somewhere between tugging at my pants and flattening my sweater, my feelings shift.

In collecting myself, I remember that it takes two to almost make out with your ex on the floor of a cabin, while your best friends are banging upstairs.

Ronan may have pulled back sooner, but I'm not the only one who was taking it there. I'm not the only one who started this.

"Can we talk at least?" I ask as he stands, stretching his jeans from inside his pockets. He hangs his head, blowing out a heavy breath, before glancing toward the bottom of the steps.

"They can't hear us," I say, walking two paces toward him, but he counters my movement falling back two steps. I sigh at the distance he puts between us and challenge him by moving closer again.

Ronan sucks his teeth, folding his arms across his chest, frustrated, I'm sure, for more reasons than one. "What do you want to talk about?"

I watch as his biceps are pushed forward beneath his fists and force myself to speak from my head, not my crotch. "I don't know... us? What almost happened here?"

"There is no us," he says quickly. "Not anymore." He creases his brow and looks to the floor. "And what almost happened here, would have been a mistake."

I pull my head back, shocked by his honesty. "A mistake?" I know he's probably right, but how can he be so hot and cold?

"Don't act so surprised, Chloe. This is what *you* wanted." His tone goes from frustrated to downright angry, and I meet his rage with defense.

"What I wanted?" I repeat, raising my voice, and the way his eyes shoot to the stairs, reminds me that we're taking a risk even talking about this here. "What I wanted," I continue quietly, whisper-yelling at this point, "was for us to stay together. For nothing to change."

"Well, that's not how it works."

"But that *was* how it worked! It worked just fine. Then you had to try to adjust our whole course, and now look at us!"

"Oh, so it's my fault?"

"It's not anyone's fault!" I shoot back. "But you knew where I stood. That was never a secret. I loved you. I loved *us*. I didn't think we'd end up here."

"You didn't think we'd end up here," he repeats under his breath. "I asked you to marry me, Chloe!" he yells, and we both pause, him listening for our friends upstairs, me unprepared for him to say that out loud. "I asked you to marry me," he says again, this time barely above a whisper but just as intentional. "And you said no."

"I didn't say no." My voice comes out sounding about as weak as my argument.

"No, you didn't. You said nothing." The look he gives me is one of defeat. "And I'm still trying to decide which one is worse."

I want to explain. To scream at him that I said nothing because I was caught completely off guard. In the moment, saying no felt wrong because I loved him and because deep down I knew that if I did, we would never recover. But saying yes... that was terrifying *because* I loved him. And because from my experience, marriage also means we would never recover. Ronan knew about my family's history and the stupid Carlson Curse, and he knew that I wanted to wait to get married—that I may not want to get married at all. I told him all of the stories—all of the ways I was afraid we'd end up.

Mom and Dad were college sweethearts. If you ask Dad, they met when he flexed his intelligence to the beautiful girl who sat behind him in class. As the story goes, Mom tapped Dad on the shoulder with her pencil and asked for help on one of the math problems. Dad turned around in his seat, flashed her the Carlson smile, and gave her the answer without missing a beat. If you ask Mom for her side, she accidentally hit Dad with her pencil while she was smacking it on her desk to the beat of a song in her head. When Dad turned around, she acted like she needed help with the problem so she didn't look crazy, and then pretended he was right when his answer was wrong.

Regardless of who you believe, there's no denying that it was love at first sight. Dad proposed to mom right out of school, and they were married no more than six months later. Mom got pregnant right after their first anniversary, and the three of us came every four years after that. For nearly two decades, my parents' lives consisted of diapers and dance, soccer games and sister fights, but none of us ever thought they were unhappy.

I'll never forget when they told us on my fall break freshman year of college, that they were getting a divorce. Cara had just rented a new apartment, and Casey was getting settled in at the hospital. All of us were going through big life changes—apparently, Mom and Dad included. *"Roommates,"* they called themselves when they tried to explain what was happening. They said they got married so young, and spent their twenties and thirties raising their beautiful girls, that when the dust settled and their lives no longer revolved around us, they found that there wasn't much else left between them.

Cara, always the dramatic one, cried on the spot. Casey kept quiet as she usually does, internalizing whatever she felt. I left the table, all I ever knew, exploding around me. Divorce was so new to me back then. I was young and naive, and I refused to believe that the parents I knew weren't crazy in love. They smiled, and laughed, and we did family Halloween costumes! How could that have all been for show?

Mom later explained that it wasn't. That she did love Dad, and she cherished our family, but that there was a difference between loving your life and *living* your life.

"Your dad and I have almost three decades worth of incredible memories," Mom said. *"But people grow, and not always together. Change is scary, girls, but so is living a life unfulfilled."*

The curse continued when Cara got married about five years later to a guy named Jake that she met at work. They realized they were having a difficult time getting pregnant just a few years in, and rather than looking for help, he told her he was actually fine with not having kids. Cara, of course, was devastated. For her, having children was, and is, nonnegotiable.

Casey met her ex online when she recognized being a nurse didn't mean leaving much time for an actual social life. They hit it off right away, and six months into dating, he proposed out of nowhere. Either enthralled or exhausted, she jumped at the ring, and they learned shortly after that marital struggles don't just go away because you rarely see each other.

All that to say, it's not that I didn't want to spend my life with Ronan, I just made a promise to myself—that would never be me. I'm not a little kid. I know curses aren't real, and my family's not jinxed, but there is nothing phony about the pain that I've both witnessed and been through when it comes to divorce. Maybe it's silly to hold onto the idea that separation is inevitable if you have my last name, but with Ronan, it wasn't worth the risk. I would have loved him forever without any ring and without the chance of us ending too.

I want to tell him all of that. To talk about why I froze on the spot, but before I have a chance, Ronan surprises me all over again. He pulls me to him, putting his hand in my hair, and brings our faces so close that our noses are touching. "They're coming," he whispers, and our lips crash together—a collision of angst and regret—and once again, I say nothing at all.

6

Before

I should have said no to this stupid coffee date, but the guy on my app had a puppy in his profile. A tiny, fluffy, freaking adorable puppy, and I think I'm more pissed that the dog didn't show up than the owner himself.

I pull down the sleeves of my chunky knit sweater, a complete waste of a cute, cozy outfit and pick up my phone from the table. The last thing I messaged Derek from Flutter was that I was on my way to Busy Brewz coffee shop. When I walked in the door, on time I may add, and was the only person out of college but not quite in the nursing home, I figured he was just running late. Forty minutes and three mocha cold brews later, I have officially been stood up.

I, once again, wasn't expecting to hit a home run on this date, but I thought grabbing coffee, maybe a pastry, and walking his dog around town would be a fun start to my Saturday morning. Turns out, even those things are too much to ask, and letting me know you aren't going to make it—simply out of the question.

I open our chat, see the message was read, and instantly rage-type a paragraph damning him to Hell. Before I hit send, I reread it and realize that this "horticulturalist" is not worth even one more word of my time. Honestly, I probably dodged a bullet with this one because we all know the only thing man-bun was growing was some cheap ass weed in his mother's garage. I erase my unsent message and unmatch his profile. Then I delete the app altogether.

I stand from the table, grateful that I'm now the only one in here, minus Frank. He is a gay, bald barista with fabulous arms and even better hands when mixing caffeine. If there *were* more customers, it's not like they would necessarily know I got ditched, but with the way Frank has willingly refilled my coffee for free, I'm not sure it's worth the risk. Tossing the last gulp of my third drink in the trash, I walk out of the door and onto the sidewalk. I pause outside of the strip mall where Busy's is and inhale deeply, letting the morning air flood my lungs. In with the good, and out with the bad boy from six miles away with the new rescue puppy and dark, flannel shirt.

I look to my right and see Bella's Boutique isn't open quite yet, so there goes my chance at retail therapy. Looking further down the row of storefronts, I notice that basically nothing looks open—another downside to this brilliant morning date idea. I'm just about to head home when I look to my right and see Enzo's, not open, but lit up inside.

I walk over and peer in the window. The restaurant that Ronan owns with his older brother Mikey is one of the best pizza places in town. The decor is cool, the food is delicious, and the workers aren't too bad themselves. It's a staple around Maple Grove, and the fact that I know the owners, just makes it even better. From where I'm standing, I see Mikey behind the counter preparing pizzas for the day. He's wearing a white Enzo's shirt and jeans, and he's tossing dough above his head, catching it only to stretch it out more.

Mikey is your typical Italian. He's tan with brown eyes, a full beard, and he talks with his hands like his life depends on it. Unlike his younger, Irish, adopted brother, Mikey was gifted in the height department and stands easily over six feet tall—which is probably why he can see me creeping in the window, even from the back of the shop.

I see Mikey smile as he walks over to the door and unlocks the deadbolt. He holds it open and ushers me in before locking it again behind us. "What the hell are you doin' here this early in the morning?" he asks, walking back behind the counter to continue his prep. His apron is already covered in flour, and there's a smudge on his forehead right next to the scar above his eye.

"You don't even want to know," I say but what I really mean is, I'm embarrassed to talk about it.

"Well, okay then," he says, spinning another pizza in the air, and like a dog with a frisbee, I follow every move. "We don't have any food ready just yet, but Ro is back in Jay's old spot if you want to say hi."

My sweater suddenly feels too cozy, heat seeming to rise up my chest. At this point, everyone knows Ronan and I hang out, but I'm not sure anyone knows what we are to each other. I know I definitely don't have a clue, so I find myself wondering if Mikey just knows that we're friends or if maybe Ronan has said something else.

"Yeah, okay, thanks," I say, and I leave him to his pizza magic as I head towards the kitchen.

Before Jay lived in his house with Claire, he stayed in the back of Enzo's in an old utility closet that Ronan and Mikey converted into a studio apartment. When he aged out of the foster care system at eighteen, Jay had nowhere to go. He stayed with the Carusos for a while, but when the boys opened up Enzo's, they made it so he could have his own space in a place he could afford.

The apartment is small. There's only room for a bed, a toilet, and a small kitchenette with just the essentials. It wasn't much, but it was enough for him, and I know he was grateful that they made him a home. Now, Jay has majorly upgraded to a house in a neighborhood a few blocks over. He and Claire are renting to buy it, and the apartment at Enzo's has become more of an office space for Mikey and Ro.

I make my way to the other side of the kitchen and hear strumming before I even make it to Jay's old door. As I walk closer, I make out notes to a song I can't quite put my finger on. The door to the apartment is cracked just an inch, and I push it forward to widen my view. Looking inside, I see Ronan sitting at the foot of the bed, just a sheet-covered mattress beneath him, a pillow and blanket stacked to the side. He's holding an acoustic guitar, and I never thought much of the stereotypical "musicians are hot" thing until right now.

I stand in the doorway, Ronan oblivious to my presence, as he plucks a string here and strums a chord there. He's quietly mumbling the words to the song, and the image I had of him before is quickly replaced by this exact picture.

I clear my throat, suddenly needing to have his attention, and he looks up at me without missing a beat. His fingers keep moving, the light music still playing, as he smiles at me like he's happy I'm here.

"Hey, you," he says, and I can't even hide the dumb look on my face, like I'm in awe of just those two little words.

"Hi," I say, then shake my head, trying to recenter myself. I walk over to where he's sitting and join him on the edge of the mattress. "Since when are you some big-time rockstar?"

He lets out a laugh that sounds like music itself. "Oh, I wouldn't say that," he says, all the while still gently strumming. "I just like to mess around." He looks at his fingers, adjusting them on the strings, and plays with just a little more purpose.

I listen intently, letting the sound wash over me, clearing my head and fogging my heart. As if I wasn't already confused about what the hell is happening between us, Ronan had to go and pick up an instrument.

"I like it," I say, and he smirks as he strums his final chord.

He keeps his guitar in his lap, but pulls one leg underneath him and turns his body to face me. "So, what's up?"

"Nothing, I was just in the area and saw the lights on."

He creases his brow and tilts his head. "You were just in the area?"

"Getting coffee next door."

"Where is it?"

"Where's what?"

He shakes his head laughing. "Your cold brew, Chlo."

I freeze for a second like I was caught in a lie. Only it wasn't a lie. I have truthfully consumed an unhealthy amount of caffeine already this morning. Nope, not a lie—more like an omission.

"I drank it," I say, turning away and staring straight ahead like suddenly the bare, white walls are engraved with a story.

"Mhmm," he answers suspiciously.

"I did! Like an hour ago." I pause then huff out a deep breath. "When I got stood up at Busy's."

He stares at me blank-faced, then fiddles again with the pegs of his guitar. He starts strumming lightly, this time a tune I recognize. I'm caught off guard by the fact that he says nothing. No snarky response, or *"I told you so."* Not even an *"I'll kill the guy,"* just for the sake of sounding tough.

I think back to the moments Ro and I have had over the last few weeks while he tinkers around an Ed Sheeran song. I can't help but think maybe I got it wrong. I thought that there were sparks, maybe mutual feelings or at least attraction, but he's never made a move. That one time at River's is all he's ever said about my dating life, and I assumed it was more heat-of-the-moment advice than anything. But since then… crickets. My ego can't take another hit, especially after today. Plus, Claire and Jay are too important for me to risk taking a chance, only to find out I'm alone in this.

My mind rips open as he comes to the hook about people falling in love in inexplicable ways. Why the compliments and thoughtfulness? Why remember small details? Why stay over? Why hang out on couches, leave me medicine, and cover my toes? I stare at his fingers moving back and forth up the stem of the guitar, my thoughts starting to fester.

Why does he know my coffee order and can tell when I'm lying? Why did he wait for me to finish getting ready that night when Jay and Claire were already in the car? And why did he shrug off his jacket and put it around me, surrounding my body, my heart, my soul with… him?

"Why have you never asked me out?" I blurt. My eyes immediately grow wide as I realize that question wasn't asked in my head.

As usual, Ronan is calm, risking a glance from the strings to my face then back down again as he comes to the chorus. Maybe it's a coincidence or just that after that brain dump, my mind is now silent, but the sound is suddenly amplified—almost like he's playing the lines about finding love exactly where you are, just a little louder.

He continues on, the volume returning to a casual level, and just when I think he's not going to respond at all, he does. "I'm a patient guy, Chloe."

My mouth drops open just an inch, my brow furrowing in confusion. "What does that even mean," I ask.

"It means I watch you go on dates with all these different guys—being let down, being stood up." He pauses his words, the music still flowing, while looking up at me sideways. He continues, playing one last chord and then uses his hand to stop the vibrations of the strings. "And the whole time, I've been waiting for you to figure out that I'm sitting right here."

I'm shocked. Baffled. Dumbfounded, that of all possible responses, that was the one he picked. I thought if anything, he would play stupid like, *"I have no idea what you mean."* Maybe even put it back on me like, *"I don't see you banging down my door."* But he didn't. He was open and honest and had a really freaking good answer, and I'll be damned if that's not so much better than a puppy.

I inch towards him, and before I realize it, our mouths are entwined. The song has stopped, and the now silent guitar is the only barrier keeping me from completely falling into his lap. I bring my hands to his cheeks and deepen our kiss, as Ronan brings one of his to the back of my head.

His lips are soft, his grip gentle, as he combs his fingers into my hair. I attempt to move closer without untangling our upper halves, when a screeching sound reminds me that he's still holding his guitar.

We both break apart—laughing and panting—and Ronan takes the instrument by its neck, leaning it against the frame of the bed. He reaches for me, pulling me closer, and moves a stray hair from in front of my face. "Chloe, I think you know how I feel about you."

"I—"

"Just wait," he interrupts. I turn my lips in and let him continue. "I think you do, and honestly, I think I know how you feel about me. But for whatever reason, you're scared and that's fine." He gently places his finger under my chin and brushes my lips with the pad of his thumb.

"But I don't want to throw my hat into the ring with other people. I won't." He drops his hand, and I whimper in response. "So continue to see whoever you want, but when you're done with all that, come find me." He picks his guitar back up and begins strumming a new tune. "I dare ya," he says, and he winks before his eyes leave mine.

Maybe it's the confession, that kiss, or the caffeine coursing through my veins, but I have never been so turned on in my life. And never so sure of exactly what I want.

"I'm ready," I blurt out, saying the first thing that comes to my mind for yet another time today. "I'm ready," I say more surely. "If you are."

He looks up at me, and I swear I see his blue eyes sparkle. He leans over the guitar and kisses me again, this time more gently. When he pulls away, he brings his forehead to mine and exhales heavily, like he's been holding his breath. And maybe he has been. Maybe we both have.

"I've been ready," he says, and I smile. Because maybe deep down, I have been too.

7

Now

"A re you ready?" I call up the stairs, sitting on the arm of the couch because for once in my life I'm not the one who's late. Apparently, the best man also wants to be the best dressed tonight because Ronan has been up there for what feels like forever.

After our moment earlier, Ro and I put some space between us. We kissed for the second time already this weekend, and for show or not, it left me even more shaken. To clear my head, I drew a hot bath, threw in my headphones, and blocked out the world. Ronan did whatever Ronan did, which I'm not sure of because I was neck-deep in bubbles. It was only when I was leaving the room—in my black sweater, plaid skirt, and suede knee-high boots—that I saw him rooting through the hall closet.

"What are you looking for?" I asked.

"An iron."

"For what?"

"My hair," he deadpanned.

I lowered my chin and raised my brows. "Well, it's long enough."

He shot me a look I couldn't quite read. "I like it," I added, then remembered those exact words coming from his mouth just hours before, the spot under my skirt remembering too.

"Yeah thanks," he said as he turned back around to search through the shelves.

"So, what's it really for then?" I asked, and as if I didn't already feel desperate enough, I was now making small talk about dewrinkling clothes.

"My shirt, Chlo." He turned back around, but not before I saw a slight smirk creeping up the sides of his mouth.

"Right," I said, nodding and pursing my lips. "I'll see you downstairs?"

His face settled into an easy grin. "Sounds good."

Forty-five minutes later, I sent Jay and Claire to start the car.

Now, I finally hear our bedroom door open and the sound of Ro's feet as he descends the stairs.

"Okay, yeah, sounds good. I'll come right over after I get back," he says, ending a call and shoving his phone in his pocket. "Sorry, I'm ready."

"Who was that?" I ask, before remembering who Ronan talks on the phone with now is really none of my business.

"No one," he says curtly, but the way he dismisses it tells me otherwise. "Let's go."

I hesitate briefly, startled by his response despite the meddling question. When he calls my name from the door, I grab my jacket and throw it on, my mind still thinking about who it could be.

Ronan is always open about things, which makes me wonder why he's being weird about this. If it was his brother, uncle, or had something to do with the restaurants, he would have just said that. And Jay is out waiting in the car. Who else could he possibly be talking to that he wouldn't want to say? Ronan isn't one to be sneaky, but I can't help but think that he's covering something up. Or maybe he's just hiding it from me.

My thoughts are still curious as we step outside, and I contemplate pushing the issue. It's only when I spot Claire in the car through the windshield, smiling from ear to ear like she's having the time of her life, that I remember that this isn't about me, and it's not about us. This weekend, this night, is only about Claire. Okay, fine, and Jay... but the rest of our drama will have to wait.

The only two lights guiding us down the dark driveway are the headlights coming from Claire's SUV, and of course, they illuminate Ronan in a warm, sultry glow. He looks good tonight as he walks in front of me, his hair still damp from his shower. The ends of it curl just behind his ears due to the length and sit almost to the structured collar of his jacket. His wool, gray peacoat lays on top of a black button-up shirt, presumably the need for the iron, and the entire outfit takes me back to our first official date.

Right after the moment with the guitar, Ronan took me to Prosecco's, which isn't anything crazy, but is the fanciest restaurant in Maple Grove. I wore an emerald green mini dress—sleeveless, mock turtleneck, a small keyhole opening in the back—*"stunning"* is what Ro called it. And he wore something very similar to what he's wearing now. Chinos and a black-button up, but in place of his peacoat, was a light gray blazer.

That night was everything. It was fun and easy and the first time that Ronan and I got to really talk about the two of us. We tested the physical, holding hands for the first time and letting ourselves get lost in the eye contact that we always avoided, but we also tried being open and honest. We talked about things that we'd previously kept to ourselves and asked questions about the start of us, like, *"How did you feel when we kissed?"* and *"Are you happy that we're finally here?"*

I remember sitting there sharing our answers and thinking that I was having such a good time, but I couldn't shake the pang of regret burrowing inside my chest. I felt like we had spent the last year missing out on moments like these because he was quiet, and I was too stubborn, looking for him in all the wrong places. And it's similar to how I'm feeling now.

We planned this trip as a getaway for the four of us to celebrate the upcoming wedding, but selfishly, it was also supposed to be a chance for Ronan and I to spend time together in the midst of the crazy. With all of his restaurant business, and my hectic school year, it felt like this trip was just what we needed. The holidays are always chaotic and busy at Enzo's, and this was going to be an opportunity to leave all of that behind. Looking at us now, I can't help but feel a similar stab of grief to the one from before—like we're wasting this time not being together.

We get to the car, and Ronan pauses before reaching for the handle to take a steadying breath, either from the cold or to prepare himself for the rest of the night. He takes one more and then opens the door, both of us sliding into the back seat.

"Finally ready there, Chlo?" Jay asks, looking at my reflection in the rearview mirror.

"Actually, that was my bad," Ronan says, and I catch how Jay's eyebrows crinkle.

"Everything okay, man?" There's confusion in his voice that's hard to miss. Jay knows Ro better than any of us, and even he seems to be thrown by his actions.

"Yep," Ro says. "All good. Just a little ironing situation." He smiles, but by the looks of the crease that runs next to his buttons, I can tell he didn't find the iron after all. So what was he doing up there the whole time?

He grabs my hand from off of my knee and squeezes it a little tighter than usual. Maybe it's for show or out of guilt from his little, white lie, or maybe he feels that same jab that I do.

"Alright then," Jay says, pulling out of the driveway, and I squeeze Ronan's hand a little too, a steadying focal point for all of my feelings.

Posto Felice is the closest restaurant to the cabin and the first one that popped up when I was planning this weekend. It's in this little, quaint town called Pine Village, that still twinkles from Christmas lights. I was drawn to it because of the authentic menu and the raving reviews, but either I failed to notice its size or at the time, that was a bonus.

Intimate would be an understatement. The dimly lit dining room was decorated with fresh, white roses and tea light candles and held just a few tables with seats rather close. Had circumstances been different, the atmosphere would have been incredibly romantic. Considering my current situation, the setting was incredibly uncomfortable.

Despite the obvious awkwardness though, the food was amazing, and Claire had a blast. The wine was flowing, and the owners kept sending complimentary limoncello once they heard we were celebrating. Jay relaxed, Claire indulged, and I just enjoyed seeing them happy.

Halfway through dinner, Ronan decided that he would drive home so the two of them could fully unwind. "Ro's so perfect," Claire says in her tipsy state, to no one in general, as Ronan brings the car around.

Jay rubs her shoulders to fight off the cold and responds with a hearty, "That's my boy."

The car stops in front of us, and the groom and his bride slide into the back. I get in to ride shotgun with Ro. Jay doesn't drink much, but Claire seems to be feeling good enough for both of them. Plus, I'm pretty sure Jay can get intoxicated on just Claire's scent alone. The radio plays some country-pop song, as the two of them make out behind us. I'm starting to realize that these full grown adults with jobs, a house, and a wedding coming up, seem to act more like teenagers than anything else. The joys of still being in love. I steal a glance at Ronan, who sits with one hand on the wheel and the other propped up by the driver side window.

All throughout dinner I caught glimpses of the old us—laughing with our friends, trying new dishes, Ro ordering chili flakes for the table because he knows I prefer my pasta sauce spicy. It was nice. For a second here and there, I was able to forget that my life is imploding. Until now.

Ronan leans his body closer to the window, and I can't help but feel like he's putting as much space between us as possible after being so close all dinner. I contemplate taking the rest of the ride in silence, but with Zach Morris and Kelly Kapowski going at it in the backseat, I speak up, if only for the sake of muffling the noises.

"So, how's Nico's coming along?"

Ro looks at me and then back to the road before responding, like he didn't realize that conversation was on the table. "It's alright. A lot more little things need to be done than expected, but Unc's place was simple. We want our second location to be a little more on brand."

I know what he's trying to say. I've seen pictures of his Uncle Nico's place, and it's pretty old school—doughboy statues in every corner, built-in wooden booths, cheap linoleum in the dining room. Enzo's is so much more updated, while still having that traditional flare.

There are framed photos of Italian gangsters on the walls, red leather seat cushions on strong metal chairs, black and white checkered tiling on the floor. When his uncle reached out and asked Ronan if he'd be interested in taking over his place, knowing the boys were looking to expand, everyone knew it'd be a lot of extra work. Despite the fact that starting from scratch might have been easier, Ro and Mikey agreed pretty quickly to keep Nico's alive. Family is everything to the Carusos.

"Is Mikey going to be able to handle it?" I ask, knowing the plan was for Ronan to go for these first couple weeks and then for Mikey to head over more permanently. Once they're comfortable having a crew run it successfully, the brothers will oversee everything from Maple Grove. At that point, Mikey will come home, but that could take months or even more, judging by what Ronan is saying.

Ro shifts in his seat and clears his throat before propping his wrist on the wheel. He rubs his first two fingers together. "Uh, we'll figure something out," he says, and as quick as the song changes, so does the topic. "How's school?" He fidgets with the rearview mirror for reasons, I assume, aren't curiosity about the makeout session behind us.

"Oh," I say, taken aback by the pivot. "It's, um, fine. Same old." The truth is, I've been sleep walking the halls and falling behind on my lesson planning. Luckily, the other support staff know pieces of what's going on and have been carrying the team the last couple of weeks.

It's hard falling back into routine when your other half is no longer there. I'm reminded every morning that Ro is gone when there's no good morning text on my phone. It hits me every lunch period when I have no one to call while I eat at my desk, and the short drive home is filled with dread, knowing I'm headed into another night alone.

"That's nice, Chlo," he says, and it sounds like he means it. "I want things to be good for you."

I freeze momentarily before looking down at my hands in my lap. Of course I don't want him to wish bad things for me, but the way he says it sounds so final. Like he's wishing me well for the rest of my life. Like he's already moved on, and he hopes that I can do the same.

I'm not really sure what to say, so I say nothing, but all I can think is, *a good thing—it's you.*

After a moment or two, Ronan puts his hand, palm up, on my knee. I glance down at it, soft and inviting, a familiar friend in a moment of uncertainty. That hand has been a ground wire, a strong rock, a steady force. It's been under my back, through my hair, between my thighs. Fingers that have been on me, in me, entangled in mine for the last year of my life.

I wonder why he's offering it until Claire's words echo in the back of my mind—*"Ro's so perfect."* And he is. For the ride, for the hand, for so many things.

I must hesitate longer than I thought, because he flips it over and grabs mine, no longer asking—maybe feeling the distance and tethering us together.

"You guys are so cute," Claire says, poking her head between our seats, and I'm surprised by both her presence and the fact that she came up for air. "I can't wait for it to be your turn to get married." She sets both of her elbows on the center console, breaking mine and Ronan's clasp, and rests her face between her hands.

"Chloe's not getting married, remember," Jay says over her shoulder. "Smart girl, am I right?" he jokes.

"Hey!" Claire says, sitting back up and playfully swatting at Jay. He wraps his arms around her waist and pulls her to him. "That's not nice! Besides, you never know. Ronan might just be the exception." She pushes her way between our seats again, getting merely inches from my face. "Right?" she asks, booping me on the nose with the tip of her finger. She then turns to Ro and does it to him.

Ronan sucks his teeth, now white-knuckling the steering wheel, as Claire returns to the back seat with Jay.

"Right?" she repeats to the rearview mirror, the anticipation of my response visible in her lifted eyebrows and bright, wide smile.

My eyes flick to Ronan. His are still on the road. "You never know," I say, but it comes out weak, a betrayal of how I'm feeling inside. Ro scowls at me, his face flushed with frustration, a fleeting moment of honesty before tucking it away.

"Yes!" Claire yells way louder than necessary, completely oblivious to the silence up front. I beg her in my mind to end the conversation, but instead, she brings her hands to her mouth to further amplify her voice. "RoChlo FOREVER!"

8

Before

"I t's been forever, Case, come on."

"I know. I'm sorry, Chlo. We're just really short staffed, and they needed more nurses." The beeping that I hear through the phone tells me Casey's already at the hospital.

"But you're already working Christmas! Now Thanksgiving too?"

"Trust me, I know."

"Ugh, stop saving lives and start seeing me."

"I promise," she says, sipping what I can only assume is her coffee—black, extra ice. "New Year's Day, no lives will be saved."

"Fine," I groan. "You're lucky I love you."

"Love you too, little sis." There's a voice in the background—a loudspeaker paging a doctor. "Hey, listen, I gotta run! Tell Ronan I want to meet him in the new year."

I'm still holding my phone to my ear when Casey ends the conversation. I inhale and exhale a recentering breath, before tossing my phone on my bed. "So much for that," I say, spinning around.

"I'm sorry, babe." Ronan comes over and throws his arms around my neck, pulling me close. He came right from Enzo's after prepping this morning for the rest of the weekend, and he smells like the perfect combination of basil and body wash, something musky with a hint of lemon and sage.

"I was finally going to get to see her! Stupid hospitals with their stupid doctors and their stupid patients who need stupid nurses."

"So stupid," he says. I laugh into him.

"I was just looking forward to it." My voice comes out muffled against the base of his neck.

I don't see my sisters as much as I'd like to. Cara and Casey still live by my parents, but I moved to Maple Grove after school. We're a couple of hours away from each other, and with all of our schedules, it's just hard to work out.

Cara works as a paralegal in a law firm in our hometown and is constantly running into the office. Casey works at the hospital nearby, and with her schedule, she might as well live on the moon. We hang out the most when my biggest perk as a teacher, besides molding the youth, gets put to use—three months off for summer vacation. Other than that, spare time's hard to come by, and it's now been weeks since we've been able to make anything work.

Tonight, Cara is apparently taking advantage of the quiet office and going into work. Dad is sick, and Mom's volunteering to hand out meals at a shelter, but Casey and I were supposed to have a turkey date—Her, me, canned cranberries, store-bought stuffing, and those Tastykake pies that are individually wrapped.

Ronan kisses the top of my head. "I know," he says. "But hey, now you can come to Thanksgiving with me." He lifts his brows and looks at me with the most sincere, sapphire eyes.

"You don't think it's too soon? We just started doing this... " I point between us, landing with my hand over his heart. "Just a few weeks ago, officially." He lets out a chuckle, and my palm vibrates in response.

"Chlo…" He wraps one hand around mine and mimics my gesture with the other. "This… has been like a year in the making."

"Talk about foreplay," I say, jokingly, but I can feel his heartbeat quicken beneath my touch.

The truth is, foreplay's an understatement. Despite now being together, Ronan and I still haven't—kneaded the dough? Sauced the pie? Cooked the pizza?

Banged. We still haven't banged.

It's not for lack of attraction that's for sure. I mean the way we're all over each other, you'd think we were christening all of Maple Grove, but we both decided to take it slower than we wanted to. Like Ronan said, it took over a year just for us to get together. The last thing we need is to risk all of that effort by rushing into sex. Not to mention, there's Claire and Jay to think about. Of course the two of them were thrilled to hear about us. Apparently, I was the only one who didn't see it coming, but they're our best friends, and I'm not willing to split custody of them with anyone should this go south.

Ronan gulps audibly, his eyes dropping to my lips. He releases my hand and shoves it in his pockets, minimizing physical contact before either of us gets carried away. Taking it slow sounds like a good idea until you're skin to skin with the person you're with. After that, even talking about foreplay can be seductive.

Ronan breathes out heavily. "All I'm saying is, my family knew we'd end up together before we ever did. My mom probably has a spot set up for you at the table already."

I laugh, but the thought both warms my heart and makes it race. The idea of Ro's parents welcoming me into their home on Thanksgiving is enough to fill the void that I'm feeling. The Carusos are such a tight-knit family, and that's the most important thing in the world to Ronan, especially after all that he's been through. His parents love him unconditionally, despite not being blood, and I know how much he loves them and respects their opinion. I'm worried that if they don't like me, or worse, if they don't think I'm good for Ronan, that our relationship will end before it even begins. I'm constantly uneasy about years down the line, but what if we never even make it that far?

"Are you sure they won't care?" I ask, feeling both nervous and anxious, but what better time to meet the parents than on a day entirely centered on counting your blessings?

"Trust me, Chlo. They'd be more upset if you didn't come."

We walk up to Ronan's parents' house, Ro's arm around me and mine around a bottle of red. I'm clutching the neck of the wine so tightly it just might shatter beneath my grasp.

I am not one to be nervous. In fact, I am typically so cool to a fault that my friends often have to reign me back in.

"Chloe, you can't dance on that table."
*"Oh my God, Chlo, please don't wear the **Calm Your Tits** shirt to dinner."*
"No, you can't tell a guy you love his balls even if you're referring to those of the meat variety."

But right now, I'm sweating bullets, and it's practically freezing out here.

"Hey," Ronan says, stopping just short of the door. "It's going to be fine. They're going to love you." And once again, he knows what I need without me having to say a thing.

We open the door, and the anxiety hits me. The Caruso's house smells like cinnamon and gravy, and voices drift from further inside. We take off our shoes, throwing them in a pile next to the door with the others, before Ronan grabs my hand and guides me toward the back of the house.

As we cut through the dining room, I see a formal table in the center set with china plates, fabric napkins, and stemless wine glasses at every seat. Ronan takes the bottle from my hands and places it in the center next to a mold of butter shaped like a turkey. The entire tablescape is out of a magazine, which makes the whole paper plate and plastic utensil girl in me even more tense.

Leading in front, Ro steps into the kitchen first, and all three of his family members erupt into cheers. I cower behind him, savoring every second that I'm not in the spotlight and listening to the calls from each one of them.

"Ayy!"

"There he is!"

"Mio bambino!"

They all speak at the same time, leaping toward Ronan like he's returning from war. He laughs and hugs them. Then they see me.

"Amica!"

"Chloe!

"Dolcezza! She's here!"

Again, it's like welcoming home a P.O.W. There are arms around me, someone's yelling my name, and I'm pretty sure my cheeks are pinched in passing. It's chaotic and passionate and honestly... perfect.

"Alright Ma, enough already," Ronan says, as Mrs. Caruso runs her fingers down my long ponytail.

"She's just so beautiful, isn't she? Bellisima!" She pulls me in for another hug, and I savor it as she slowly releases my nervous energy.

"Of course she is," Ronan says, planting a kiss on the side of my head. He fist bumps Mikey and grabs a noodle from a bowl on the island. "But give her an inch."

"Thank you for having me, Mr. and Mrs. Caruso."

"Oh nonsense," Mr. Caruso says, waving away my gratitude. "The more the merrier. Plus Camilla always makes way too much food." He moves to his wife and kisses her cheek.

"It's true," Mrs. Caruso says, shrugging her shoulders. "But that just means more leftovers for my three best men." She winks at her husband, then smiles at her boys.

Mikey puts an arm around his mother, towering over her in height, and lays his head on top of hers. "Damn straight."

"Okay, enough, enough, go!" she says, shooing him away. "The lasagna is in, the turkey is ready, antipasto is out. Dinner's in twenty."

Mikey dashes out immediately with Mr. Caruso close behind, only stopping to whisper in his wife's ear. Ronan takes a focused interest in digging through the meats and cheeses surrounded by noodles, as Mrs. Caruso giggles at whatever her husband says. Judging by the playful eye roll that follows, and the fact that Mr. Caruso whistles on his way out of the kitchen, I would say Ronan should be glad he didn't hear his parents' little exchange.

In this brief interaction, it's obvious that Ronan's mom and dad are completely in love. They share a quiet kind of affection—pecks and winks, and presumably, lewd comments in secret. It makes me think of my parents. Were they ever like this with each other? I remember Mom and Dad kissing goodbye or saying I love you, but did they do these kinds of things, and maybe I missed it? Growing up, I always thought my parents had a perfect marriage, but maybe they were just good at hiding the imperfections.

"Can I help at all with anything?" I ask, secretly hoping Mrs. Caruso says no, because I have no idea what I'm doing in the kitchen.

"No, no, let Ronan give you the tour."

"Works for me," Ro says, picking again from the bowl. He grabs my hand, this time leading me the other way around.

Their home, much like them, is cozy and welcoming. There are candles lit on every table top and pictures of the boys all over the walls. We pass Ronan's dad and brother sprawled on two couches, watching a game and bickering while the refs review the last play. I laugh at their argument—something about lines and flags and knees being down—as Ronan directs me up the stairs.

The steps are lined with pictures of the boys from when they were younger, like a photo of Mikey in a bowtie and sitting in a highchair covered in sauce. There's school pictures and ones of the two of them playing catch, but it's not lost on me that there are none of Ro any younger than a teen. You'd never know it in the way they treat him, or me for that matter, so sometimes it's easy to forget that Ronan has only been a Caruso for half of his life.

The second floor is a series of doors, the first of which, is a full bathroom. Apparently, this was the boys bathroom, and the brothers would argue each week about who had to clean it. "Mikey was always a smartass, saying he cleaned it for fifteen years before I came along, so it was only fair that I make up for lost time," Ronan shares.

He makes a joke about my tiny tank, asking if I need to use it while we're here, and then closes the door behind him when I nudge him on his side. The door that follows is a guest room with walls and decor of sage and soft yellows. There's a glider in the corner, and I wonder if it was a baby's room once upon a time. The next room is Mikey's.

"Mom left everything the same in both of our rooms when we moved out. The poor lady didn't even want us to leave, let alone think about changing our stuff."

I take in the room with its tan walls, maroon comforter, and a bold red, white, and green flag above the bed. It's just like Mikey—laid back and simple, with just a hint of Italian flare. There are photos on the wall of Rocky and The Godfa-ther, and beard oil on the dresser that tells me Mikey's always been hairy.

I voluntarily skip the door after that, partly not wanting to intrude on the master bedroom, and mostly because I'm more interested in the only other room left. Ronan opens the door to his teenage bedroom, and I practically snort at what sits in front of me. It's painted in cream, the bed covered in a navy blue blanket, and Converse shoes line the wall. There are a few framed photos sitting on his dresser—One of him and Mikey, one of him and Jay, and one of his whole family the day he got adopted. An old acoustic leans against the side of his nightstand where three products sit—cologne, deodorant, and gel for his hair.

"This is... " I start to say.

"Weird, I know."

"Exactly like your room right now."

Ronan looks at me almost sharply. "It is not!" he argues. "My walls are white!"

"Okay," I laugh at this one technicality. "But literally everything else is the same." He looks back to the room, then glances at me side-eyed.

"Oh, come on, the shoes, the guitar—I mean you still use that exact cologne." Ronan's face takes on a grouchy expression as he folds his arms dramatically across his chest. "It's not a bad thing!" I say, placing my hand on his shoulder. "Just means you've been *you* since you were eighteen."

"Fifteen," he says quietly, a pout on his lips. "I've had the same room since I was fifteen." I cackle now, and he cracks a smile.

"Creature of habit?" I ask stepping further inside.

"Nope." He bearhugs me from behind, and I drop my head back onto his shoulder. "I just like what I like," he whispers in my ear.

My whole body stills, the atmosphere in the room, suddenly shifting. A heat grows south matching the temperature of his warm breath on my neck. I lean my weight further into him as he plants gentle kisses along the collar of my sweater. Ronan's hands travel away from my torso towards the hem of my skirt, his fingers sliding slowly up my inner thigh. I turn my face, my mouth just brushing his, as a soft moan escapes my lips. Ronan tightens his grip on my skin before groaning and dropping his forehead to my shoulder.

"Chloe," he says, brushing the tip of his nose along the curve of my neck. "I'm not sure how much longer I can do this."

"Fool around in your teenage bedroom?" I quip.

"No," he says dryly, then nibbles my ear. "This."

Without asking any more questions, I know exactly what he means.

9
Now

"**W**hat the hell was that?" Ronan asks as we get to our room. Claire and Jay went right upstairs after we got back, the horn-dogs that they are, and Ro all but carried me up the steps moments later.

The rest of the drive that followed Claire's little interrogation was unpleasant at best, at least for the front half of the car. If I thought he was off before, Ronan became a stranger the rest of the way home. He was distant and silent, his body language screaming in comparison—all tense arms, clenched fists, and gritted teeth.

"What was what?" I ask, as he searches through his bag. He pulls out what I know is his speaker, the familiar ding filling the room, meaning it's on and connected to his phone.

"*You never know,*" he says, mocking me, at least two octaves higher than necessary. He fiddles with the volume, then scrolls on his screen, as if now is the time to test out a new playlist.

"I do not talk like that."

"Not the point!" he snaps, as a song I can't quite place starts playing through the little box. Ro sets the speaker on the dresser behind him and then faces me head on.

"Then what is the point? And what's with the background music?"

"So they can't hear us," he says as something bangs on the wall next door.

"More like so we can't hear them," I mutter under my breath, but Ronan stares at me blankly, apparently immune to my clever response.

"So..." He's waiting for my answer when the first verse of the song begins.

"Well, I don't know if I would have gone with Coldplay but—"

"Chloe!"

"I don't know!" I yell. "To make Claire happy I guess." It comes out smooth, but it's an absolute lie. I know exactly why I said it, and it has nothing to do with pleasing the bride.

When Ronan proposed, I was totally thrown. People talk about fight or flight responses, but they forget to mention that freeze is an option. When he got down on one knee, that's exactly what happened—my body was paralyzed by those four simple words. I remember searching for answers and willing myself to say something, anything, but either my mind moved too quickly or my mouth moved too slowly, because it's like they were fighting each other instead of working together.

The whole thing was a blur of confusion and hurt, and I couldn't decide if I was upset or happy, pissed off or excited. He knew how I felt, and he asked me anyway, but the way we were with each other, was I really that surprised? Either way, there were a million feelings, a million answers, but none of them jumped right to "no." If he had asked me a year ago, I probably would have been more convincing. Two, three, five years in the past, I would have answered with an overwhelming, *"Absolutely not."* So, how come when he pulled out that ring, I had nothing to say?

It all got me thinking. In my head, I couldn't say yes to Ronan because I wanted him always, but I lost him anyway when that wasn't my answer. I did love him, and I did want to be with him, but I felt anchored to the thought that I would end up like the rest of my family—alone, with my life changed and my heart broken.

Lately though, it feels like the idea of some curse is still controlling my fate, even without a marriage to ruin. Could I have gotten it wrong? The idea seems unlikely, and the proof's in the history, but maybe Ronan *is* the exception—for both me and my family.

"Well, if that was the case, buy her a goddamn butterscotch latte or tell her she's pretty or some shit. Don't play that fucking card." Ronan brings his hands to his hips and hangs his head, staring at the carpet. *"You never know,"* he says. "Don't do that to me."

I close the gap between us, the song still playing in the background about finding your lover amongst a sea of stars. "I'm sorry," I say, no longer having to yell but also not capable even if I wanted to. My voice is heavy, my heart even moreso. I look at Ronan, his body so close to mine that I could reach out and run my fingers down the line of buttons on his shirt. "For all of it."

Let's just call it what it is—today has been an absolute mind fuck. It's only day one of our weekend together, and already there's been a constant push and pull between Ronan and me. I knew it would be hard. I knew we'd have our moments, but what I didn't expect was for so many of them to involve just wanting him back.

I inch forward still, the tension pulling me towards him. I look to his eyes for any sign of forgiveness. Any indication that he'd let me back in.

"Chloe, let's... " he starts, and I lean in just slightly. I bring my hand to his chest like I've done a million times before, and at the same time, he continues. "Let's just get through this weekend."

My hand drops slowly, falling towards the floor along with my dignity, as he turns and walks to the bathroom attached to our room. The door closes, and I can't help but feel like it's symbolic of so much more.

I barely hear the shower turn on as I'm left standing frozen in place from either pain or embarrassment, the bass of the music pumping in rhythm to the beat of my heart. I want nothing more than to follow behind him, strip myself of my clothes and my pride, and join him under the heat of the water. I would give anything to wash his long hair, rinse his toned arms, and show him how much second-guessing I've done.

I walk downstairs to a quiet house minus the running water above. I search the first floor for the other two and see only an open bottle of whiskey on the kitchen island. I pour myself a drink to take to the porch, just to find Jay and Claire already outside when I open the front door.

They're sitting on the Adirondack chairs around a steady flicker of flames, and although I planned to soothe myself in the rock of the porch swing, I move to where they are. As I near the fire pit, I hear Jay talking about his current project with the car he's rebuilding, and see Claire nodding along like she has even the slightest idea what he's trying to say.

"Got room for one more?" I ask, sipping my whiskey. Claire leans over, tapping the chair next to her, sloshing her drink just smoothly enough that it doesn't pour over. "How are you two still going?"

"Well, technically, this is like my third drink," Jay says, and Claire's eyes grow increasingly larger.

"This is *not* my third drink," she replies, and Jay and I laugh to each other. She shrugs it off, then leans really close to my chair. "Are you and Ronan okay?" she whispers.

My mouth runs dry. I take another sip of my drink to buy me more time. "We're fine," I say cheerfully, hoping she's too drunk to notice the shake in my voice.

"Are you sure?" she half-slurs. "Because I heard Coldplay coming from your room and that just feels like… weird vibes." She squints, then hiccups so hard that this time her drink does spill over the rim.

"Okay," Jay says. "Time for bed."

"Noo," Claire whines. "I'm talking to my best girl." She reaches for me, and I take her hand in mine.

"We have all day tomorrow," I say, and Claire's eyes light up then fall peacefully down.

"The spaaa," she says as she drags out the last sound.

"That's right. So you better get some rest."

"Mhmm, can't wait." She goes to turn and smacks right into Jay who, like the caveman he is, picks her up and cradles her like a baby in his arms. I'm giggling as Jay looks at me, his expression unreadable between the glimmer of flames.

"Have a good night, Chlo," he says, turning towards the house.

I'm trying to decide if it's sadness that I heard in his voice when Claire yells from over his shoulder. "RoChlo FOREVER!"

I practically shudder at the repeated expression and reach over to grab the blanket that Claire left behind. When I look back up, I see Ronan opening the door at the same time that Jay reaches for the knob, stepping aside to let them in. Once Jay steps over the threshold, Ronan moves onto the porch, closing the door behind him. He has on a hoodie, joggers, and a beanie that covers all but the ends of his hair as he walks to the chair across from me.

"Hey," he says. I hesitate to make eye contact, focusing my attention on the glass in his hand.

"Hey." I adjust my legs so they're under me and wrap the blanket around my body.

"Listen, about earlier... " His voice trails off, my eyes moving to his wrist perched on the arm of the chair, where he's rubbing his fingers together.

"Don't worry about it."

"Chloe."

My eyes move to his for the first time. "Seriously, Ro. It's fine."

As much as I was begging for him to talk to me earlier, I'm just exhausted. Today has been a shitshow of highs and lows, and I can feel each one of them weighing on me physically. It's funny how a relationship that started with words blurted out, continues to end with things left unsaid.

He adjusts the fabric on either side of his ears, and I'm reminded that Ronan in a hat is one of my favorite things. Whether it's baseball or beanie, there's something about a hat on a guy—this guy in particular—that just liquifies my insides.

"So, how are your parents?" I ask.

There's a tug on my heartstrings as I realize that I may have had my last Mr. Caruso bearhug or Mrs. Caruso pinch on the cheeks. I think that's part of what makes things like breakups so hard. You suddenly have to go without things you have become accustomed to. Like you've had your "last" of something, and you didn't even realize it.

"They're good. Dad's been by the shop a few times, working his mouth more than anything else."

I laugh, thinking back to all of the times I've heard his dad's stories. They're almost always about something that's not important at all, but it's the way he tells them, like their the most exciting thing in the world, that really captures your attention. Your typical Italian, Mr. Caruso talks loud and fast, and his hands fly around like he's signing the words. I've heard the same few stories over and over, but right now, I'd do anything to hear them just one more time.

"Sounds about right," I say smiling. Ronan smiles too, and it's the first time I think I've seen him genuinely happy here.

"And your mom?"

He pulls his leg up so his ankle sits on his knee and plays with his shoestring as he talks. "She's fine," he says. "She misses you."

At first I think ash has flown up from the fire and landed right on my chest, but then, I realize that the sudden sting that I felt came from inside. I have gone my whole adult life missing my family, and now for the past three weeks I've had to add Ronan's parents to that absence.

"I miss her too," I say. My voice comes out drained because that's exactly how I feel.

I love my mom, and I'd pick her to raise me in every lifetime, but she's hours away, and this past year, Camilla has been there to fill her void. We hadn't gotten around to it yet, but I always thought her and Mom would get along great. Now, I guess we'll never find out.

Camilla, which she insisted I call her, is just so... warm. She's kind and attentive, and she really listens to you. She loves you with food and with grace, and I never once felt like an outsider with her. If she was even a fraction as welcoming with me as she was with Ro, I can see why he would fall as in love with her as he did. Why he would feel so at home in her arms.

Ronan nods his head but looks a million miles away. He finishes off the rest of his drink and sits forward resting his forearms on his knees. "Listen, Chlo, I know this is weird," he exhales loudly. "But let's just get through one more day, and we'll be on our way out of here. Maybe we'll talk about things once we're back but not here."

I rub my lips together and tilt my chin up. He's right, it is weird. But I feel that blaze again throughout my whole chest. Nothing with Ronan and I has ever felt weird. Confusing maybe, but never strange. I hate how so much is different now. It's the craziest thing, going from seeing one another everyday, finishing each other's sentences, and being half of a whole, to asking about our lives and catching up over awkward conversations.

I mean, right now we're practically strangers... except that we're not at all. No, we don't talk or hang out like we used to, but I know that he's nervous because he's messing with the pad of his thumb. I know he got that beanie from his grandma last Christmas and that the hoodie he's wearing is missing the string because he and Mikey were wrestling, and his brother pulled it out. I know he hates that he's keeping this secret from Jay and that it's killing him that his mom says she's missing me. He hates to see his family upset, and I know that just adds to everything else.

No, we're not strangers, and I don't want to be. I don't want to just get through one more day. I want to spend this time with him. Laughing about his dad's stories instead of hearing about them secondhand. Snuggling by the warmth of the fire instead of one building inside of me. I don't want to just *exist* together. I want to *be* together.

But I think I ruined that.

"One more day," I say, gulping down the rest of my drink, and it's like the whiskey's taunting me as it burns going down. "Got it."

10

Before

"G ot it!" I say, laying out the dough I just stretched onto the counter covered in flour. It looks more like a thought bubble than an actual circle, with a few holes here and there, but it's my best attempt so far.

Ronan comes up behind me, hovering over my shoulder, and resting his hands on the counter on either side of my body. "That looks... almost edible," he says. He smells like a full day's work because he's been here at Enzo's since they opened this morning.

"Well, fine then," I say, primping the edges. "More for me."

He pushes off of the counter and comes up beside me. "Move over, and let the boss handle this." Ro bumps his hip against mine and stretches in front of him like he's warming up for a fight.

The last few nights he's been working until closing, which gives us essentially no time to see each other. I'm out the door first thing in the morning, and Ronan's prepping for the dinner shift by the time I get home. To make up for lost time, I've been popping in when I don't have a ton of school stuff to do, and he's been attempting to teach me how to make my own pizza. It's going about as well as expected, but I like being a part of what's important to Ro.

He grabs another ball of dough from off of the tray at our work space with what I now know is a dough knife. He throws the ball into a bowl full of flour, flipping it so it's coated all over. Using his fingers, he fans out the dough so it grows slowly into the shape of a pie. He works it with his hands, pulling and stretching, all of his movements graceful and fluid. Watching Ronan make pizza is like watching Picasso make art. None of it makes sense to me, but it's refined and effortless, and the finished product is always a masterpiece.

When the dough is a mini version of the pizza it will become, he slides it onto his hands, tossing it high and rotating it above his head like it's an extension of himself. I watch *him* watch *it*, from under the rim of his hat. The now-stretched disk lands delicately on top of his knuckles. On the second throw, he extends his arms, releasing the pizza and sliding his hat to the back of his head. It's not meant to be sexy, but every woman knows the spin of the brim is like turning on the heat, and to do it mid-motion, is like the hottest thing I've ever seen. Ro catches it again, and this time, it's the exact size of the pan he lays it on. The dough is a perfect circle and a flawless canvas for sauce and cheese.

"Here," he says, sliding the tray in front of me. "In case you want to save yours for later and slum it with mine."

I step in front of his pan, taking my time to inspect his work. "Okay, I'll give it to you. This one's... alright."

He snickers and holds his arms out as if to say, "go ahead."

I reach for the ladle of sauce and drop it onto the dough. Moving it in circles, I attempt to spread it the way I've seen Ronan and Mikey do a hundred times before, but the handle is long and the cup is heavy. It stutters against the dough instead of running smoothly like it does for them. Ronan steps up, placing his flour-dusted fingers over mine and guides it to do what I wanted in the first place.

"All in the wrist," he says, as the sauce comes out in even, red rings, working their way from the middle towards the outer edge.

There's something about the way the ladle now moves fluidly in my hand that's mesmerizing to watch. It's effortless and satisfying, and when Ronan leads my hand back to the stainless steel container that the sauce sits in, I hear myself exhale a breath I was unexpectedly holding.

Ronan tenses at the sound, his fingers that were once on mine, now beginning a slow glide up the edge of my forearms. I freeze where I stand, both of our arms still extended towards the sauce, his other palm on the edge of the counter. I'm wearing long sleeves, but between the tight material and my hyper-sensitivity to anything Ronan, I feel his touch like it's branding my skin.

His fingers continue until they brush my shoulder, sweeping my hair off to the side. I naturally relax into his touch, my head tilting to open up the crook of my neck. Ro plants his lips on the inside of my collar, then trails them towards my jaw, not quite making contact with my skin.

I feel his warm breath travel upward, goosebumps breaking out under my shirt, until he nibbles gently on my ear. A soft whimper escapes my lips, and I feel him twitch beneath me. At this point, I'm leaning on him head to toe, my weight pressed against him as he braces himself, reaching under my arms to grip the counter. If I thought pizza was arousing before, it is completely intoxicating now that I am pinned between it and Ronan's firm body, hard against me in more ways than one.

I reach up and behind him, my fingers stroking the spot of skin left exposed under the brim of his hat. I turn my head so it lays on his chest, his muscles rising and falling beneath me. I kiss his collarbone, and before I can do it myself, he tilts my mouth up to meet his, placing my chin in the curve of his thumb. A low groan comes from the back of his throat as he tightens his grip ever so lightly, pulling me to deepen our kiss.

I spin in his arms without breaking our connection, and I feel him just above where I need him to be. I bring my hand to the rim of his backwards hat, and tug on it roughly, lifting his face from mine. Licking up the side of his neck, I land on the soft spot under his jaw, sucking just enough to leave my mark.

"Chloe," he whispers. His voice comes out like the sweetest beg, and I feel it right between my thighs.

I reach around his waist, loosening the knot of his apron that's folded and tied low on his hips. It drops to the floor, the perfect cushion, as I fall to my knees on top of it.

Grabbing the button on his jeans, Ronan looks me dead in the eye. He's needy, and I'm looking to please, as I undo his zipper and let gravity pull his pants to the ground.

Ronan brings his hand to my cheek, then slides it firmly into my hair, as I bring his boxers down to his feet. He springs to life in front of me, just as eager for me as I am for him.

I lick delicately at first and then suck him hard, before pulling back completely, teasing him with just my breath before swallowing him whole. He pulls at my hair and bucks into my mouth, still bracing one arm on the metal behind me. I relish in the sight of him, weak under my touch, a power building in me that's new to us both. We've done this before, but this is the first time I don't plan to stop here.

Taking all of him one more time, I pull free from his grasp and rise to my feet. He looks at me curious, his gaze heated and hopeful, and I tell him all he needs to know with a lick of my lips.

"Jesus Christ, please explain to me why we waited so fucking long to do that," Ro says, pulling me to him, both of us crammed into this one tiny bed.

"Something about making sure we don't ruin our friendships with Claire and Jay by rushing into sex."

"Well, those two better know we're the best fucking friends they've ever had because withholding from that feels criminal."

I blush into the crook of his arm, still panting from the events that proceeded. And it's true—what just unfolded was borderline pornographic.

I would have done it right there on the floor of the kitchen, but something about sanitation and codes freaked Ronan out, so we opted for the bed in Jay's old apartment. It's almost sweet that our first time was in the same place where we decided to take our relationship to the next level, but I can promise, nothing about that was mushy at all.

The short walk from the kitchen to here, honestly, might have been the best part. Ronan stopped every few seconds to pin me to the wall, strip me of layers, or drop to his knees. I had come undone more than once before even making it to the room. It was rough and wild, and if I thought Ronan was laid back and calm, now I know where he finds his edge.

"Well, we never have to wait again," I say, turning to wink at him.

"Like right now?" he asks. "Round two?"

I roll my eyes, but in reality, if I wasn't so hungry I would totally go again. I haven't slept with as many people as some may think, being that I used to go on so many dates, but without even pulling out my notes, I know that what just happened here was hands down the best I've ever had.

My stomach rumbles, and Ronan looks down at it. "Or not," he says through a chuckle.

"Hey, that's not my fault." I trace the lines of the peaks and valleys of his chest. "We never actually finished a pizza."

"That's probably for the best if you're talking about yours." I flick him playfully in response. "I'm just saying, maybe leave the food to the professionals."

"Whatever," I laugh. "You've had more practice."

"Just a few years."

"Speaking of, have you always wanted to be a *professional*?" I say the last word in a mocking tone, and Ro gives me a lighthearted nudge.

"Not at all," he says. "To be honest, I had no idea what I wanted to be. When my parents died, I was only fourteen. What kid that age has any clue what he wants to do with his life? I went from playing video games and throwing a baseball back and forth with my friends, to packing up all of my things into a duffle bag. I left my childhood bed to sleep in a house full of people I didn't know, with other kids who were just as miserable as me."

"Was that hard?" I ask, immediately regretting the question. Of course it was hard. One second Ronan was an only child with two loving parents, living a completely normal life for a young teenager, and the next day he was an orphan with nowhere to go.

Despite my stupidity, Ro looks at me with sincerity, a reflective gleam in his eyes. "For a while, I was so numb to it all. I don't know if I could even say it was hard, you know? I just sort of let life happen to me. I felt so out of control because I had no control. My parents were gone, I was taken away from my friends, my school, and the only home I'd ever known." Ro pauses and takes in a deep breath. "I pretty much put my head down and got through life one day at a time. It wasn't until I met Jay that I realized, just because my parents were gone, that didn't mean I'd never have a family again. When I got adopted, I was so happy. Kids at that age just don't get chosen like they do when they're younger. So, I held my breath through the whole process of settling in with my parents and Mikey and just walked on egg shells until I was eighteen. By then, I guess everything had become my new norm, and I realized I should probably get my shit together and figure out a future."

"So, you picked this?" I ask, propping my arm onto his chest and resting my cheek against it. Ronan has talked to me a little before about everything in his past but never like this. It's nice to just listen and take in what parts of his story he's willing to give me.

"Well, at that point Mikey knew he wasn't going back to college, and Dad was already way out of the game with Uncle Nico. Mikey was just going to move there and work for him, but I had money that my parents left me, and to be honest, I just didn't want him to leave. Even before the accident, I never had any siblings. I wasn't going to just let him get away that easily. I knew the basics from Dad's stories and visiting Unc and thought, *fuck it. Let's just do it ourselves.*

It took a couple of years to get it all moving. Dad helped us with everything on the back end, and my inheritance was more than enough to cover the start up costs. The first year or so that we were open was rough, learning the ways of the actual business—the menu, the marketing, managing employees and funds and all that—but Mikey and I had a blast figuring it out together, and surprisingly, we started turning a profit before we even realized it."

"That's incredible," I say. "You guys have accomplished so much, and you haven't even killed each other yet!"

He laughs, and I feel it beneath the palm of my hand. "Not yet, but we want to try to expand in the next year or so. That'll be the real test. Can we be profitable more than once? Or was this first time just a fluke?"

"You'll be great," I say. "Plus, this time you'll have me."

He snuggles me closer and kisses the tip of my nose. "I sure hope so," he says. "You will."

"Well... " He looks back and forth between my eyes, and it's almost like a calm washes over him. He lifts his hand and brushes a stray hair from my forehead. "If that's the case, I'll consider myself the most successful guy in the world."

11

Now

I woke up with an arm around my waist, a thigh across my leg, and something poking into a place it most definitely shouldn't be. I blink hard, looking around at the white, oak walls, rustic decor, and natural sunlight from the windows. Finding the mounted fish on the wall, I remember that I'm in a log cabin miles from Maple Grove, with Claire, Jay, and...

"Ronan." I say it out loud without even meaning to, shocking myself and waking him up.

"Huh?" Ro says, nestling his face further into my neck. I look over my shoulder as he flutters his eyes. He then rubs them with the palm of his hand, and I watch as he realizes he's spooning me in bed.

"Oh, shit!" he says, removing apparently three body parts from mine and pulling the comforter into a pile on his lap. "Damn, I'm sorry." His expression reads as something similar to embarrassment, but because he's Ronan, his reaction is way too subtle compared to how I'm feeling.

"It's fine," I say, sprinting from bed towards the bathroom. "I'm just going to, uh, shower." I pull the door closed behind me and brace myself against the rim of the sink.

It's fine, I repeat to myself, staring at my reflection in the mirror in front of me. *So we woke up cuddling. It's just out of habit. And his other... issue... is totally natural.* I turn on the shower to warm up the water.

After our talk at the fire, Ronan and I decided to call it a night. We walked silently into the house and up the stairs, moving through our bedtime routine in sync with one another like we've done a hundred times before. It was only after faces were washed, teeth were brushed, and jammies were jammin', that we reluctantly started to speak.

"So, I'll sleep on the floor?" I'm not sure he meant for it to come out a question, but he looked at me like he was waiting for an answer.

"It's okay. I think we can manage a few hours of sleep in the same bed without killing each other or getting it on."

Ronan raised his eyebrows. "Getting it on?" he said with a slow smile.

"Shut up, you know what I mean."

"I know what you mean," he repeated. "We can sleep next to each other and keep our hands to ourselves." His eyes scanned my body so fast I almost missed it.

"Right," I said, swallowing hard.

Ronan cleared his throat and gestured towards the bed. We both walked to our designated sides and slipped under the covers. I rested both hands on top of my stomach, not quite sure if we were going right to sleep. Ronan tucked one hand under his head, and we laid there in silence for what felt like forever.

"Well, goodnight, Chlo," he eventually said, and I felt him roll over to his side of the bed.

Lying next to him and not talking about our days or kissing goodnight, felt like drinking black coffee. It was somewhat familiar but without all of the good stuff—the same buzzing feeling in a less enjoyable way.

Now, it's the same. It's not the first time I've woken up as Ro's little spoon, with his body draped over mine and him... excited to be there. But it's also different and foreign—and no longer my place.

I take one more look in the mirror and think, *I can do this*. So what if his little (definitely slightly above average) friend was just on me. That thing was in my mouth like three weeks ago. And besides, today I get to spend all day with Claire. A massage, a facial, and time in the sauna, all with my best friend in the world. I just have to survive the next hour first.

I search for a towel but come up short, assuming Ronan used the last one yesterday. It seems in his attempt to wash off my apology he forgot to leave a towel for me. Rolling my eyes, I run my hand down my face and exhale an exasperated breath. I turn the knob of the door and as it opens, I am met with Ronan's bare-naked ass. I mean that thing is right there, and it's toned and firm, but it's paler than he is.

"Oh my God!" I yell, covering my eyes. "Really, Ro?"

"Shit!" he yells, stepping into his boxers. "I thought you were in the shower." He fumbles to get his leg into the second hole and all but falls to the floor. "I was just going to change and go use Jay's bathroom." Typical, two-shower a day Ronan, has to change from his sleep boxers into his morning boxers at the exact time that I exit the bathroom.

"Don't worry about it," I say, still holding my hands over my eyes. Again, I've seen all of him before, but not while I'm still trying to forget the way we woke up. "I just need a towel." I stand there, holding my pose until Ronan speaks.

"Here," he finally says, his voice merely inches from me. I lower my hands and see him standing there in just his boxers and jeans, shirtless, with sleep still in his eyes and the most perfect kink in the side of his hair. He holds out a towel and our fingers barely touch as I take it from his extended hand.

"Sorry again," he says, turning to leave but not before I see goosebumps on his bare upper-half.

Claire comes downstairs for our trip to the spa, and her face is glistening even before our facials. "Why are you damp?" I ask her, pouring coffee into a second to-go cup.

Luckily Ronan is still in the shower, so I'm trying to leave before he comes down. I'm having a hard enough time shaking the previous image of him without witnessing anymore. There is no need for me to see his muscles gleaming from a steamy shower and him walking around with just a towel wrapped around the V of his—.

"I'm sweating," Claire says, interrupting my thought, and it's only now that she's closer that I notice she's not only clammy, but she's borderline green.

"Hungover?"

"A smidge."

She brings the egg sandwich I have wrapped in a napkin up to her nose and gags before even taking a sniff.

"A smidge, huh?" I laugh. "Are you still okay to go to the spa today?"

She holds up a finger, turns on the sink, and chugs straight from the faucet. Wiping her mouth with the back of her hand, she closes her eyes and takes a deep breath before answering with a resounding, "Maybe."

"Claire, we don't—"

"No," she cuts in, pulling her hair to the top of her head. "I'm good. A spa day will be perfect."

I watch as she moves, collecting her things, stopping every so often to regather herself. Five minutes later, she throws her bag over her arm and winces as it lands on her shoulder.

"All set?" I ask, trying to hide my amusement.

"All set."

We walk down the driveway as I mess with my phone, trying to plug the address to the spa into my Maps. When we get to the car, Claire loses her jacket.

"This place is everything," she says, her breath visible in the morning cold. You'd think she'd be chilly, but the way she inhales like she was drowning before, tells me it's more refreshing than frigid.

"I think you're just really hungover."

"My insides feel like they're trying to escape."

"That'll do it," I say, but I must admit, this cool, vacant air is energizing. I felt it when I first arrived, and having been this hungover, I can see how it might be exactly what she needs to detox herself and reset the tone for the rest of the day.

We get into the car, and I crank up the heat, then crack the windows just enough to bring the outside in. Claire and I spend the ride talking about nonsense, listening to music, and attempting to distract a certain someone from her queasy stomach. Thirty minutes and one cautious pull over later, we make it to The Opal Oasis.

The building in front of us is made of white stone with floor to ceiling windows lining the front. As we walk through the doors, we're hit with the sound of a steady, trickling waterfall that flows down the side wall. The stream runs into a pool layered with stones to match the spa's name. They reflect the light from the windows, playing different colors into the water. There's dull, zen music that sounds like chimes played in nature, and the smell of lavender that makes Claire dry-heave.

"Oh my God," she chokes. "What is that smell?"

"I think it's supposed to be relaxing."

"Well it's not," she says. "It's nauseating."

"I'm sure you'll get used to it."

Claire is fanning the smell away from her nose when a woman with glowing skin, a crisp white tunic, and a name tag that reads **Giselle** comes to the desk.

"Welcome to The Opal Oasis," she says, her voice as tranquil as the music itself. "Do you have an appointment with us today?"

"We do," I say. "Under Carlson."

"My little Swedish meatball," Claire says, squeezing my cheek, but the second the word *meatball* falls from her mouth, she turns a suspicious shade of gray and cups her hand around her mouth.

"Oh, dear," Giselle says, clearly appalled by the situation at hand.

"Bathroom?" Claire mumbles from behind her palm.

The lady points to a door off to the side, luckily just a few feet from where we're standing. Claire rushes to it, slamming the door behind her, surely break-ing several norms of spa etiquette along the way.

"She'll be fine," I whisper in an attempt to wash the horrified look from Giselle's face. She smiles politely and hands me two robes and our day's itinerary.

"Here is your schedule for the day," she says peacefully. "Snacks and drinks at your designated time, or cucumber water at any point of the day, can be found in the Crystal Cafe through the door to your right. Lunch will be served to you poolside, and any down time you may have can be spent in the women's suite, the cafe, or the gardens out back."

I nod calmly, soothed by the sound of her voice, as Claire rejoins us looking surprisingly close to her natural color.

"Thank you," I say to Giselle who responds with a smile, looks at Claire, and then promptly glides away.

"She hates me," Claire says.

"Probably."

Claire smacks my shoulder. "Hey, as my maid of honor, you are not supposed to agree with statements like that." She snatches the itinerary from my hands.

"Well, as the bride," I say, grabbing it back. "You're supposed to be spending today pampering for the wedding, not decorating the toilet bowl."

"Ha ha, very funny. For your information, I'm feeling much better. And that bathroom has heated floors. My knees are pleasantly warmed."

"Well, alright then," I say, weaving my arm through hers. "Puke and rally—spa edition."

By the end of our day, Claire and I are both feeling relaxed and refreshed. Somewhere around the seasonal facial, Claire started to get her mojo back. It might have been the twenty minute sauna that expelled all of the alcohol out of her system, but by lunchtime, we were back in business.

Our food was delivered to our indoor cabana by the pool. After scarfing down our cool winter salads with candied pecans and goat cheese and chasing them with pomegranate and pear infused tea, we were ready to hit the hot tub until it was time for our massage. Soaking in the jacuzzi, Claire and I finally get to talk about the wedding, just the two of us.

"So, how do you feel?" I ask Claire, laying my head back on the ledge and letting the jets work their magic on my stress-riddled shoulders.

"So much better. I mean, damn, I know I had too many drinks, but it's nothing I haven't done before."

"Maybe your old age is showing," I say. "But I meant about the wedding, you goof." I crack an eye open and catch Claire giving me a fake death stare from across the tub.

"Oh, that?" she asks. "That I'm not worried about." She brushes it off like I asked her the weather and slides slightly lower into the bubbles.

"You're not nervous at all?" Again, I know as the maid of honor I'm supposed to be the one steering the bride away from negative thoughts, but I can't help it. Claire just seems so cool and collected for someone who is completely changing her life in the span of a week.

"Not at all," she says. "I love Jay."

"Well, yeah, but that doesn't mean you aren't anxious about getting married."

"I mean, sure, I'm hoping there's no rain and that Aunt Shirley doesn't dance on the table, but as far as the actual marriage, why would I be anxious? I'm going to be with Jay either way."

Exactly, I think. *So why even risk it?*

"Are you ever afraid it'll change you guys? Ruin what you have?" I cringe as I say it, knowing these are not the words that should be coming from my mouth. But how can Claire and I think so differently about something when we're so much alike?

"The same way a piece of paper can't save a relationship, it can't destroy it either, Chlo. I know your family doesn't have the best track record, but your relationship isn't just left up to fate." I look at her sideways. "Or a curse," she adds on. "You aren't your mom or your sisters, and Ronan's not your dad either. Yes, you Carlsons have had a string of bad luck—unfortunate coincidences maybe—but you can't let that define your relationship, or your entire future, with the person you love."

"I know," I say, but even I'm not convinced by my quiet response.

Claire slides around so we're sitting next to each other. "I'm serious, Chloe. One day, hopefully soon... " She squeals a little on those last two words. "Ronan is going to ask you to marry him, and I hope for all of our sakes that you're brave enough to say yes."

Panic rushes through me, and I'm suddenly feeling overheated, but it has nothing to do with the hot tub I'm sitting in. "Because it would mess up our friendship?" I ask. Just hearing it out loud is enough to bring me to tears.

"What? Of course not. Nothing could come between me and you, and nothing could come between Ronan and Jay. We're family, Chlo, and so are they. What I mean is, you guys are better versions of yourselves when you're together. You're still your sweet and silly self, but you're also focused and motivated. Plus, you haven't let your phone die because you left your charger in the car once this past year."

I laugh with tears slowly forming behind my eyes. She's right. Ro does make me better, and I haven't felt like that version of myself for almost a month now.

Claire takes my hand under the water. "Same goes for Ronan, you know. He was successful before, and confident, and he has that fine ass…"

"Yes!" I yell realizing that—A. I said it out loud and B. I still can't believe I didn't notice that man has a peach until yesterday.

"But you make him fun and allow him to let loose in ways that even Jay has never seen before. You both bring out the best in each other, and that's what makes a marriage last—or fail."

At this point, tears are streaming down my freshly peeled face, celebrating how Claire sees us and mourning that she won't ever see it again. I look up at Claire whose face mirrors mine. "Wait, why are you crying?"

"I don't know! I just got really emotional." She wipes her snot with the back of her hand. "Why are *you* crying?"

I fumble over my words, easily hiding it as powerful sobs. "I just, I—that was so nice to hear."

Claire throws her arms around my neck, and we both let it out—Claire's wedding emotions getting the best of her and my pent up tears finally releasing from the last few weeks. I hold my best friend, imagining the sight of two twenty-somethings embracing in a hot tub, one in cheetah print and the other in fire engine red.

"We are totally in the opening scene of some porno right now," I say, pulling away from Claire and laughing at the thought.

"Perv." She laughs too, and the sincere look on her face makes it so the truth almost comes pouring right out of me.

I want to be honest. I want to hear her advice. Let her tell me what she thinks I should do. But I can't.

Not yet.

Not until after this week.

12

Before

This week has been absolute chaos. Between finishing up at school before break, trying to see Ronan while he's swamped at work, and the random snow storm that snuck in out of nowhere, my lateness has taken on a whole new level. This is why, on December 23rd, me and all of the other batshit crazy people are scouring Center Springs mall for our last minute gifts.

Parking was... well... like trying to find parking at a mall near Christmas. Now that I'm inside, I get the added joys of navigating pedestrian traffic on probably the most stressful day of the year. Let's just hope everyone's in the holiday spirit.

I start at the place I always do at Center Springs—Auntie Anne's Pretzels—because nothing says shopping-fuel like soft, buttery dough coated in cinnamon sugar.

I get in the line that is somehow just a few people long, when I see an all too familiar bicep sticking out of the queue, bulging under the weight of a bag. I move from my place to join the person who's second in line and get quite a nasty look from a teenage thug-wannabe who's in spot number three. Thankfully, my new line buddy is the equivalent of Hercules—if he had tattoos and a military style haircut.

"Jam Man!" I call, tapping Jay on the arm. I stand close beside him, making a point to the kid behind us that I'm in cahoots with the inked god in front of him.

Jay turns to me, his face a permanent scowl, probably due to the fact that he's here in the first place. His eyes flit to me and then to the pretzel stand. His cheeks turn a nice shade of rose when he realizes he's not only been caught at the mall alone, but he's standing in line for a sweet, little treat.

"What are you doing here?" he asks, glancing around frantically. "Who are you with?"

I snap in his face, drawing his attention away from the crowd and back down to me. "Calm down there, buddy. I'm just shopping like everyone else here. And it's just me." When those last words leave my mouth, Jay's whole body relaxes. "What's your problem?"

"I thought you might be with Claire." His eyes dart to the bag that hangs from his hand.

"Excuse me, but did you just now, on December 23rd, buy your future wife her Christmas present?"

The scowl is back but directed towards me. "Maybe," he says.

"Interesting," I say, drawing out the word like I might be able to use this to my advantage.

"Don't you'dare say anything." He points a finger at me.

"Oh, I won't. But I'm keeping this little secret... " I tap my temple. "Right here."

Jay rolls his eyes as the kiosk worker calls us up to order our pretzels.

"Two cinnamon sugar, please," I say. "He's paying." I wink at Jay playfully, knowing full well the big softie would never have let me buy my own anyway.

"Wait a second," Jay says, handing his card to the clerk. Her red and green elf hat jingles as she moves to the register. "Who are you shopping for?"

"Uhh… Ronan," I say, muffled under a cough. Jay looks at me blankly. "Ronan," I repeat clearly. "It's been a crazy week, and you know I do everything at the last minute. Claire, and you of course," I lie, "were easy. But I had to think about Ro's, and I had no ideas until earlier this week." I grab the bag of pretzels from the counter and continue my rant as we walk away from the stand. "I was going to come after school one day, but it snowed so I didn't go anywhere. Then he was actually home one night so I spent time with him instead, and now—"

"Jesus," he interrupts. "You sound like Claire, rambling like that. Relax. Your secret's safe... " he mimics my movement of tapping his temple and winks. "Right here."

"Fine, we're even." I roll my eyes, and we spend the next five minutes in sugary bliss as we scarf down our pretzels.

"So, what'd you get?" I ask, reaching for Jay's bag once I have thoroughly licked my fingers clean.

"Nothing," he says, pulling it back.

"Oh, come on. Let me see."'

After a quick tug-of-war, he finally submits. I crack open the bag, and my mouth falls open. Looking at Jay, who's wearing a sheepish smile, I cock my head to one side and look him up and down.

"What?" he asks.

"Oh nothing. Just trying to decide if a regular-sized coffin will hold your dead body when Claire kills you for this or if you need a specialty one made for behemoths."

Jay pulls the bag back from me, the weight of its contents causing it to swing back and forth.

"She wanted it!" he argues before I speak again.

"Don't," I say.

"We need one!"

"You just got engaged! And you're not eighty-five."

"It was on sale!"

"It's a vacuum!" I yell, and the knockoff gangster from in line shoots me a look from the bench where he sits eating his snack.

Jay looks around, already hating being somewhere this crowded, let alone drawing more unwanted attention. He speaks in a way that's overly calm—his way of telling me to dial it back. "It's a nice, *expensive* vacuum."

"It sucks up dirt, and it's not even cordless," I say, emotionless. Jay practically growls at me but then pauses and waits for me to continue. "Do you want some help, J-Bone?" I ask.

He hangs his head and attempts to hide both his shame and the vacuum. "Yes, please."

We wandered around the mall for the next forty-five minutes, bopping between stores for Claire and ones for Ronan.

Jay decided to keep the vacuum but also bought Claire a cozy, chic robe and cute matching slippers for when she stays up late or wakes up early to work on her writing. I opted on cologne for Ro because even Jay said he's had the same one since ninth grade. I'll pair it with the graphic tee that I got him last week online that says, **DILL WITH IT** where the "I" in **DILL** is shaped like a pickle. He'll love the whole thing.

Now, as we walk towards the exit, leaving the chaos, Jay slows to a stop. "You know, don't let this go to your head or anything," he says smiling, "but Ro's crazy about you."

I bat my eyelashes. "Obviously."

"I'm serious," he laughs. "That kid has always been so focused on work that I didn't think anyone would be able to get his attention. But then you came around, and for the last year, he's been captivated by you."

"I don't know if I'd say captivated."

"I would," he says. "And these last two months, forget it."

I blush and play with the cuff of my sleeve. As much as I held my breath at the beginning, Ronan and I are really happy now that we're together. I already knew that I was falling hard, but it's nice to hear Jay solidify that it's mutual for both of us.

The last time I had a serious boyfriend, it was freshman year of college. At that point, what even qualifies as serious? Nate James (With Two First Names), as everyone called him, walked me to an occasional class and made out with me at basement keggers. Were we madly in love? I guess I thought I was at the time. But did it feel even remotely close to how I feel with Ronan? Absolutely not. Since then, I haven't been serious with anybody. There were the occasional second or third dates, and then there was Connor—Or should I say Seth? He was the guy who took me to Cabo over Spring Break a few years ago, only for me to find out he was a liar and a criminal who stole people's credit cards to pretend he was rich.

All of that to say, it makes me happy to hear that Ro feels the same—that he's into me as much as I'm into him—but it also terrifies me to know that we both feel this way. It's only been a few weeks. Sure, we've had plenty of warm up, but it's hard to imagine where we'll be in a year, and for now, my views on my future haven't quite changed.

"Oh, Jay… Don't try to butter me up so I forget you almost bought my best friend a vacuum cleaner for Christmas," I say, ignoring my nerves.

"Oh my God, she wants— you know what? Never mind." He picks up speed as we walk through the exit. "Merry Christmas, Chlo!" He yells over his shoulder, but at the last minute, he turns around and winks before heading to his car.

"Happy HoliJays!" I call back, and even I cringe as it comes out of my mouth.

"Do you like it?"

"Are you kidding me?" I say, sitting in front of my tiny tree, pulling the yoga bag from the box it was wrapped in. It's spacious enough to hold all of my stuff, with exterior straps to slide my mat into. It has a side pocket for my water bottle and a separate wet-bag pocket for my sweaty clothes after hot yoga. Add in that it's an adorable white and teal chevron, and you'd think I designed it myself. "It's perfect."

"Good," Ronan says from the spot next to me, and for the third time since he's opened it, he smells his new cologne. "It's like you dipped nature in cinnamon, then lit it on fire."

"That is oddly specific."

He shrugs. "Guy stuff." We look at each other and both start laughing.

Waking up on Christmas morning with Ronan was everything. For years I woke up at my mom's, which is fun and all, but it loses its appeal once you're well into your twenties. My parents, despite now living in separate households, attempt to keep our childhood traditions alive. Dad comes over for cinnamon rolls, and there are always joint gifts for us under the tree. We spend the morning unwrapping presents and laughing at the ones that Dad thought were funny. We pick at appetizers and listen to carols, and it always ends with full bellies and Mom's favorite version of *The Grinch* on TV.

I like spending the holiday with my family, but this year with Ronan around, I thought it'd be nice to wake up together. I'll call my parents later, along with each of my sisters, and my group chat will flood with goofy pictures. Casey will send ones at work in Santa scrubs or reindeer antlers, and Cara will take one of herself looking grouchy in the festive pajamas Mom will inevitably pick out. I'll miss them, but we'll see each other on New Years. So, for now I'm enjoying just being with Ro.

"I can't believe we got his and her t-shirts without even knowing it," I say, holding up the graphic tee Ro got me that says **SASSHOLE** across the front.

"Talk about perfect," he says, and I wind the shirt up and whip him with it on the arm.

"You love my sASS," I say, emphasizing the last three letters. Ronan leaps on top of me, pinning my arms above my head and the strap of my yoga bag underneath my back.

"I love a lot more than that," he says smiling. I know how he means it, but my chest grows so tight that I have to look at the space between my body and where he hovers above it, to make sure he's not physically pinning me there as well.

Ronan's eyes wander my body beneath him before finding mine again, looking back and forth between the two. "Hey," he says, tilting my chin up to him. "Where'd you go?"

I part my lips to speak, but nothing comes out. I feel my face change as my mind catches up to my body's response.

"Chlo," Ronan says tentatively, rolling onto his side. I miss him suspended above me like the warmth of a fire that you can feel without touching, my arms now abandoned behind me without his firm hands on my wrists.

My thoughts are reeling from this one simple banter, in spite of my body that's still in comparison. I think about this moment, our morning, my conversation with Jay. The last week, the last two months—hell, the last full year. I study the

94

ceiling, the memories flying behind my eyes like they're on a conveyor belt that just ends out of nowhere. A slow tingle of anticipation makes its way up from the pit of my stomach, and I feel it all happening just a moment behind, my head just a follower to my body that's leading.

"Chloe," Ronan says as if it's not the first time he's tried to get my attention. I turn just my face towards his, the rest of me still lying flat on the floor. "When I said that, I didn't—"

"I love you," I say, rotating my body so we're now chest to chest. I brace my weight on my forearm, Ronan's head pulling away from the hand it was propped up on.

He looks at me, a mixture of shock and pure joy, but he doesn't say anything back. I sit up, suddenly very aware of the fact that he may not reciprocate my statement. This wouldn't be the first time I just blurted out my thoughts. It is, however, the first time I've said those three words to a guy since Nate James (With Two First Names), who seduced me into it. He surprised me with tickets to our campus concert that he purchased for $12 at the Student Center. I mean, how else does one respond to that kind of romance?

Unlike Nate though, Ronan led me here by just being himself. So, this *is* the first time I've said I love you to someone based solely off of how I felt. It just never occurred to me, until now, that he may not feel the same.

"Did I make things weird?" I ask. "I feel like I made things weird." Ronan sits up to join me, shaking his head.

He blinks slowly like he's lost in a thought. "I just can't believe you said it first." He snorts out a breath when my mouth drops open. "Miss I'm-Scared-of-Commitment, not so scared anymore?"

"Whatever! I take it back then." I go to nudge his shoulder, but he grabs my wrist before I make contact with his arm.

He scoots closer to me so we're just inches apart. "Can't do that," he whispers.

"And why not?" I ask, pursing my lips and folding my arms across my chest.

He leans in and brings his forehead to mine. "Because I love you too... you little sasshole."

13

Now

We pull into the stone driveway of the cabin and see the boys outside, their backs to us in jeans and hoodies. They're off toward the back of the land, huddled around a low tree stump with chunks of wood at their feet in every direction. They don't even notice us pull in as we turn off the car and study the scene.

"What are they doing way out there?" Claire asks.

"And what's with the wood?" I say. Ronan turns sideways to step back from the stump, and it's only then that we see the dull metal Jay is holding by his side. "Is that an—"

"Oh, this is too good," Claire interrupts, and we both lean forward for a better look. Claire is half on my dashboard as I pull on the steering wheel to hoist myself higher—one of the many downfalls of being this small. I'm almost to my knees when I see Jay swing a long, wooden handle with a rectangular head into the air, and at the same time, my body leans on the horn.

My car honks, loud and long. I fumble myself back down to the seat, as Jay spins his body toward us, releasing the ax that then goes flying behind him. My hands fly to cover my mouth, and Claire busts out laughing. Now that his body's facing us, we can see there is a large log standing upright on the tree stump.

"What the hell do they think they are, lumberjacks?" Claire spits out through laughter. My mind instantly goes to Ro in a wide open flannel with a big, bushy beard, and now I'm cackling too... and somewhat turned on. My eyes find him on instinct. He's staring at Jay, half amused and half shocked, as Jay searches for the tool that went rogue on the ground.

Claire opens her door and steps out, and before even closing it, she catcalls to Jay. "Nice moves there, Paul Bunyan!" Jay finds her, his face quickly turning from stern to light-hearted, as he throws up his arms in defeat.

I join Claire outside of the car, attempting my best whistle. Ronan and Jay look at each other and snicker before walking towards us in the driveway. "That thing swinging back over there, Errington?" I pull my bag from the car and throw the door shut.

"We were doing just fine before you two showed up," he says, and he looks at Ro like, *can I get an amen?*

"Poor baby," Claire says, falling into his arms. "I'm sure you showed that thing who's boss *right* before we got here."

Ro looks back at the scraps of wood surrounding the stump. Some are thick wedges and some tiny splinters—none of them remotely resembling useful logs—and all of them proving Claire wrong.

"We figured we'd give the man thing a try since you guys were having a girl's day." Ronan brushes his hands on the side of his pants. He looks down at himself, mud on his sleeve and sweat at his collar, then looks at Claire and me. We're cozy in loungewear, relaxed and rejuvenated, our faces glistening with nearly invisible pores. "Maybe we should have had a girl's day instead."

"Seriously," Jay says, throwing his arm around Claire. "You guys look refreshed and recharged. We're a mess, and I'm sore as hell."

"Well, you have a few hours of recovery time before we head back to Pine Village," I say as Jay wipes his brow.

"Come on, babe," Claire says, tapping his chest. "Let's get you iced and cleaned up." They walk in together, arms wrapped around each other, as Jay gimps dramatically holding onto Claire's shoulder.

"Pussy!" Ro calls, and Jay flips him off from behind Claire's head.

"How about you?" I ask Ronan, brushing my foot back and forth in the dirt. "Ax throwing not really your thing?"

He takes off his beanie and runs his hand through his hair, the front of it slicked back from the sweat at his forehead. "I think I'll stick to throwing pizzas instead." I chuckle and nod, adjusting my bag in the crease of my elbow.

"Here, let me take that," he says, tugging on the strap.

"No, it's fine," I say. "You're probably tired." He insists, pulling it down lower until his cool hand brushes the inside of my wrist.

I all but throw my bag from his touch, his chilled fingers more like matches to the sensitive spot on my skin. It falls to the ground, its contents spilling onto the stones.

"Shit, sorry," Ro says, leaning down toward my things.

"Stop apologizing," I say, and my cheeks grow warm, remembering his reasons for doing it before.

"Sorry." He looks up at me, smiling slyly, putting the contents one by one back into the bag. I reach for my still damp bikini, but Ro grabs it first, holding the top up by the strings. He raises his eyebrow in my direction as I snatch it from his grip.

"Some spa day," he says teasingly, but the way I feel his eyes on the place it would cover, is far from funny.

I gather the rest all together and shove the handful, still half-covered in gravel, back into place. "It was great, thank you very much."

He chuckles softly. "I'm glad you guys had a good time." He shoves both hands in his pockets, and I use mine to secure the straps of my bag high on my shoulder as we turn to walk towards the cabin.

"And how was your day?"

"It was good," he says nodding. "Watched the game, ate some food—"

"Hacked some wood," I interrupt.

He laughs as we climb the stairs. "We sure as hell tried," he says, and instinctively we both stop on the porch.

"I'm sure you gave it all you had," I say, looking into his eyes, the blue somehow brighter in this damn cabin air. He has a smudge of dirt on his cheekbone, and it takes everything in me not to brush it away.

"I did," he says looking down at his feet. He lingers there until his eyes rejoin mine, and I swear they're now a shade darker than they just were. "I did," he repeats. "I always do."

Ronan and I left things in a weird place... again. I don't know if I was reading too much into it, but—*I always do?*—What the hell was that supposed to mean? Was he insinuating that he gave his all to our relationship and that *I* didn't in comparison? Or was he just really freaking into splitting those logs with a razor sharp weapon? Regardless of his intentions, we came into the house and went our separate ways. He and Jay stood around the kitchen talking shit about the wood that fought back, and I took my yoga mat onto the porch.

Today was so peaceful, and it was nice to spend time with just me and Claire. It didn't really hit me until I was focused in tree pose, which is incredibly hard in this many layers, that today may have been the last time for a while that we spend just the two of us. Between the wedding, her honeymoon, and me back at work, I know we'll catch up, but it won't be the same. I'm not going to be dramatic. I know we won't stop being friends, but Claire will want to spend her free time with Jay. They'll be in that new marital bliss that everyone talks about, and I'll be an entirely new form of third-wheel.

Not to mention what will happen when the truth comes out about Ronan and me. Jay will obviously side with Ro, and Claire will tell me that nothing will change, but that just can't be true. She may be around more at first, helping me through it, but eventually life will fall back into place. Our foursome will become a trio of my best friend and her boys, and I'll be at home with comfort movies and my damn apple nachos.

Now, laying in corpse pose for entirely too long, I decide that this means I just have to make the most of the next fifteen hours. Tonight, we are heading back to Pine Village, the little town in the middle of nowhere with Posto Felice, that seemed to glisten against the black of the sky. We decided after dinner last night that we had to explore it but that we *(Claire)* weren't in the right mindset to really enjoy it. We left tonight open with nothing planned, so we put our outing off until then.

I roll up my mat and head back inside. Despite the cold, I've worked up a sweat, so I strip off my jacket and sweatshirt on the way up the stairs. When I get into our room, I hear the shower turn off, and I purposely slam the bedroom door shut so Ronan knows that I'm here. Neither me, nor my blood pressure, are capable of risking another accidental mooning.

I'm down to my tank top and leggings and am desperate for a shower, when I look at my phone and see I'm also short on time. I hear Ronan start the sink for his post shower ritual of brushing his teeth. I realize I may not have enough time to be respectably late if I wait for him to finish the other steps in his routine—deodorant, hair gel, cologne—so I tap on the door.

"Hey, I'm sorry, can I just get in there?"

The lock unlatches, and the door creeps open. Steam filters out into the room as the picture of Ronan before me comes into view. His hair has yet to be done, a stray wave falling onto his forehead. His skin is still wet, either from the shower or the haze, and a towel hangs loosely around his hips. With the sheen of the water, his body is enhanced, each curve and every indent, made more stark and prominent. The sparrow tattoo that he and Jay got when they were young, flaps its wings over his chest muscle as he casually lifts his arm to rest his forearm on the doorframe.

"Stop apologizing," he says, the corners of his lip curling up slowly.

"Sorry," I say sarcastically.

He steps to the side and motions for me to come in. "I can finish when you're done." He goes to pull the door behind him, but I grab it first and hold it open.

"It's okay," I say, before I have a chance to regret it. I don't know if it's my newfound motivation to make tonight awesome, our short window of time, or my subconscious obsession of how he looks in that towel, but I decide that him staying is for the best.

"We don't have much time. You can keep getting ready," I pull open the shower curtain. "I can shower with you." Ronan's eyebrows lift. I step one foot in the tub. "I mean with you in here." He sucks his teeth. "Well not in *here*. Just..." Ro crosses his arms and leans his hip on the sink. "You know what I mean."

"I know what you mean." He smiles, but there's curiosity behind it. He reaches for his deodorant as I throw the curtain shut and close my eyes.

I take a deep breath before yanking off my tank top. Reaching for the bottom of my sports bra, I start to worry. Between my sweat, the steam, and it already being a bit too tight, I struggle to work the fabric up my back, which happens way more frequently than I'd like to admit. Worry turns to panic as I tug and pull. It only rises a couple of inches, now awkwardly stuck higher in some spots than others. I spin around unnecessarily, like turning the radio down when you're looking for your turn, and wind up banging my elbow on the wall of the shower. I sigh dramatically.

Ronan's voice slips through the curtain closer than it should be if he were still at the sink. "Everything okay in there?"

"Uh, yeah," I say, crossing my arms over my chest. I tear at the elastic on either side of my ribs. "Totally fine."

"Chlo... "

"Yeah?" My tone sounds like I'm eager for questions despite wanting to discuss literally anything else but this.

"Are you stuck?"

"No." I answer way too quickly, my voice so much higher than normal.

"Chloe... "

When I don't say anything, Ronan's fingers slide between the curtain and the wall. "I'm opening this," he says as he cautiously slides it ever so slowly like he's waiting for my objection.

Having done all I can—left it all on the field—I use a lack of protest as my sign of permission, the elastic of my sports bra now crammed up my arm pits. The loops at the top of the curtain skate over the metal bar that it hangs from, breaking the divide between Ronan and me. I surrender to him, completely defeated. We've been here before. Usually it's more of a joke than a near-death situation, but by the pink rising up my exposed chest, I'm extremely close to dying of embarrassment this time.

"Turn around," he says gently, but my face must show reluctance because he feels the need to explain. "Just turn around. I'll lift it up and close the curtain. You can face the wall the entire time."

All I can think is, *thank God I didn't start with my leggings.* This is humiliating enough. Doing this pantsless would be down right mortifying. I exhale loudly, then turn towards the wall, lifting my arms above my shoulders. I feel Ronan step into the tub, his body now mere inches from mine.

His hands first touch the top of my ribs, and as if there's a sensor under the skin, my flesh ignites into goosebumps. I hear Ronan inhale at the same time that his fingers work their way under the band of my bra. Ronan shimmies the fabric up past my shoulders and over the length of my arms. I feel him blow out a soft, slow breath, the air landing like ash on my skin.

I bring my arms to my chest, covering what he has seen a million times before. I look over my shoulder to see Ro staring at my back, only it's more like he's thinking in a fixated spot than actually looking at my figure. "Thanks," I say, my voice barely above a whisper.

Ronan slowly lifts his head until his eyes find mine. My heart rate rises with every inch, and his chest expands more and more with each breath. He brings his hand to my elbow and leans his weight closer to me, closing what little gap lies between us. I follow his movement with only my eyes, my body frozen because I'm scared of what's happening and terrified that if I move... it'll stop.

He brings his mouth so it's almost touching the curve of my neck, then passes his parted lips past my skin, landing his forehead in their place instead.

I lean the side of my head against his, my body still covered, but his bare chest is now pressed to my back. I breathe in the scent of a sweet-smelling campfire—the cologne part of his routine already done.

"Chloe," he exhales, raising his head. "I don't know how to do this."

I swallow, then lick my lips, my mouth suddenly wet and dry all at once. "Do what?"

"Pretend I don't still want you."

The second the words leave his mouth, I know I'm breaking rule number one. Nobody's here, and we definitely don't have to, but if you ask me, no situation has ever called for a kiss more than this one. "Then don't." I drop my arms and spin so my chest is on his. He clenches his jaw, his arms still by his side, as he tries reading my face for more explanation.

I bring my lips so they hover just over his, tempting us both. "I dare ya," I say, and the second I do, his lips are on mine.

We stay interlocked, our kiss deep and passionate, our hands roaming to make up for lost time. Ronan gathers my hair to one side and attempts to wind it around his hand like he has so many times before. He laughs into my mouth when for the third time, it spills from his fist, the cut now too short to make it all the way around.

I, on the other hand, push both of my hands into his hair, pulling and combing the unfamiliar locks—exploring them like uncharted land. Every time I tug it gently in my grasp, Ronan makes a guttural sound, and I make it a goal to coax it from him again and again.

Dropping his hands from my hair in defeat, Ro drags his fingertips down the length of my spine. I arch away from his touch, feeling him beneath the thin towel that's all that sits between us. I trail my hands down his chest, then trace the V that leads to the edge of the fabric. My fingers dip just barely underneath it, when there's a pounding on our bedroom door.

"Ten minutes!" Jay yells from the hallway. I still completely at the sound of his voice, my fingers now clutching the knot on the towel.

Ronan, whose hands now rest at my hips, squeezes me harder and lets out a groan. He stares at me like he's searching for something or maybe just taking me in one more time. I look back, a combination of questioning and longing, knowing that if this were a month ago, he'd tell Jay he could shove that ten minutes wherever he wanted—we'd be done when we're done.

Now, instead of doing that, he kisses me gently one more time, then steps out of the shower, closes the curtain, and walks away.

14

Before

"Last chance to walk, " I say, turning to Ro. We're standing on the front steps of my childhood home, and I'm graciously offering him the chance to run from meeting my mom and two sisters.

"No way, I'm good," Ro says, and he truly looks confident. There's no jitters, no sweating, no nervous fingers—typical Ronan—calm and collected.

"There is just like... a lot of estrogen in there."

Ronan sticks out his bottom lip, nodding his head. "Sounds perfect, honestly."

I smack his arm, almost hitting the flowers he's holding. "Well, alright then, smartass."

Pushing open the door, I'm hit with a blast from the past. This always happens when I walk into Mom's— the smells, the sounds, the shoes in a pile. It's suddenly ten years ago, and everything's perfect. I kick off my boots to add to the others, and Ronan does the same, tossing his Converse next to what I can only assume are Casey's sneakers.

She was always the tomboy—soccer cleats instead of ballet slippers, sweatpants versus skirts, Nikes over Uggs. She liked to blend in, and she liked to be comfortable, where Cara was the girlie girl. There were never too many sparkles and always not enough bows. She liked clothes that made a statement and by default, made her the center of attention. It's funny because you would think as three sisters, we would all share our clothes, but between the age gaps and the differences in styles, we usually all ended up with new things. I, personally, was always right in the middle. I like certain frills but also prefer to be cozy. I like bold statement pieces but pair them with more neutral staples. Basically, I'm the best combination of the other two girls.

We head towards the family room, and the usual vocals trail through the halls—Cara's theatrics, Casey's loud voice, and Mom's soft laugh in the rare pockets of silence. I smile at the sound, but I can't help but think that there's something that's missing.

It's funny, I always feel like a teenager walking into this house. It's all so nostalgic and seems so familiar, like a time warp bringing me back to my youth. Then, my biggest concerns were having enough time in the shower and not snoozing my alarm for my 8am class. But now there are reminders that it's not all the same.

Dad isn't gone. In fact, he's right across town, and he'll even stop by later today, but his absence is a void in this house. It's dulled over time, a now muted alarm, but it's there all the same—everything's different. I reach over to Ronan, placing my hand in his, and my heart fills with appreciation for him... and for us. I give it a squeeze, as a thanks and a warning, and then bound around the corner to where my family is waiting.

"Ahhh," we all scream. An echo of shrieks and yelps consume the room, and my sisters leap off the couch and run over to us. There's a group hug of squealing, the three of us jumping and spinning, and then suddenly there's four sets of arms in the mix.

Somehow Ronan gets pulled into our embrace, and when we separate, he looks a little afraid for his life. "I told you we're a lot," I say laughing, then I go in for one more hug from my sisters.

There are eight years between the three of us, and that lends itself to some undeniable differences, but my sisters and I have always been close. Cara doted on me like I was her baby, and Casey bossed me around because she finally could. I was pushed around and fawned over, and I loved every second of it. Of course, there were years where our lives didn't overlap like they once did. Cara went off to college, and I wasn't even in middle school yet. Casey learned to drive, and I was just finally comfortable riding my bike around town. We always came back together though—an inseparable bond between the three of us girls.

There were other times, of course, where we were like animals. Cara was home over break, Casey was in the thick of high school, and I was the annoying little sister. Our cycles would sync, and we'd be feral and nasty, and Mom would do everything but lock us in a room and force us to figure it out. But at the end of the day, I always had them.

Now, things are a little bit different. We don't all live near each other, our jobs are insane, and Cara swears that somewhere over time, our age gap was lengthened. Apparently there's no way she's the only one almost forty. We have different interests, friends, and personal lives, but when we're together, none of that matters.

"To be fair, you did warn me," Ro says, making it a point to push his hair into place and straighten his sweater like he got mauled by lions instead of us three.

"Ro, this is Cara and Casey. Girls, this is Ronan." They exchange pleasantries, each girl hugging him again, this time less viciously.

"Okay, he is way better looking than you let on," Cara whispers, but because we're all in a group, everyone hears.

"What now?" Ro asks, spinning towards me.

"Taller too," Casey adds. She turns to Cara. "So, do you think she under played the size of—"

"And that's enough," I chime in. Ronan looks at me, eyes wide and brows raised, with a suspicious smile forming on his lips. "You be quiet." I wink and lead him away from my sisters, who I have to remember to kill before I leave. We head back towards my mother who stands from the couch.

"And this is my mom."

Ronan picks the bouquet off the arm of the sofa, that would have otherwise gotten crushed in the moment. "It's nice to meet you, Ms. Walters," he says, hugging her and offering the flowers.

Ro made it a point on our way here to ask what he should call my mom. I never really thought about it, being that I wasn't necessarily bringing Nate James (With Two First Names) home to meet my mother in between frat parties. Plus, to me she was still Evelyn Carlson. He asked me her maiden name and said he'd take it from there, but hearing it now, that void creeps back in.

"Oh, please, honey, call me Evelyn." Mom takes the flowers and brings them up to her nose. She breathes them in slowly, a gentle smile spreading across her face.

My mother is beautiful, inside and out. She's pleasant and kind, and she spent her life being a role model for three little girls. She does everything for everyone and never asks for anything in return. She is patient and our biggest cheerleader, and from the way she is smiling, she is... honestly happy.

One of my biggest worries after Mom and Dad's news was that something about them was going to change. I was blindsided by their little announcement and instantly felt like there was more I was missing. My parents were fun, attentive, and as calm as you can be with a house full of hormones. They spent time with us and supported our dreams. I guess I was scared that because their marriage wasn't what I thought it was, that everything else wasn't real too.

I was afraid that Mom wouldn't be happy or that Dad would be lonely, and like any teenager, I thought they were too old. Too old to change course. Too old to start over. Why would they waste the life they had left being potentially miserable? Was being together really that bad? But looking at Mom, her eyes bright, her cheeks a light pink, she doesn't look miserable. She looks content.

"My mom says peonies mean good luck, so I thought with it being New Year's... "

"Peonies are perfect," Mom says. "And we could all use a little extra luck from time to time." She leaves, presumably to put the flowers in water, and we both turn back to Cara and Casey.

"Speaking of New Years," Cara says. "What are our resolutions this year?"

"Well, mine is to get my ass out of that hospital. I swear, it's all I do." Casey looks to the sky, shaking her head. "If another man over ninety makes one more pass at me... "

"They still have you in geriatrics?" I ask.

"Yeah, and it's getting old."

"Ba-dum-tss," Ro says, earning a laugh from us girls.

"Well, mine is breaking this freaking curse," Cara says.

"Here we go." Ronan rolls his eyes. "Not you too."

"Oh, so she told you about the curse?" Casey asks, but she's looking at me.

"Relentlessly," he says. "But I don't buy it."

"I don't know. With our track records... " Casey says, gesturing to Cara. "Not to mention hers." She points to Mom who is coming back from the kitchen. "Feels pretty real to me."

"Oh, you two better not be going on about that stupid curse again," Mom says, waving away our conversation. "Ronan, don't believe a word they say. Their father and I got married so fast my head spun, and we still got over twenty good years from it. There is no Carlson Curse. You two just need some of that luck Ronan's spreading." She winks at Ro and pats the couch, telling him to take a seat.

"Well, whatever it is," Cara says. "I need it to change. Your big sis isn't getting any younger." She leans her head on mine, a quick reminder that I am quite literally the littlest sister.

"So, what's your resolution, handsome?" Mom asks, turning towards Ronan.

"I'm not sure I have one," he says. "I just know I want to make big moves this year." Ro stares at me, and my head goes to the restaurant plans that he's talked about before. But the way that he's looking not at me but through me, makes me feel like maybe there's a little more to it. I go to speak but as my lips part, the front door opens, and Dad's voice drifts in from afar.

"Hello!" he calls, and I'm taken right back to him coming home from work after a long day at the office, all of us girls rushing right to him.

Similarly now, we all turn towards the doorway, only instead of running to him and grabbing his legs, we wait for his arrival, Cara yelling, "We're in here!"

Dad rounds the corner, and he scans the group of us, his gaze settling on me. "Hey, Dad." I go to him, and he wraps his arms around me like he hasn't seen me in years. Much like my sisters, I don't see my parents nearly as much as I'd like to, but it hasn't been that long. Dad has just always been known for his hugs.

"You must be the boyfriend," Dad says, eying up Ronan, but he can't hold a straight face for even a minute.

Ro stands, walking over to Dad and extending his arm for a handshake. "Ronan, sir. It's nice to meet you."

Dad turns to us girls. "Did you hear that? He called me sir. Your old man's still got it."

"Oh, yeah, Dad. That's it," Casey snickers. Cara joins her, and I just shake my head and smile.

The six of us spend the next couple of hours talking about a little bit of everything. Ronan tells my parents about Enzo's and makes them promise that they'll come up soon and have a meal. My sisters and I try to map out a few times in the next couple of months where we can carve out time to see each other, and we all joke about stories from when we were younger.

It's not lost on me that so many people who go through a divorce can't coexist like my parents can. We're lucky that our family wasn't left completely broken, despite how much it felt like that when it was all still so fresh. Mom and Dad can still come together and spend time with their kids, laugh about memories, even meet my boyfriend. It's a nice silver lining, but I still wish this wasn't how it had to be.

"Okay, your parents are cool as hell," Ronan says when we get back in the car. I wish we could stay longer, but Ro has Enzo's, and I'm back to school after today.

"Your dad invited me to go golfing with him, but I'm not sure he knows how terrible I am."

"Please. There is no way that Jimmy Carlson is at all decent at golf."

"Perfect. Maybe he'll make me look good in comparison."

"You look good all by yourself," I say, reaching over and planting a kiss on his cheek. "Thanks again for coming with me and for driving all this way."

"Of course, babe." He places a hand on my knee. "I'd do anything for you, Chlo."

I look over at him as he glances back at the road. I take in his features, his bronze lashes and five o'clock shadow, like cinnamon dusting the upper part of his jaw. His eyes tend to glisten, the blue lighting up under the glow of the moon, and his lips are parted just slightly—welcoming, but only for me.

Ronan is good. He is patient and steady, and I've never met someone so pure in my life. Watching him interact with all of the people that mean the most to me today, was healing in a way I didn't even know that I needed.

"I love you," I say.

He studies me affectionately before responding. "I love you too, Chloe." I place my hand on his and then realize something.

Today is the start of a new year, a new beginning, and a brand new chapter. It's the start of three hundred and sixty-five days to spend however I want, with whoever I want. Three hundred and sixty-five opportunities that I plan to spend all with him.

And I can't see there ever being a year where I feel any differently.

15

Now

Pine Village is literally something out of a Hallmark movie. The little town is like a winter wonderland that is apparently decorated for all the cold months. There are cobblestone roads just for walking around and shops in every direction. Pop-up booths are scattered throughout with hot chocolate, cookies, and warm, classic cocktails, and there's a soft hum of instrumentals playing in the streets. We've been meandering around for just under an hour, and Claire and I are already in love.

"This place is like heaven," I say over my steaming hot toddy, either the alcohol or the atmosphere putting me in extra good spirits.

"Agreed," Claire says, stifling a yawn. "We should totally move here."

"No shot," Jay cuts in. "Could you imagine me revving my hot rod around here?"

Claire purses her lips in defeat. "Okay, fair." She walks another couple of feet before pausing. "I know! You guys move here!" Her eyes bounce back and forth between Ronan and me. Ro keeps walking, but he stutters just a step, and I assume it's because she's talking about us.

"Get out of here," I say, knowing Claire's joking anyway. "You know we can't do that. I have school, and Ronan has Enzo's."

"Yeah, but he could totally open his next shop here after he gets Nico's all done. I mean look at this place." She continues walking and spins around, her arms out wide, gesturing to the setting we're in. "A cute little pizza place would be perfect right here."

Ronan glances over his shoulder to her. "Cute?" he asks in a nonchalant tone.

"Oh, you know what I'm trying to say. Just leave Nico's to Mikey, and you come to Pine Village and open the next big—or tiny and adorable—pizzeria."

Ro clears his throat, and I notice his fingers on one hand brush gently against one another as he throws his cup away with the other. "Let's not get ahead of ourselves."

"Sure, but as your business developer—"

"Nope."

"Your friend then."

"Still no."

"Okay, fine! Suit yourself." Claire sighs dramatically then stops in her tracks. "Guys, look!" she says, pointing at the door in front of us. The sign hanging on it says **Novelteen Books**. "A young adult bookstore! I can't believe it." She pulls on Jay's arm. "We have to go in. Maybe I can convince them to carry my book!" Jay ushers her forward, and Claire makes happy claps as she walks towards the door.

"We'll wait here," I call over to them. The last thing Claire needs when she's trying to be professional are her two best friends trailing behind her. She smiles at me from over her shoulder, then pulls the door open and saunters in confidently.

Ronan and I look at each other uneasily. "Want to keep walking?" he asks. I nod, happy for the movement to distract me from the rest of it.

We begin walking in sync, passing just a few stores in front of us, when another pop-up stand catches my eye.

"Oh my God," I say, stopping at the photo booth next to me. "Do you remember... "

"Mystic Island," we both say together.

Ronan laughs, and I start to blush, thinking back to Valentine's Day last year.

We made plans to have dinner at a new restaurant a few towns away. The reservation was for 6pm, but of course I ran late so we didn't get there on time. We pulled into the strip at 6:25pm, but Ro walked to my door in no rush at all.

"Shouldn't we hurry?" I asked, stepping out of the car. Ronan took the time to tuck my hair behind my ear, then led me to the storefront next door. "What are you doing? We're already like a half an hour late." I surveyed the business, **Mystic Island** written in bold lettering across the window. Ro pulled open the door, the delicious smell of popcorn and liquid cheese filling my senses, the pinging and beeping of games in the background.

"The reservation's at seven," he said from behind me, and at the same time, a machine with buzzers and triggers yelled, "Big Ticket Winner," at maximum volume.

"But you said six!" I turned around to see Ronan pointing at his watch.

"And how'd that work out for us?"

My mouth dropped open, while simultaneously forming a smile. "You're sneaky!"

"I'm smart." He dropped a kiss to my forehead and reached into his pocket. When his hand reemerged, he was holding a small stack of ones.

"Woah, what kind of establishment is this?" I joked, the singles dancing from the breeze someone let in through the door.

"They're for games," he said wryly, glancing around.

"You totally planned this."

"Something like that."

We proceeded to spend the next thirty minutes blowing through the pile of money. On our way out the door, I spotted a photo booth tucked away behind vending machines on the wall near the corner.

"Aw, man! I can't believe we missed that." I pouted, and Ronan dangled a dollar bill in front of my face.

I breathed in a dramatic gasp. "My hero." I snagged the single, then pulled him into the booth next to me.

I inserted the money, and four empty frames popped up on the screen. After hitting the start button, the timer in front of us began its countdown from ten. It repeated this two more times, totaling three of the four poses complete—a smile, a kiss, and our tongues sticking out. When the last countdown flashed on the glass, I started to panic.

9...

8...

"What else should we do?"

7...

"Flash it," he said.

I still have those pictures somewhere in my room. The first three at least because Ronan somehow snuck off with the fourth.

My focus on the photo booth is broken when Ronan's hand taps me on the elbow. "Come on," he says, nodding towards the box in front of us. The long, black curtain is open, inviting us in, but I'm still surprised by his offer.

"You just want to see boobs." I instantly regret opening my mouth, remembering the sports bra incident from earlier when mine were pressed against his smooth, damp chest. I can feel my face grow warm as I watch Ronan swallow hard.

"Maybe." He plays coy, but the way his jaw tightens when he says it, tells me he's remembering too. "I'm kidding. Just get in there."

Ro guides me toward the booth, and I slide across the bench inside. He sits down next to me, his thigh gently brushing mine, and pulls the curtain closed. I watch as he reaches into his pocket and produces a crisp dollar bill from the slit in his wallet. He waves it in front of me, taunting me to take it. I look at him over the swaying money, his eyes relaxed and rested on mine—a glimmer of the way he used to be. There's a slight stirring in the pit of my stomach as my fingers graze his when I pull it from his grasp.

I place the money into the slot, and the screen in front of us springs to life. Ronan reaches past me to choose a frame lined with snowflakes, four empty

116

middles just waiting to be filled. He waits for the page to load, and when the start button flashes, he looks at me for confirmation. I nod uneasily, the tension in here and the pressure to produce four pictures in under a minute, rising to the surface.

The timer begins its countdown, and I look at Ronan in a frenzied panic. "I hate this!" I say. He laughs, pulling me towards him and smiling for the camera.

I look at our reflection and can't help but think we look so good together. My stark blonde hair compliments the natural highlights in his. My big, bold smile, a contrast to his soft, easy grin. Even my small frame sits so comfortably against the crook of his arm, the rise and fall of his chest matching mine. The timer counts down, and our first frame is filled. An ordinary picture of the two of us smiling that means even more than it normally would.

Almost instantly, it starts again. I look to Ronan for direction for almost half of it, until he turns away from me and contorts his face into a cross between a hideous ogre and a grumpy, old man. Without thinking, I make the first funny face that comes to mind, poking my tongue out and crossing my eyes. The finished product pops up on the screen, and we both bust out laughing at the ridiculousness of the picture in front of us.

Ronan looks me up and down, casually at first, the curiosity of our next move written all over his face. But as the ten pops back up on the screen, the humor subsides, intensity rushing to take its place. Ronan's eyes seem to darken and begin pulling me in, the sudden shift sending a chill up my spine.

People make references to circumstances where small increments of time seem exceptionally long—running on the treadmill, holding your breath, the time it takes responders to get to the scene of a crime—but I am almost certain that these photo booth seconds beat them all by a mile. I know logically that we have about five seconds left, but the way that time passes while we're making eye contact—studying one another, longing for each other, or at least me for him—feels like an absolute eternity. And I never want it to end.

The small space inside suddenly feels even more crowded, like we're two passengers on a loaded train. Almost simultaneously, Ronan and I inch just a tiny bit closer. When only a few seconds must be left on the screen, Ronan's eyes drop to my lips just for an instant. By the time he brings them back up, they're hot and hooded, and mine follow suit.

The camera flashes, and we both look at the photo. I breathe in audibly as he exhales heavily, the image in front of us, almost erotic. We're looking at each other, a picture of lust and desire, and that stir in my stomach from before suddenly drops further south.

The seconds begin their final journey to zero, and Ronan and I can see ourselves looking at each other in the camera, a mirror of passion and honesty. He watches me move my gaze towards him, my face now turned away from the lens, and he slowly mimics my movement.

Our eyes meet one final time, the briefest of instants, before our bodies intertwine. The memory of earlier floods back to me as if this moment is just an appendage of that one. Only this time, there's no roaming. No wandering hands mapping their course. This time, each movement is intentional. My hand on the back of his head, deepening our kiss. His grip on my knee, pulling me all but onto his lap. I move my hand from his hair to his hip, pulling it toward me, my body stretched across his, begging for friction. Ronan groans the second my fingers slide under his jacket to the skin by his belt, and his palm slides down to the hem of my sweater dress.

I can assume the timer has already run out, the image done previewing up on the screen, but neither of us seem to have any intentions on leaving. I dip my fingers into the waste of his jeans, and have a feeling of deja vu from doing the same to his towel. Ro sucks my bottom lip, scaling the length of my leg.

Before I have time to think or protest, his hand skips my thigh like it's jumping a curb. Almost instantly, a heat ignites the flesh underneath and like a moth to a flame, his fingers draw closer. I reach for his belt but freeze mid-motion as he pulls away the only fabric between his hand and my most sensitive spot.

"Ronan," I whisper into his mouth, and at the sound, his palm makes contact like his name was permission.

And maybe it was.

His middle finger slides down my center then curls back up like he's taking in all of me. I shudder at the movement, needing him more, and like reading my mind, he slips it inside. I pull back from our kiss, my forehead to his, and watch as his chest heaves in short, gasping surges. I'm lost in a trance of the rise and fall and don't even notice when I let the weight of my leg drop to the side, completely opening myself up to him. Ronan sucks in a breath at the sight of all of me, and I know we should be more cautious, but I don't even care.

He finds me with the same pad of his thumb that he was nervously rubbing such a short time ago, and it's the perfect reminder that we're better together. Just the thought adds to the pleasure that's building inside of me, and as Ronan moves his parted lips to the space by my ear, I feel myself teeter right on the edge.

My hand drifts from the spot it was frozen to where I can feel him from outside of his jeans. He leans into me, and when he moans into my ear, then whispers, "I missed you," I lose it completely.

Ronan continues the in and out, the brushing and stroking, until I collapse in fulfillment. He slides from within me, leaving me hollow, and it's only then that I see the screen in front of us and remember where we are. Still coming down from my high, I move to reset myself, as Ronan places kisses up the side of my neck.

When my sweater is back down where it belongs, I reach again for the area just under his zipper. Ro turns more towards me. His movement naturally pushes my hand into him with more pressure than before, and at the same time, the curtain behind him slides open.

"There you guys are!" My head snaps past his shoulder, and I see Claire standing there completely oblivious to what preceded her entrance. "We've been looking everywhere for you!"

"Told you," Jay says. "Always all over each other."

Ronan inhales a deep breath, his eyes closed only to me, then releases it as he slides just his face towards our friends. "And what if it wasn't us in here?" he asks, changing the subject and fidgeting with the waist of his jeans.

"Well," Claire says. "Then I would just tell whoever it was the good news. They're taking my book!"

Both Ronan and I light up for Claire. "That's amazing!" I say.

"Congratulations," Ro says, seeming genuinely happy. He turns back to me, his smile fading slightly but still clearly there. "You're incredible," he says, and for a second I think he may be talking to me.

16

Before

"It is incredible that there is still snot coming from your nose," Ro says just inches from me, his head in full tilt like he's interpreting art. "Where is it all coming from?"

I pull the sheet up over my face, sliding further into the bed. "Stop, I'm disgusting," I say, my voice sounding somehow more nasally than I feel. "I told you not to come over!"

I woke up this morning with the spring head cold that has been going around at work, taking out teachers and students one by one. My throat's on fire, my temples are throbbing, and my sinuses are—as Ronan so eloquently explained—leaking mucus like a broken faucet. I have been in bed all day, binge watching Ryan Reynolds movies and refusing to move for anything other than tissues and the bare minimum amount of water needed to keep me alive.

Ronan texted me throughout the day to check in and to push me to eat something. Apparently the three saltines I had left in a sleeve didn't count as breakfast or lunch in his eyes. Now, it's been four movies and almost twelve hours, and he decided coming over was the only way to help.

Ronan laughs and tugs at the sheet once, then twice, until he rips it down altogether the third time. My hands fly to my miserable face, only separating at my wrists so I can breathe through my mouth because now I'm a mouth breather on top of the rest of it.

"Oh stop it." He pulls at my wrists so I'm forced to lower them completely. "I brought you some soup."

My creased brow starts to relax as I peer into the bag from Enzo's that Ronan is holding out in front of me. "Minestrone?" I ask hopefully.

"Your favorite." He pulls out a plastic spoon and a to-go bowl that's still warm from the paper bag. "You need to eat."

"I need a new head."

"Well, I'm fresh out of body parts stored in a jar." As if on cue, my stomach makes this strange gurgling noise like it's thanking him for the sustenance he's offering.

I open the lid cautiously, a welcoming steam wafts out, waving me in. I push the spoon around and am happy to see it's loaded with carrots, zucchini, tomatoes, and the little tiny noodles that I love—because the shape of the pasta really does matter. It's only when I attempt to inhale the fresh ingredients that my anticipation fades, the movement of the vapor turning from a cheerful invitation to more of a taunt. "I can't even smell it," I whine.

"Eat," Ronan says, without missing a beat, and I huff like a child throwing a tantrum.

I'm the worst sick person. I know people always joke that it's men, but it's not—it's me.

Chloe Carlson
Age: 26
Height: 5' 4" (on a good day)
Position: Horizontal
Complaints: Infinite
Accomplishments: Worst Sick Person Ever

I begrudgingly fill my spoon and slowly slurp the contents into my mouth, only adding to my lack of attraction. I swallow, my face falling even further in defeat. "I can't taste it either."

Ronan sighs like he knew this was coming and takes the spoon from my hand. He dips it back into the soup and brings another spoonful to my lips, his eyebrows high and smile low, in what I like to call his *no bullshit face.*

"Eat," he repeats, and as it usually does, his stern and protective side kicks on the heat, my once sickly senses suddenly more alive. I know it's not normal to be thinking of sex at a time like this, but I can't help it—it's Ronan. He does things to me even when I'm revolting.

I raise my eyebrows just once, almost challenging him, then lean towards his hand. I attempt to allow him to feed me in a way that's smooth and seductive, but out of nowhere, as if my body's way of reminding me I'm repulsive right now, I sneeze uncontrollably. Broth is sprayed all over Ro's face, and a baby noodle I can no longer love, lands in his lap.

"Oh my God." My hand flies to my mouth as if it's not two seconds too late from showering my boyfriend with minestrone soup. "I'm so sorry." My voice is almost inaudible between my congestion and my palm, not to mention my embarrassment. To top it all off, I can barely breathe now that my only open airway is blocked by my hand.

Ronan laughs to himself, his eyes closed to keep the droplets of soup from entering them. He wipes his face with his free hand, then puts the bowl and spoon on the table next to the bed.

"Damn, Carlson," he says, scanning his clothes. "Good aim."

A laugh escapes behind my blockade, and I lower my hand before I lose air completely. At least we can add that to my stats. "I've been practicing," I whisper. Ronan peers up at me with a blank expression minus the slight lift in his cheeks.

"Why don't you go wash up," I snicker, placing my hand on his knee. "Thanks for trying."

He uses his shoulder to wipe off beads of broth still left on his chin. "I think I will," he says. "But you're coming with me."

He moves to the edge of the bed. I open my mouth to argue, but before I form words, Ronan stands, extending his arm for my hand. "Come on."

"But I'm sick," I say.

"The steam will be good for you."

"But my bed... "

"Will be right here when you get back."

"But I'm so gross." I once again pull the sheet up so it covers my face.

"So... you're opposing a shower?"

I drop the fabric and stare back at Ronan all out of excuses. Then, I reluctantly place my hand in his. I peel back the covers with my free hand before Ro grabs that one too and lifts me to standing. A shower does sound kind of nice and showers with Ronan are sort of my favorite.

"You'll feel better when we're done," he says and again, all of my senses start working. *They do say that orgasms help with a headache...*

I trail Ronan as he walks the few feet it takes to reach the bathroom, my body a cross between weak and excited. Ronan is so humbly sexy. He takes care of himself and smells really good, and he never leaves the seat up in the bathroom. He brushes *and* flosses, and he always subtly makes the whole day feel like foreplay—a cheek brush here, a lower-back graze there, complimenting me, feeding me soup.

It doesn't hurt that he's sincere in everything he does—his movements deliberate, his actions intentional. So when he tells me I'm going to feel better, I believe him. I'm just not sure if he means it in the same way that I'm assuming, and although he looks fine, this cold is kicking my salacious ass.

When we get to the shower, he turns it on, letting the water run until it's a more comfortable temperature. He turns to me, stripping himself of his shirt, and I look at him with sleepy, yet lustful eyes.

"Don't look at me like that." He unzips his jeans and glides them to the floor. I follow their path and then head back north.

"Like what?" I ask his crotch before catching myself and tearing my eyes from where I was staring.

He laughs, reaching for my double XL sleep shirt that says **NOT ADULTING TODAY**. "Like we're about to have wild sex in the shower."

My face scrunches up. "We're not?" I ask.

"We're not."

"Are you sure?" He pulls the hem of my tee over my head and takes a quick breath in when he sees that I'm completely naked underneath.

"How about now?" I begin to smirk right before a coughing fit ruins the moment, and I gag on my own spit for what feels like forever.

"Definitely not now." He kisses me on my temple, then tests the water, and I guess I have the answer to my prior question.

I smother another cough before he guides me into the shower. I watch as he takes off his boxers and then melt into the hot, flowing water. Goosebumps break out all over me as the temperature of the water hits my chilled skin.

Ronan steps in behind me and plants a kiss on the back of my head. "I'm sorry," I say, tilting my chin up and allowing the water to cascade down my front.

"For what?" He gathers my hair in his hands and brings it all to one side, tossing it to the front of my body and reaching for something behind him.

"Well, mostly for sneezing minestrone all over you," I say. Both of our bodies rumble as he laughs, my back now flush against his chest. "But also, this would be way more fun if I wasn't such a gremlin."

Ronan's hands find my shoulders, and slick with soap, he massages the area up to my neck. A second set of goosebumps spreads on my skin where his hands knead away the tension from my day spent in bed. "You're not a gremlin, Chlo, you're sick." He slides his hands down my back, continuing to rub my aching muscles, washing my body as he does it. "This is what I'm here for."

I relax into his touch, allowing his fingers to work out my stress. "Still, if I wasn't so snotty, this would be really seductive." I spin around, facing him, the water now saturating my hair. "And either way, it's really sweet." I lean up to kiss him before remembering I'm sick. I lower myself back down, right as Ro is leaning to meet me.

"Woah," he says, pulling back after I do. "What was that fake out?"

"I can't kiss you. I'm sick!"

"Oh, so you would have sex with me, but you can't kiss me. Is that it?" He shakes his head playfully. "Like a piece of meat." I nudge him in the chest that's now beaded from the spray of the water. "Not to mention you already all but sneezed in my mouth."

I cringe knowing he's right and mentally add that to the list of reasons his lips can not touch mine tonight. I throw my arms around his waist and hide my embarrassment into his chest. "Please can we just never talk about that ever again?"

Ronan huffs out a breath. "Talk about what?"

"Exactly."

He leans back, creating distance between us. "Just kiss me."

"But I—"

His lips press to mine. "I don't care," he says with his mouth still against me.

It's an innocent kiss, not greedy or heated. A kiss that leads to nothing more. Just one that says *"I love you,"* and *"I'm here."* I sink into him, thanking him through the breath I release.

He pulls back slowly, my lips still puckered and my eyes still closed when he says, "Now, turn around."

My eyes shoot open. "Wait a second, I thought... "

"So I can wash your hair, you animal." He winks and gently twists my shoulders.

"Tease," I say playfully.

He tugs on the ponytail he makes in his fist so my ear now sits next to his lips. I breathe in a quick gasp. "But you just wait till you're better."

For a third time, goosebumps form all over, but this time it has nothing to do with his hands or the water.

Ronan was right. The steam of the shower, plus his touch and sexual innuendo, were exactly what I needed to perk up a little. My sinuses cleared, at least momentarily, and it felt nice to wash the germs off of me. I even braved the minestrone once more, and this time I was able to conquer it all.

Afterward, Ro and I changed my sheets and snuggled into a nice clean bed. Now, we're laying together, with *Just Friends* on in the background, laughing at Ryan Reynolds in a fat suit.

"Hey," Ronan says out of nowhere. "What would you think about Mikey and I opening up a second location?"

I sit up on his chest, the memory of us in this same position coming back to me from the time at the restaurant when he told me about how that was their goal. "I think it's a great idea," I say. "You guys are killing it at Enzo's, and your food is amazing. You'd be doing people a disservice by not opening more."

Ro laughs to himself. "I don't know if I'd take it that far."

"I would. I'm serious! That soup, although aggressive today, is my favorite from anywhere, and don't get me started on your meatball subs."

"Yes, we all know how you feel about my balls, Chloe," he jokes.

"But why are you bringing this up now?"

"I got a call from my uncle on my way over. He has a shop over in Grand Oaks that he just can't run like he used to. He tried to pass it off to my cousin, but he doesn't really want anything to do with it. So, he has to sell it to someone."

"And he wants that someone to be you?"

"Yeah, me and Mikey if we want it. His offer kind of came out of nowhere though, so I'm not really sure what to think. We always talked about opening a second location, but I pictured doing it the same way we did it the first time—finding a spot, designing it from scratch—this would be more like rein-venting Nico's, rather than creating our vision from a clean slate." I consider what he's saying and nod along. "What do you think?" he asks.

"I think," I say, gathering my thoughts. "That it may not be the exact way you pictured it, but a good thing has fallen into your lap, and you guys need to trust yourselves. If this is what you want, you'll make it happen. I have no doubt about that." I lay my head back into the crook of his arm. "Plus, you guys have an entire village backing you. I don't really think failing is a possibility."

Ronan lies still for a moment as I consider my answer. If you change the context, it's almost like you can apply what I'm saying to really anything. We all have that one fear that stands in the way of creating the future that we truly hope for. Sometimes it's easier to talk ourselves out of something, rather than run the risk that it might not work out. It's also easier to see that perspective when it's someone else's life, rather than your own.

"Thank you," Ro says, resting his head on top of mine.

I turn up to him and peck his cheek. "Always," I say. He smiles and then out of nowhere, he sneezes, just barely missing my face.

17

Now

The drive home from Pine Village was... invigorating.

After Ronan and I were interrupted in the photo booth—something I could never imagine I'd say—we headed back to the cabin. Claire swore she was exhausted, either from the morning she had, the day at the spa, or just the excitement of securing her book a spot at the store.

She said she pitched her book, *The Adventures of Alice and Owen,* the story of two childhood best friends who grow up taking on life's hardships as a team, and the owner was instantly sold. They spent the next twenty minutes talking about their own life stories and describing how to market the book on the shelves. Apparently Claire now has her reason for returning to the village—author signings, meet-and-greets, and general promotion—and in getting there, she gave Ro and I a solid half hour to... spend together.

"You're welcome by the way," she said as we walked down the street.

"For what?" Ronan asked.

"Now we all have an excuse to do this again." Ro and I peered over at each other, knowing she meant our weekend together but thinking of what had just happened with us.

Once we got home, Claire decided to go right to bed, barely able to keep her eyes open, and the rest of us chose to hang outside by the fire.

I headed out first, leaving the boys to get drinks and am now sitting here, scrolling on my phone in my lap. As I mindlessly toggle different social media, I find myself looking at my own profile riddled with pictures of Ronan and me. I click on the first one I notice. It's a photo his brother took of us last winter—him and I laughing as we're covered in snow.

Under that is a black and white selfie that I remember taking like it was yesterday. It's in Ronan's apartment. He's on the couch, and I'm in his lap, smiling wild and cheesy, only inches from the camera. I remember thinking the photo was funny and captioning it underneath with: **Talk about a close up!** What stands out to me now though, isn't my face. It's Ronan's in the background, looking at me. His expression is the same as it was tonight when we walked to the car after the previous incident. All weekend it felt like when he looked at me, all I could read was hurt and resentment. Tonight though, stealing glances at one another as we moved towards the car, it was like layers of that negativity were slowly peeled back.

I hear the boys step onto the porch, and I scroll one more time through the pictures on the screen. My eyes land on the one of the torn photo booth strip from Mystic Island last year, and I laugh out loud.

"What's so funny?" Jay asks, two drinks in his hand. Ronan walks beside him, carrying a drink for himself and his acoustic guitar.

"Oh, just a memory," I say, smiling at Ro. He returns the gesture in the form of a smirk, and it's not lost on me that tonight he chooses the seat next to mine instead of the one across from me like before. "You brought your guitar?"

Ronan sets his drink on one arm of the chair and his phone on the other closest to me. He settles the guitar in his lap and begins turning the pegs, plucking here, strumming there. "Sure did. What's a campfire without a little Kumbaya?"

"Please don't actually play that," Jay says, and Ro huffs out a snicker.

"I guess I'm taking requests then." He leans back in his chair and sips his drink.

As much as I want to chime in and tell him to play one of the Johns—Legend or Lennon—I don't want to push my luck. Since our moment in the photo booth, I haven't gotten any feelings like Ronan is upset or ignoring me. There have been no awkward looks or bitter remarks. For once in the last three weeks, things feel better between us, and I am not risking that now by asking for opinions about my broad taste in music.

"Nah man, just anything but Kumbaya," Jay says.

Ro glances at me and then sets down his drink. He adjusts the guitar in his arms and begins strumming a familiar tune. My gaze moves from his hands to his eyes, but his are already settled on mine. He looks back down at the strings. The same song surrounds me that he played during our first kiss in the back of Enzo's more than a year ago. My heart starts to race as I think about the old times that we shared over the same instrumental—our first kiss and the times it came on in the car when Ro would turn it up loud and sing it to me. Then I think about now and what it could mean that this is the song he chose out of all of them.

I feel my focus move to Ronan's profile as I watch him follow his movements on the neck of the guitar. I knew what happened earlier meant more to me than two ex-lovers having one final fling, but I wasn't sure what it meant to him. Now, observing his expression as he plays our song—the song that he picked—his eyes look thoughtful, not saddened. The ends of his perfect lips are turned up instead of pressed into the straight line that they've been in since we got here.

He begins humming along with the acoustics and turns to me over his shoulder. I cast a shy grin, knowing my face is full of the same hope that I'm feeling inside. He matches my expression, and it's like the weight that has been sitting on my shoulders since our break up melts away—thanks to one look. Thanks to one song. I don't know what this means for me and Ronan. We had one brief, lust-filled experience and now one significant song by the fire, but after the ups and downs of this trip and the devastation of the last few weeks, I'm holding on to any possibility that it may mean something more.

Ronan rounds out the end of the song, turning to me when he hits the last chord. By now, my heart beat is so strong I'm scared he can see it. I narrow my eyes at him softly, and he answers only with his lips that turn in, but it's something. At this point, I'll take whatever he gives.

"What even was that?" Jay says, his candor breaking the moment. "Sounded pretty fucking good."

Ronan just laughs and reaches over the chair to lay his guitar on the ground, and at the same time, his phone lights up next to me. I'm not trying to look, but my eyes are drawn to the glow, and before he sits back up, I see the text on the screen. My heart that was racing suddenly stops altogether.

MAGGIE: Call me :)

When the guitar is safely next to the chair, he sits back up and sees the same light that I do. I bring my attention back down to my phone and act fully invested in the screen I pull up. From the corner of my eye, I see Ronan glance quickly in my direction before rushing to shove the device in his pocket. Watching his reaction makes my heart sink deeper into the pit of my stomach. My mouth floods with saliva like I'm going to be sick, and I'm suddenly suffocating under this blanket and sweater dress.

I fidget in my seat. My head feels light, but my legs are heavy. I want to leave, but I'm not sure if I can. I clear my throat in an attempt to get rid of the lump I can't seem to swallow. Ronan looks at me again, and I somehow manage to paint a fake smile. He reaches for his drink and brings the rim to his mouth, taking a long, slow sip while staring at nothing.

Jay sits forward in his seat, his eyebrows raised in Ronan's direction "What?" Ronan asks as if he's lost in thought.

"That's it?" He gestures towards the guitar. "One and done?"

"Uh, yeah, man," he stutters. "For now."

Jay rolls his eyes. "Fine. Then I'm heading in. I only have one more night with my girl in that comfy ass bed." He stands and extends his fist to Ronan who meets it almost reluctantly.

"I'll come with you," I say. Ro's head snaps to me. "Tired," I add in his direction. I force my legs to move from beneath me and somehow manage to do so without falling over.

"Chlo?" Ro sits forward, his brow furrowed with curiosity. I avoid his eyes as I wrap up the blanket.

"I'll see you inside," I say.

Walking in, Jay rambles on about the heaven-sent mattress that they have in their room, but I'm barely listening as my mind races, my night—my life—imploding… again.

MAGGIE: *Call me :)*

It's been less than a month since Ronan and I broke up. I can barely get through work, and he's getting texts from girls that... aren't me. What's worse is, like a thunderstorm on a sunny day, it came out of nowhere and in the middle of one of our best moments this weekend.

The last thirty-six hours play back to me—the good, the bad, the downright awkward—and suddenly small things start to stick out like clues that I should have seen this coming. Of course Ro's been distant, but I chalked that up to hurt or resentment, and maybe I was wrong to think that's all that it was. Then there was the phone call from yesterday.

"I'll come right over after I get back."

Could he have been talking to her? The thought makes me sick. Ronan going to any apartment that's not mine but especially hers. Sitting on a different couch... sleeping in a different bed. He was in such a hurry to brush right past it, like he knew if he was honest, a war would erupt. My brain starts reeling, and now everything is starting to make sense. The backpack of clothes like he didn't care to impress, the long hair, the smooth face—all of it... her. I trudge up the steps as nausea takes over and am barely able to say goodnight to Jay as we part ways in the hall.

As I slide leggings up under my dress, I remember Ro's hands brushing my thighs. I pull at the hemline, and the sight of the fabric bunched at my hips reminds me of Ronan beneath it. Suddenly, I'm no longer nauseous but so goddamn heated. Here I am, sitting around the fire, listening to Ro serenade me after what we did earlier, thinking that we've finally reached a turning point. Instead, I learn that Ro has been talking to Maggie, and everything that's happened between us has been—what? Some kind of game? Drawing me in, then pushing me off. Touching and kissing, then pulling away. Calling her one night then in me the next—Who does he think he is?

I turn off the light and climb into bed, not even bothering to take off my dress. I pull out my phone and open a new message to group text both of my sisters.

ME: I need you guys.

It's late so I don't expect a response, but I instantly get one from Casey. I realize she's probably working the night shift tonight, and I'm grateful for my workaholic big sister.

CASEY: Everything okay? If it's about Ronan, don't worry. It'll all work out.

What I want to do is say, no. Everything is not okay, and it is definitely not working out. I want to tell them both that I'm coming home, and I need them to drop their own lives to help me put mine back together. But I can't.

Not only do they have their own stuff going on, but I have Claire and Jay's wedding this weekend, the rehearsal dinner Friday, and a week of work between now and then. Despite my now twice-broken heart, we're all grown ups, and burdening my sisters isn't going to help.

ME: I'm fine, and you're right. Just miss you both.

CASEY: Miss you too, little sis.

CARA: Ditto!

I chuckle at Cara's response as tears collect behind my eyes. My sisters are the only ones who know about the breakup. We've talked twice as much since, and it might be the one silver lining of losing my relationship.

CASEY: Look at it this way, Chlo. You might not have him, but at least you aren't almost forty.

CASEY: Ditto, Car? Really?

I laugh again, but before I can respond, the doorknob twists open. I plug my phone in and set it on the bedside table, then pick at my nails, waiting for Ronan to appear.

He comes into the room and strips off his sweater. "Hey. You're still up?"

"Mhmm," is all I say back. The moon casts a glow in through the window that lands on Ronan like a lighthouse pointing out danger ahead.

"You alright? You seemed to kind of take a turn out there." He unzips his pants, and the sound vibrates between my legs, my own body betraying my heart.

"I'm fine." I repeat the same response that I gave to my sisters. Both times it was an absolute lie.

He climbs into bed and lays on his side, perching his head onto his elbow. "Can we talk about earlier?"

Anxiety swirls deep in my belly, the butterflies from before, now drunk with rage. Is he really going to talk about her? "About what?" I spit out.

"The photo booth," he says, and I hate that this specific memory is now tainted with the idea that I may not be the only one Ronan has been with.

"We don't have to." My response comes across blankly, but I can feel the tears forming behind my eyelids again.

"I want to." He holds my chin in his palm, and I can still smell myself on his fingers, like I've branded them so they're only for me. But they aren't.

The thought brings back the nausea from earlier, and between that and the resentment that I'm feeling towards everything, I think the only safe thing to do is go to bed. Then I can wake up tomorrow and just go the hell home.

"Well, I don't think I do," I snap, and I roll away from his hand that still sits at my face, the spot where he was, now warm from his touch.

"Chloe," he says, but like he did earlier with the text on his phone, I pretend I don't notice and bury it away.

18

Before

"**Y**ou're not even pretending to listen to me!" Claire throws her balled up straw wrapper and hits me right on the nose.

"Hey!" I say, bringing my attention back to her. "What was that for?"

"I'm trying to tell you about my tutoring session today."

"And I'm listening," I say, but as I do, I feel myself getting lost again in the sight that's behind her.

"So you heard me?"

"Uh huh."

"All of it?"

"Mhmm."

"Even the part about the gorilla that broke into the library and ate all of the vending machine snacks?"

"Sure," I say, nodding along. "Wait, what?"

"See!" Claire yells. "Will you stop staring at Ro for like two freaking seconds?"

At the sound of his name, I glance past her again, and this time she moves her head to block my view.

"Okay!" I throw my hands up in surrender. "I'm sorry. I wasn't actually listening, but look at the guy!" Claire turns around on her side of the booth, fixing her view on Ro across the restaurant.

"He looks like Ronan."

"Exactly." She glances at me, and I shoot her a wink.

Ronan is standing behind the counter at Enzo's, an apron wrapped loosely around his waist, his navy baseball hat backwards on his freshly cut hair. He's chopping up vegetables in a crisp, white shirt, his forearms flexing as he lifts and lowers the knife. The view is nothing I haven't seen before, but I never get tired of watching him work. There's something so sexy about a guy in an apron—especially when you know what he's packing underneath.

Behind me, the door opens, but I can't stand to break my stare for even an instant. Ronan looks up, first smiling at me, and then lighting up and waving to someone who must have walked in behind us.

"Who is that?" Claire asks as her eyes follow them in.

"Who?"

"Oh my God. Two freaking seconds!"

I go to look, but I don't need to turn far because the mysterious customer is now strolling past our table. My gaze meets a petite waist, just a sliver of exposed skin peeking out below her tank top. The girl continues moving forward, and I continue watching her. She has flowing dirty-blonde hair that lands just below a small, perky butt and hips that sway back and forth as she walks.

"Who is that?" I whisper, and Claire throws her hands in the air.

"If I knew, would you even hear my answer?"

I squint and tilt my head sideways. "Ha ha, very funny."

She approaches the display window, resting her elbows casually next to the register, and Ronan drops the knife where he is, rounding the counter to meet her. He wipes his hands on his apron and throws his arms around her neck, squeezing her in a warm embrace.

"Seems like Ro has a type," Claire says, and I too gently smack the back of her head. "Ouch!" she yelps. "I'm just saying. Long, blonde hair, short and tiny..." She sees my face and adds on, "Devastatingly beautiful." I roll my eyes for two reasons. One because of her brown nosing, and two because she's right. This girl is gorgeous, and by the way she's looking at Ro, she thinks he is too.

I continue watching their little interaction, him leaning his palm on the counter, her talking way too closely to him. I nearly leap from my seat when she does that fake, giddy laugh that girls do and slaps him playfully on the arm.

If it wasn't for the fact that Ronan looks in my direction and smiles, I would have started practicing my kneading skills on her face.

Claire turns back towards me. "Seriously, who do you think that is?"

"We're about to find out," I say, as Ronan leads all five feet of Ms. Porcelain-Skin over to our table.

"Hey," he says, and because he likes his balls attached to his body, he kisses me right on the lips. It's a quick peck, which is different than normal, but the way his little friend's eye twitches briefly, tells me it was enough to do the trick. "This is Maggie. Maggie, this is Jay's fiancé, Claire and my girlfriend, Chloe."

Maggie looks at me with big, milk chocolate eyes and long, dark lashes that frame each one. She smiles without showing her teeth, the corners of her full lips meeting in deep, charming dimples. I flash her a grin, feeling Ronan watch our interaction. Despite my annoyance, I have no intention of letting this random girl be the reason I lose my cool girlfriend card.

"Hi," Maggie says, but she's looking at Claire.

"It's nice to meet you," she says back, and before I have a chance to chime in, Ronan speaks.

"Maggie and I actually know each other from when I was a kid."

"That's right." She does that giggle again and places her hand too comfortably on Ro's shoulder. "I've known this guy since he had long hair and no beard and when he thought it was cool to ride me around on the pegs of his bike."

"Oh my God. I forgot about that," Ro laughs. "Maggie lived right down the street from me. Since I didn't have any siblings to play with, I would just show up at her house when we were eleven or twelve and beg her to hang out with me."

Maggie smiles up at Ronan, this time with full teeth. "You didn't have to beg. If you didn't come to me, I would have come to you." Ronan shakes his head still laughing about the memory, completely missing the tone in her voice. I look at Maggie who's still staring at my boyfriend like he's a rare steak, and she's a hungry lioness.

"Wait," he says, moving his hand to the back of his neck and running it over the fade at his hairline. "It was not that long back then."

"Longer than now!" she replies. "And I liked it."

"So, what? You guys haven't seen each other in like fifteen years?" Claire asks, and I remind myself to thank her later for getting to the details.

"No, she used to live around here actually, so we saw each other from time to time, but then she became a big city girl."

"It was just better for work," Maggie says. "But I'm actually moving back now. Well, closer at least."

Ronan pulls back his head in surprise. "Oh, no way."

"Yep. I'm going to be working at my mom's office. It's just a few towns over." The way she speaks only to him, I feel like I'm watching an intimate conversation between two people, rather than sitting in a pizza shop talking in a group.

"That's awesome, Mags."

My body tenses at the nickname and the way that it so easily flows from his lips. Almost two years I've known Ronan and he's never mentioned her before, but here he is abbreviating her name like they talk all the time—like he does to mine. I can't help but feel a pang of jealousy at the idea that Maggie and Ronan's relationship has over a decade on ours, and the fact that her hand is once again touching my man's arm, really sells it for me.

"Well, I better get going," Maggie says, finally removing her fingers from Ronan's forearm. She leans in for a hug, and Ro wraps an arm around her shoulders. "It was good seeing you." Her eyes linger on him for a second too long to be considered friendly, before turning to Claire and me. "Nice to meet you guys."

"You too," we both say simultaneously. But was it really nice? Or was my time designated for staring at my boyfriend, interrupted by some home-wrecking Bratz doll?

Maggie saunters out the door, and before it even shuts fully, Claire says, "Soo... who the hell was that?"

"That was Maggie. You literally just met her."

"Did you guys date before or something?" she asks, and I sit slightly forward in my seat.

Ronan chuckles. "Me and Maggie? No way. We were just friends as kids and then after I—well after my parents died, we lost touch for a bit until she and her mom moved around here. After that, we saw each other here and there until she went away. But I guess now she's moving back."

"Interesting," I say. Claire looks at me, her expression eager for what's coming next. She pulls her drink closer to her and sucks on her straw in anticipation.

"What?" Ronan asks.

"Oh, just that you didn't notice the drool gushing from her mouth when she looked at you." Claire nearly spits out her soda as I look at Ro blankly, minus a slight lift in my brows.

Ronan laughs and slides in next to me. "I'm sorry," he says, pulling one leg up so his body's turned sideways in the booth facing mine. "Are you jealous?"

I roll my eyes, and they land on Claire who looks mildly impressed that Ro called me out. "Um, obviously not." My voice comes out warped, and even I don't believe it.

"Chloe Carlson, you're jealous. She's jealous," he says to Claire.

"No I'm not."

"She is," Claire nods.

"Oh I know." Ronan leans into my ear and whispers. "I kind of like it."

I feel myself blush as he instantly eases my anxiety. I playfully push him away but am happy when he pulls me to him once more. I rest my head on his shoulder, his arm draped around mine. "Whatever, I'm not jealous. But she totally wants you."

"She does not."

Claire nods again, "She does."

You didn't have to beg. If you didn't come to me, I would have come to you," I say, repeating Maggie's words in a breathy and sultry voice.

"Did anyone else feel dirty just hearing that?" Claire asks, fanning herself. We both start laughing.

"Alright you two," Ro says lightheartedly. "Maggie was a good friend growing up, and there's uh, not many people from when I was younger that I still have around." Ro grows quieter and removes his arm from my shoulders. Rubbing his thumb and pointer finger together ever-so-slightly, he continues. "We're obviously not as close as we used to be. I mean, I barely see or talk to her anymore, but her and her mom were always good to us."

It's one of the first times that Ronan's ever alluded to his parents. He tells stories about his younger self or talks about *before* the accident or *after* the accident, but he never mentions them specifically—Mom, Dad, them, us. He just always seems to talk around it.

Another stab of jealousy hits when I realize Maggie has been to a place that I'll never get to go. I love Mr. and Mrs. Caruso, but I will never get to meet Ronan's birth parents. I'll never get to see his childhood home or introduce my mom to his mom like she has. Maggie holds a piece of Ronan's past in her heart that I never will—memories that we will never share.

The idea of her being around here again too, is enough to bring my meatball sub from lunch right back up. I reach for my drink, my mouth suddenly dry, and at the same time, Ronan scoots out of the booth.

"Where are you going?" I ask, and as ridiculous as it is, I sound about as clingy as I feel.

"Back to work?" He thinks it's funny, but what's not funny is the fact that my afternoon went from staring at Ronan with sex on the brain, to staring at him in desperation.

He leans down and kisses me on the forehead. "I'll see you later, okay?"

I nod and fake a smile. Thanks to Maggie and Ronan's stupid history, I feel distant from Ro, and him walking away is the last thing I need.

I feel my face drop, and Claire seems to notice because she reaches over and takes my hand. "Come on. Let's go get coffee next door."

I get to Ronan's apartment once I know he's home from Enzo's. He texted me earlier saying he was bringing home dinner and to meet him here when he got off.

After leaving earlier, I talked with Claire, and we decided I was being ridiculous about the whole Maggie thing. Okay, so she is stunning, moving back here, and clearly into Ronan, but Ronan's not into her. Besides, I trust him. If he says that nothing is happening, then that's that. Regardless, I'm happy for the chance to see him tonight. After a stressful couple of hours, being with him and eating leftover pizza sounds like the perfect night to me.

I knock once on his door before cracking it open. I'm hit with a dull lemon smell and the glow of a flame from the kitchen island. As I open the door fully, Ronan sneaks behind the other side. He scoops me up before setting me back on my feet and kissing me hard. I sink into his mouth, both of my hands finding the small of his back, and despite wanting all of his kisses, this one was especially welcomed.

When he pulls back from me, my eyes flutter open, and I see a smug little smile on his adorable face. "Hey, you," he says, stealing one more peck on my cheek. I look at him suspiciously before glancing around him. The island is set with two dinner plates, neither of which contain end-of-the-night slices.

"Hi?" I say as if it's a question. I walk towards the food, the smell pulling me in. There's lightly coated chicken in a buttery sauce and perfectly toasted broccolini right next to it. "This looks like the best day-old pizza I've ever seen."

Ronan swoops in behind me, taking me once again in his arms and resting his head on the back of my shoulder. "You seemed weird when you left the restaurant today. I thought I'd make you a real dinner instead."

I spin around in his embrace, placing my hands behind his neck. "You noticed that?" I ask shyly, suddenly feeling really embarrassed.

"I notice a lot of things," he says with a wink, and I'm taken right back to that time at River's Rum.

I drop my head to his collarbone, flushed at both the memory from before and my behavior from today. Ronan has this way of making me feel seen without feeling needy. Like he just gets me and isn't looking for an explanation. It's sweet and romantic, but it leaves me feeling more vulnerable than I ever have felt before.

"Hey." He pulls back on my shoulders. I look up at him, my nose scrunched and lips pursed in a shameful expression. "You have nothing to worry about," he says. "With Maggie or anyone else."

"But she's hot."

"You're hotter."

"She's got these lips—"

"That have nothing on these." He plants a gentle kiss on my pout.

"But those eyes! They're like a cartoon's!"

He tilts my chin up. "But I don't look at them like I look at yours."

I melt into him because I know that he's right. I saw it today. Maggie stared into Ronan's eyes like a lost puppy who finally found their way back home, but the way Ronan is gazing down at me now, doesn't even compare to how he looked back at her.

"She just knows so much about you and your... " I play with the hem of his shirt, feeling guilty for even bringing this up. The fact that Maggie can say she's been there through it all really bothers me, especially considering Ronan seems to avoid it with me at all costs. "Your past," I continue and slowly bring my eyes back to his.

His jaw is tight, but his expression is the opposite, looking at me almost in wonder.

"You want to know about all of that?"

"I want to know all of you, Ro. And then some."

He holds my face in the palm of both hands. "I love you, you know that?"

"More than Mags?" I ask jokingly, emphasizing the nickname.

"More than anyone." His lips find mine, then he places his hand on my back and leads me to the stools that line the kitchen island. "Let's talk over dinner."

As I walk to my seat, I see to-go containers next to the oven. "Hey, you brought this home from the restaurant," I say, pointing to the evidence.

"I never said *where* I made it." He smiles, and I can't resist kissing him just one more time.

"It's perfect, and I'm starving."

"Then let's eat, and you tell me what you want to know."

I sit down and spend the next couple of hours eating Ronan's delicious chicken piccata and asking him questions about his parents, his life before the accident, foster care, and everything in between. He tells me about how before they died, he and his mom and dad were as close as they could be at an age where it's pretty much written into your DNA to hate everything about your parents. He tells me how he and his mom used to watch old movies before bed and how his dad used to take him to a baseball game every year on his birthday. He even shares that the last thing he and his parents talked about before their accident was snacks of all things.

"I mean can you imagine? They tell me they're going to the store and without even realizing it, the last thing I say to my parents is, '*Yo, can you buy Doritos?*' "

"The red kind," we say at the same time, and we both smother a laugh before he continues.

Somewhere around hour two, we catch up to the part that I know already. How he had no living grandparents, aunts, or uncles, and how Marcus, his case manager, met him the day after it happened. He tells me how the time in foster care before meeting the Carusos was tough and having no one to lean on was even harder. Jay, he says, was the one person who he connected with in the year he spent bouncing around to three different houses.

"So, that's pretty much it." He clears away the wine glasses that we broke out after dinner and sits back down, pulling my legs onto his. "Feel all caught up now?"

"It wasn't about feeling caught up," I say. "I just want to know you. That stuff is important to you, and I didn't like that I didn't know it before."

"And that Maggie did."

I bite my bottom lip and let my eyes wander away from his face.

"I get it," he says, rubbing my feet. "But you have nothing to worry about. She might have known me in the past, but you're my future... " He pulls me up by my arms so I'm sitting in his lap. "And my right now."

"Mmm," I say, moving my mouth so it's just inches from his. "Good. Those are my two favorite things to be."

19

Now

The morning of our last day at the cabin, I wake up pretty much as expected—mentally drained and ready to get out of here—minus one thing. Ronan is gone. His side of the bed is empty, the bathroom door wide open. My only thought is that he's downstairs, saying his goodbyes to Claire and Jay first.

I slept surprisingly well, all things considered. The emotional turmoil from last night probably took more out of me than I realized. The night began so unexpectedly with Ronan and I sharing a kiss in the shower. A real kiss, not one for Jay or Claire, or to continue this charade that we're playing. A real, genuine kiss, that was greedy and charged but also so natural. Then the photo booth happened, and it was as if this whole time, our bodies were just waiting to find their way back to each other.

The way the night ended came without warning as well, especially considering the direction it was headed. Ronan and Maggie? So much for "just friends." And could he have mentioned that before he entered me in a dark, metal box?

I wipe the sleep from my eyes and roll over to grab my phone. I scroll through my messages, reading the ones that my sisters continued sending back and forth in our group chat. Cara tried to defend that *"ditto"* is cool because Patrick Swayze says it, and Casey came back with the fact that if she thinks Patrick Swayze is cool, she really is getting old. I'm giggling to myself when the door creaks open.

I squeeze my eyes shut, trying to gather the energy to deal with the Ronan situation, when I feel a warm body slide in behind me. I almost buck away. The audacity that he thinks he can just snuggle me after I now know he's been talking with her, is borderline insulting. But just before I have a chance to throw an elbow backward and into his ribs, a feminine hand, with long, dainty fingers and chipped, pink polish, slides onto my arm.

"Hey, baby," Claire says, her imitation of Ronan weirdly spot on.

I laugh, shifting to my opposite side to face her. "Why does it feel like you've been practicing that?"

"Nope, just gifted." Claire winks. "Listen, we're gonna get going. Between that hangover yesterday and the excitement about the book, I'm wiped and feel a little fluey or something."

"Oh, perfect. Thank you so much for spooning me with your germ-ridden body."

"Welcome," she says sarcastically.

"You better not be sick this week."

"I won't be. I'm sure I'm just tired." She kisses my forehead. "Thanks for a great weekend, Chlo."

Claire slides out of bed, and I sit up, leaning back on the headboard. "Call me later," I say, turning my attention back to my phone.

"I will. And hey, tell Ronan we'll see him in a few days and that we're sorry we missed him."

My head snaps from my screen back to Claire. "What do you mean?"

"He already left." She says it matter-of-factly, despite the emotions that rise up inside of me, like she expected that I knew this already.

Because she did.

"His car's not in the driveway. Did you not know?"

"Right, no, I knew," I lie. "I just, uh, forgot." I hold up my phone. "Got stuck in a black hole."

She studies me briefly before saying, "Cat videos?"

I nod. "Always cat videos."

She chuckles, but I notice her gaze lingers on me for an extra beat. "Hey, you okay?"

I look back at my phone, afraid that if she sees my eyes, she'll see all of it—the breakup, the lies, the photo booth, Maggie—everything. "I'm good!"

"Okay," she says hesitantly. "Then we're taking off, but I'll call you?"

"Perfect." When I hear the door pull shut, I finally move my eyes to where Claire once stood. Ronan is gone, not downstairs. He actually left. And now Claire and Jay are leaving too, and I'm, once again, alone.

I think back to last night. To me and Ro, to the text, to rolling over instead of confronting him like I probably should have. Okay, so I was mad at him and avoided it all by going to sleep, but that doesn't mean he was supposed to leave without saying goodbye. How is he the one who gets to be upset?

I get up from the bed, looking around and realizing I wouldn't have even noticed Ronan was gone if Claire didn't tell me. All that is missing is his little, old backpack. I change out of my dress that I'm still in from last night and throw a hoodie over my leggings. Lifting my duffle bag onto the bed and packing up my things one by one, I replay the weekend in my mind.

In some respects, the last two days were exactly as I expected—full of ups and downs and awkward conversations. But in other ways, they were nothing like I thought they'd be—small moments with Ro and quick glimmers of the old us. I definitely didn't expect to hook up with Ronan, in a photo booth or otherwise, let alone find out he's been talking to Maggie, all in the same night.

The memory of the whole thing feels like the break up all over again. In some senses, I was pleasantly surprised, but in others, the rug was ripped right out from under me. They say the first stage of grief is denial, and I think early last night I started that process. Being with Ronan felt like a time machine had taken us back to a month ago, and, if you ask me, I wasn't the only one who momentarily forgot we broke up. Either way, it felt like we were headed back in a positive direction, and for just a second, I thought we might come out of this weekend better than we started it.

But hours later, after seeing his phone and his reaction of hiding it, that confidence turned to anger—stage two. As I gather my belongings, I'm not sure I'm quite done with that yet. Stepping into the bathroom to collect my toiletries, I'm right back to the shower from yesterday. Nobody asked him to help me. I damn sure didn't ask him to confess he can't stop wanting me. Okay, I dared him to kiss me, but the feeling was clearly mutual. Skimming the shower, I can almost feel his gentle lips on mine. Even after the first heat of the moment, he still sweetly kissed me again. Now, I'm not just angry, I'm pissed. It's one thing for Ronan to lead me to believe that we still have a chance, but it's another for him to do that while he also plays the field.

Throwing my mascara into my bag, I stomp back to the bed, toss my things into my duffle, then rip my phone from the charger on the wall. I open my contacts and scroll to the R's. My thumb hovers over the stupid heart emoji that I forgot to remove from Ro's name as I think of all of the things that I want to say to him,

I thought Ronan was different. I thought what we had was so special that it would take more than three weeks for him to move on. For him to find someone new... for him to run to her. I thought kissing in the shower, hooking up in Pine Village, spending the car ride home exchanging glances, would change things between us. I guess I thought wrong.

I press down, all of my rage channeling into the tip of my finger, and bring the phone to my ear—right to voicemail. I call once more, and the same thing happens. I groan out loud and hit end, just as the automated message plays for the second time. I might be mad, but I'm not desperate, so instead, I blacken my screen and throw it next to my bag.

I take one final look around, and like how it always goes when a vacation is over, the room suddenly seems so vacant compared to how it did before—As if somehow, my knockoff boots by the door or my graphic tee thrown over the dresser, filled the room more than I realized.

I throw my bag over my shoulder and slip my phone into my pocket. I descend the stairs and loop around the first floor to see everything has already been picked up and put back. I set the owner's keys on the kitchen island and move towards the entrance.

As I walk out of the door of this storybook cabin for the last time, I wish I could say it worked its magic. That the remarkable decor, endless land, and air that seemed so invigorating, was able to piece my life back together. But I guess that's just not how it works. *Life's not a fairytale,* I think to myself, *no matter the*

setting. And sometimes the characters just don't get to live happily ever after.
"Married or not apparently," I say out loud.

I walk to my car, and a feeling of dread drapes over as I realize that I can't even blame the Carlson Curse for my miserable calamity. I unlock the doors and pull the driver's side open, deciding no—all of this is Ronan's fault.

I'm almost home when *Sorry* from my road trip playlist, is so rudely interrupted by an incoming call. I glance over to see Ronan's adorable—and smug and terrible—face pop up on my screen, the small green answer button just begging me to take it. I hesitate, my eyes scanning back and forth between the road and my phone dock, trying to decide what I should do. Best case scenario, Ronan is calling to tell me he made a huge mistake and he wants—no—*needs* us to get back together. Worst case scenario, he's calling to invite me to his and Maggie's wedding because she screamed, "Yes!" and took the damn ruby ring when he offered it to her.

The phone rings again, and I come to a crossroads. I could answer it and hear what he has to say, or better yet, give him a piece of my mind. Or, I could let it go, put it off, make him wonder for a change. I make a decision, and before I have the chance to change my mind, I tap the red circle next to it, Justin Bieber's voice once again filling my speakers.

"Ooh, ooh," I sing. "Is it too—"

I'm interrupted again by another call from Ro, and this time, it barely rings once before I hit decline. Sure, I'm probably being petty, but after his yo-yoing this weekend, I think I'm entitled to a little time to sort out how I feel. It is kind of nice to see him desperate to reach me again, but maybe Justin's right. It is too late for an apology.

Ten minutes, and two more ignored calls later, I pull onto my street. I desperately need to stretch my legs, but I am feeling quite satisfied knowing that my call log now lists four incoming calls from Ronan in the last fifteen minutes.

Swiping out of my Maps, I see the back of a familiar baseball cap in front of my building. I roll down the passenger side window closest to the curb and also see a worn, black sweatshirt and gray joggers that I recognize.

"Ro?" I call out, leaning across the middle console. Ronan whips around like he's surprised to see me at *my* apartment and then rushes to the car.

"Where the hell have you been?" he asks, opening the door and taking a seat.

"Well, that feels like a trick question." *I* know that *he* knows I'm coming home from the cabin.

He lifts his hat and rakes his hands through his hair, and damnit if my mouth doesn't water as he does it. Setting his hat back on top of his waves, he continues. "I called you four times."

"I know," is all I say.

"So, what the fuck, Chloe?"

"Woah! Who are you to show up to my place, highjack my passenger seat, and then talk to me like that? Not to mention after—"

"Jay and Claire were in an accident." Instantly, a lump forms in my throat, and by the way that I feel, it might be my stomach.

"But... what... they were just... " I can't find thoughts that make sense, let alone turn them into comprehensible words.

"They're okay," he says, and I could slap him for not leading with that. I blow out a breath and lay my head on the steering wheel, only for the horn to be hit, jolting me back to reality. *I've got to stop doing that.*

"So, what happened?" I ask. "Where are they?"

"Apparently, Jay hit a patch of black ice, and the car slid off the road and into a tree. They're at Center Springs hospital. Luckily they weren't too far from home."

"The hospital?" I yell, and Ronan holds up his hands to tell me to slow down.

"Jay has a broken rib from his seatbelt, and his shoulder got all messed up from the impact. It was on Claire's side though, so she took the brunt of the hit." My heart rate picks up, and I feel my eyes go wide. Ronan timidly places his palm on my knee. "She's fine, Chlo." And this time I really do slap him... in the arm... hard. He jolts back from the contact, exhales, and closes his eyes. "I should have started there. I'm sorry."

Those two words ring out from earlier, and they should mean more, but all I can think about is my best friend lying in a hospital bed, covered in bruises. "So, what's wrong with her?"

"I'm not really sure. The hospital gave me more of Jay's story because I'm his emergency contact. I'm sure they called the Dawsons for Claire." I gulp, my eyes frantically searching for, I don't know what, but it's like all of the sudden, I need to find something—to do, to fix, to help.

"Chloe," Ronan says sternly, his eyes concentrated on mine, his face serious. "Everything's going to be fine." *How can I believe him? It feels like nothing is fine.*

When I don't respond, Ro leaves the car, and before I have a chance to wonder where he's going, he's tugging at my driver side door. I slowly move my hand to unlock it. My body feels like it's disconnected from my brain, the two things both barely working and not at all together.

When I tap on the button, Ronan throws the door open and reaches in to pull me out. I watch as his hand finds mine, and I trail its movement until my limp arm is fully extended. I allow him to drag me out until I'm standing just inches from him. Looking up, I know my eyes are glazed over from the shock that I feel. He looks back at me with a tight jaw and razor sharp eyes. I always said that Ronan was who I'd want in a crisis, and now here we are. It seems I was right.

We stare at each other, his stoic expression a stark contrast to mine full of worry, until he pulls me to him, wrapping me up in his reassuring arms. "We're gonna go see her," he says quietly, and as if my body was waiting on those words alone, I sink further into him, relishing in his embrace.

If only for now.

20

Before

"Just leave it by the door for now! Hurry up!" Ronan calls to me from the couch. As far as he knows, I just filled the giant cauldron in my hands with candy from the bags that cover the kitchen island. What he doesn't know is that I finished doing that five minutes ago, but I've been sitting here munching on gummies and chocolate ever since. Moving from where I've been propped on the counter, I dispose of the evidence, then head to the entryway to set the bucket by the door.

I make my way to the couch where Ronan is sitting with a bowl of popcorn in his lap and his feet on the coffee table. He's scrolling through Halloween movies, trying to decide on one he knows I'll agree to. Sitting next to him, I curl my feet under my legs and reach for the snack. I finally roll enough pieces of popcorn into my hand to fill my whole palm, when he grabs my outstretched arm.

"What are you doing?" I gasp, my fingers unwillingly releasing a few of the kernels.

He pulls me closer to him, bringing his nose to my lips. "Why do you smell like candy?"

My eyes double in size like a kid who stole from the Halloween bowl, rather than a grown adult who did such a thing. "I don't," I say through all but closed lips. I try to breathe my sweet breath sideways and slide away from him, but his grip is too strong.

"Yes, you do. You smell like nougat and caramel and... " He sniffs again. "Chocolate."

I sink into him in defeat. "Okay, okay. I had a piece." He looks at me doubtfully. "Okay, four pieces... but what did you expect? You know you can't put me in charge of things like that."

"You're unbelievable." He brings his hand to his chest, releasing my wrist, and fakes devastation. "Those are for the children!"

"Oh, whatever." I say, pulling the bowl of popcorn from his lap. "We have like ten bags. What did your mom do? Buy out the stores?"

"It's edible. Are you really surprised that my mom got too much?" I laugh, but it's true. Ronan's mom loves you through food, so anything you can eat, she always has tons.

When Ro asked me to hand out candy with him on Halloween, I thought he was kidding. We both live in apartments, so I wasn't quite sure who would be trick-or-treating by us. It made much more sense when he explained that it would be at his parents' house. Apparently, Mr. and Mrs. Caruso go to his uncle's costume party each year, so Ronan or Mikey typically hang here to pass out candy in their quaint, little neighborhood.

"I'm sorry," I pout, and Ronan pulls me to him by my big, baggie pullover and plants a hard kiss on my lips.

"You should be," he winks, and I pull on the string of his sweatshirt because I know that he hates when they're uneven. He glares at me playfully as he messes with them, then brings me even closer to him. I nestle my body so it's snug against his, burrowing into the soft fabric of his hoodie, the strings of which are back to being perfectly balanced.

Do we have to dress up?" was the first thing I asked when Ronan presented this idea. I used to live for Halloween and would go all out with costumes, but that was when I was single and out at the bars. Although part of me would still love to put on a skimpy skirt and pretend glasses and threaten to keep Ro after school for detention, now that we're together, I can technically do that any day of the week. The idea of pushing through crowds and drinking red, sugary shots from tubes, just sounds like a lot of work and a several day hangover. I'd much rather be cozy in leggings. Needless to say, I was thrilled when Ronan responded with, *"If by dress up you mean pajamas, then sure. Definitely dress up."*

So here we are, snuggled on the couch, sitting in sleep clothes, and getting ready to hit play on *Edward Scissorhands*. I reach for the remote, and just as the intro appears on the screen, there's a knock at the door.

Ro and I both look at each other, finally settled, but as much as I want to watch the movie, I'm also loving the idea of handing out candy to all of the kids. I jump from the couch, Ro following behind me, and open the door.

He comes up beside me with the cauldron in tow, and standing in front of us are three little girls that look to have about the same age gap as me and my sisters. They're in sparkly dresses and silver, faux diamond crowns and those fake, plastic, kid heels that clack when they walk.

"Trick-or-treat!" they squeal in unison, the middle one holding the youngest one's hand. I open my mouth to greet them, when Ronan suddenly pushes right past me.

"Woah," he says, crouching down to their level. "Chloe, are you seeing this?" He looks back at me, a surprised look on his face. I play along by smiling, though I'm not quite sure where he's going with this.

"Real princesses," he whispers loudly enough for the girls to hear. They giggle in response, the oldest one growing a smile so long, it barely fits on her face.

"No way," I say. I stifle a laugh and kneel next to him. "Do you think they live in a castle?"

Ro's face lights up like he heard something magical. "I don't know!" He turns back to the girls and asks eagerly, "Do you guys live in a castle?"

The three sisters snicker again, the middle one bringing her hands to her mouth to cover her bashful expression. "No, silly," she says. "We aren't *real* princesses. They're costumes!" She moves her hands to the hem of her dress and spreads out the fabric to show off the skirt. The oldest one playfully rolls her eyes, dramatic like Cara, who also thinks she's more mature than she is.

"Hey! *I'm* a real princess!" the youngest one says. She leans in to Ronan to tell him a secret, although like most young kids, her whisper sounds the same as her regular voice. "She's just jealous because I have a wand." She whips out a bedazzled star on a stick, nearly smacking Ronan right in the chin.

He dodges the blow, smiling at me. "Well, I think you all look beautiful," he says to them, and my heart does that flutter it does when guys do things like respond well to children.

"Me too," I chime in. Ro holds out the candy, and each girl politely takes a piece for themselves before he grabs an overflowing handful and drops several more in each of their bags.

The girls' faces light up. "Thank you," the oldest one says, the other two darting away with their sacks in the air.

"You got it... Your Majesty." Ronan stands and takes a damn bow, and my ovaries all but shriek in response.

We wave to the parents, who are waiting across the lawn on the sidewalk, then head back inside. Ronan shuts the door and walks right to the couch, like the scene I just witnessed was completely normal and under no circumstances left me in pieces.

I sit next to him, somehow even closer than before, my entire being swelling with pride for this man. "You were so good with them," I say, and I realize now that I have never seen Ro with anyone so little. Of course, with it being my job I'm sort of built for the task, but not everyone could act so naturally otherwise.

"I love kids," he says, tossing a handful of popcorn into his mouth. He's so casual about it, as if it should be expected, and that alone makes it even more charming.

"So you want them?" I ask awkwardly. "Kids."

Ro looks at me, slowly chewing his mouthful of kernels. He keeps steady eye contact until he swallows. "I do," he says, running his tongue across his top teeth. "Do you?" He asks it hesitantly, bracing himself for the answer.

"Of course," I say quickly, grateful for his response. I grab another handful of snack and pop a rogue piece in my mouth. "At least three. I don't care what they are, but I want them all close together. Like maybe, oh, I don't know, every twenty to twenty-four months."

Ro laughs, reaching for the glass of water that sits on the coffee table. "Very specific," he says, and I tilt my chin down just once, noticing he doesn't even flinch at the thought.

When I was dating before and I told guys that I was in no rush to get married, a lot of them sighed huge breaths of relief. Even those who wanted to get married quickly, thinking a wife would solve all of their problems or at least get them out of their mom and dad's basement, weren't looking to have kids any time soon. They assumed that because I didn't plan for a wedding, that I also had no intention of having children. Too many times I had to remind them that we live in the 21st century and that, believe it or not, the doctors don't actually require a marriage license before they deliver your baby.

Kids have always been in the plan for me, and when the curse started running its course, that was the one thing that stayed the same. I just needed to find a guy who was also on board with my plan. My students are the best part of my job, and having sisters was the best part of my childhood. The only thing I always wished was that we were just a little closer in age. That way, the gap between us wouldn't have been just another factor, on top of distance and jobs, that tend to keep us apart.

When Ro and I started dating, I could quickly see that he would make a great dad. He's patient and understanding, even-tempered and supportive. He's also fun, loving, and surprisingly affectionate. Honestly, he sort of reminds me of my own dad sometimes, which is something I'd never want to think about otherwise. If we're talking about parenthood though, then I'm okay with the comparison because when it comes to fathers, I've got a good one.

I guess I just never thought to bring up the topic with him before. If there's one thing I've learned over the past almost-year of my first *real* relationship, it's that I'm hesitant when it comes to anything that potentially progresses things along. It doesn't make sense because with Ronan, I don't want to hold back. I just think somewhere in my subconscious I might be a smidge afraid of the future. As Ro pointed out, maybe to me, commitment feels just a little bit scary. So, things like meeting his parents, asking to know more about him and his past, talking about kids, don't necessarily come naturally—despite that I want all of those things and more with him.

"Well," Ro says. "Three works for me. But I think I'd like to adopt at least one of them."

My mouth falls slightly open, the ease of his tone speaking volumes in itself. He's so comfortable talking about all of this. Is that because he just knows what he wants? Or because he knows what he wants... with me?

In all honesty, I never even contemplated adoption, but of course it's something I would love to consider. I almost feel silly for not thinking about it sooner, especially with Ronan. I know how much others choosing that path changed his life.

I stare at him in wonder, my heart physically aching for him in the best possible way. Sometimes I forget that this guy has been through hell and back, and yet, he still carries himself in the way that he does.

"Adoption," I say, thoughtfully. Now that it's been put on the table, I'm thinking about me being a Camilla to another little Ro. Taking in a child in need, being there for them, taking care of them... loving them. The idea is now permanently stamped into my mind, and I'm not sure I'll ever think about my future the same after this conversation. To have my child one day look at me, speak about me, think of me, the way Ronan does with his mom and dad—that just feels like the ultimate dream.

"I'm definitely okay with that," I say, and I mean it. I give Ronan a soft kiss on the lips, lingering there while I let my heart overflow with the love that I have for him and the way that he is. After a few seconds, I open my eyes, and pop back abruptly, "If you mean with me, of course."

Ronan rolls his eyes, setting the bowl on the table. He adjusts himself so he's sitting up straighter. "Yes, Chloe," he says, grabbing my cheeks with both hands. "I mean with you." He leans over me, and I fall back under him, my body now sprawled across this half of the couch. Suspended over me, I take his sweatshirt strings in my hands and pull him to me, his breath smelling like buttery goodness. He plants a kiss on my lips, the salt from the popcorn still on his tongue as he sweeps it over mine.

I move to continue, but Ro pulls back out of nowhere. He stills, narrowing his eyes at me, then says, "If *you* meant with *me*."

"Hmm," I say as he hovers above me, and I make a point to act unsure. After two seconds too long, I wrap my legs around his hips and pull him to me so his body is flush with mine—thigh to thigh, chest to chest, mouth to mouth. "Yeah," I say. "I think I can make that work."

He kisses me again, but I can feel his teeth on my lips as he smiles through our embrace. I revel in the moment, both of us so happy, so sure, so set on the future. I wrap my legs tighter around his lower half, and his smile fades as he hums into my mouth. He slides one hand under my hip and pulls me to him, when suddenly, there's another knock at the door.

21

Now

Ro and I pull up to Center Springs hospital, and I all but fall out of the car while it's still moving.

The entire ride here, we sat in an audible silence—talking with no words at all. Ronan's left leg tapped rhythmically, the pointer finger on his right hand grazing his thumb over and over, his body's way of saying he's nervous. I, however, sat completely still. My anxiety and worry occupied all of my energy, my lack of motion speaking volumes compared to my normal, high-energy self.

We park the car, and I sprint across the lot. I bang through the hospital doors and hear Ronan jogging up behind me. We walk to the front desk, where a nurse in powder blue scrubs with a jet black ponytail flips through a pile of paperwork.

"Excuse me," I say quickly, and when she doesn't look up right away, I clear my throat and adjust my stance in agitation.

The girl raises a finger to tell me to wait, and I slap my hands on the counter. Opening my lips, I feel Ro's hand on my shoulder, gently guiding me back. I gesture to the nurse, shaking my head with squinted eyes, and he moves me aside, stepping up to the desk.

"Hey there," Ro says. I don't think he's necessarily trying to be charming, but his voice comes out like he's here to rescue her from her tower, rather than find out the room my best friend is in.

Of course, the nurse drops her papers this time and slides her pen into the band in her hair. "Can I help you?" she asks.

"We're here to see two patients, Jamison Errington and Claire Dawson."

"You're family too? Her parents just left."

"Jay's my brother," Ronan says without hesitation. "Claire's his wife."

The woman nods and types something into her computer. "And you are?" she asks, looking at me.

"I'm *his* wife," I say to her, but I'm looking at Ro. He nods slowly, a distant but understanding look in his eyes.

He turns back to the desk as the nurse clicks her mouse one final time before saying, "It looks like there was a... request... for them to be put in the same room." The nurse says *request* like she's leaving out details, and Ro and I look at each other, a knowing smirk on both of our faces—Jay. "So, room eight for both of them."

I grab Ronan by the arm and beeline it for the main doors that lead to the individual rooms. "How did you know Jay would have said Claire is his wife?" I ask, pushing through the entrance.

"It's what I would have done."

I nod, my gaze falling to the floor. I know he's right. It is what he would have done. It's what I would have done. Hell, it's what I did when the nurse asked me who I was at the desk.

The thought scrambles my brain even more than it already was before, and the numbers on the wall seem to pass in slow motion until we get to six, seven, eight. When we reach their room, I pause at the door, my previous adrenaline drained.

I'm not sure why I feel so scared to go in. Ronan has assured me they're fine. I know what happened, but for some reason, I feel incapable of moving forward. As if he's reading my mind, Ro drops his arm from mine and interlaces our fingers instead. For a second, I wonder if he's doing this for the sake of preserving the act we've put on, but a gentle squeeze and a brush of my knuckles tells me he's just genuinely here for me. He takes one step in, his pull on my arm encouraging me to do the same.

I stride forward, eventually rounding the half-wall that stands between the door and first bed, the basic, white paint littered with warnings about germs and flyers for call centers. The first thing I notice is that the room is dimmer than the fluorescent lights that run down the hallway, and the second thing I see is Claire's face.

She looks tired, and there's a gash near her right eye, but other than that, she's her smiley self. I run to the far side of her bed, my eyes finding Jay on the way over. His arm's in a sling, but otherwise, he seems to be his normal self too, face serious and eyes locked on Claire.

"Hey, Chlo," she says, when I finally reach her, and as if she triggered a dam with just that hello, the tears flow that I have been trying to hide. "Hey, it's okay. I'm alright." She wraps her arms around my body that is now falling onto hers. I feel her wince underneath me and spring back to standing.

"I'm sorry," I say, realizing as petite as I am, she must be hurting from the crash. I brush her hair back with my hand. "You're lucky, you know that?"

Claire takes a deep breath. "I know. It could have been so much worse."

I nod my head, wiping tears from my cheeks. "Well, yeah," I whimper. "But I just meant because if you would have been any more hurt than you are, I might have had to actually kill you."

Claire starts laughing, grabbing her chest, the reaction clearly borderline painful. "You're right," she says. "Next time I'm in a car accident, I'll think of you."

"Thank you," I say. I look over to see Ro and Jay smiling at each other. Ronan extends his right arm to take Jay's left hand in his. "Good to see you, brother."

"Thanks for coming."

"Of course. We got here as soon as we could."

"So, what happened?" I ask.

"Fucking black ice. I tried to avoid it, but the turn was too tight. We drifted right off the road and into a tree not far from the street."

"It wasn't your fault," Claire says. By her tone, I can tell it's not the first time she's said that to him.

"Yeah, man," Ro says. "That shit just happens, and everyone's good. That's all that matters." Jay lays his head back on the pillow, clearly still thinking about all the *what-ifs*, when there's a light knock on the frame of the door.

A doctor enters the room in green scrubs with a white coat on top. A stethoscope hangs around his neck, and there's a clipboard in his hand. "Well, hello there," the man says as he approaches the bed. The badge that hangs from his coat reads **Dr. Klein**. He's older—maybe my dad's age—and his smile is friendly, which is exactly what we need. "Visitors?" he asks, looking between Jay and Claire.

"They're family," Claire says, grabbing my hand.

"Practically a cult," Ronan says, and Jay snorts a laugh.

"Alright then," Dr. Klein says to the chart in his hand. "So, Jay, it looks like you have a broken rib and a torn tendon in your right shoulder from the impact of the seatbelt. You'll feel some discomfort and may need some physical therapy on that arm, but with a little time, both should heal up nicely."

Claire heaves a sigh of relief, reaching over the gap between their beds with her free hand to grab Jay's. He smiles at her as the doctor continues.

"And Claire, in addition to some bruising across your chest, and a pretty nasty gash by your eye from the window, you also have a mild concussion as we mentioned before."

"So, what's that mean?" I jump in. Dr. Klein finds me and gives a reassuring smile.

"Just that she should take it easy. Limit screen time and bright lights for a while and ease back into things like driving and exercise as she starts to feel better."

"Are you sure that's all it is, Doc?" Jay asks, with obvious tension in his jaw.

"We'll do a CT scan now, just to be sure, but I think you got lucky." He smiles at Claire, who looks at me side-eyed and chuckles to herself. *Lucky.*

"Oh," the doctor adds. "And don't worry. Because we'll be focused all the way up at the brain, the scan is totally safe for the baby." He surveys the room and nods, his lips turned in. "We'll see you in a little bit," he says and walks out the door.

The four of us remain still, the same dumbfounded expression on all of our faces. "Baby?" Claire whispers, the first of us to break the silence. Her head first rolls to Jay, who's stone-faced, staring straight ahead, and then turns to me. "Baby?" she says again, almost inaudibly.

I move my gaze that was once on Ronan's, both of our eyes wide and our eyebrows raised through the roof, to Claire's, whose are distant, her brow furrowed. I picture the girl in front of me, my best friend in the world, holding a newborn—my future niece or nephew. "A baby," I whisper back in wonder, and her expression instantly softens, a slow smile spreading across her face.

We let out a quiet shriek, bringing our foreheads together as Ro pats Jay's leg. "Yo," he says through a breathy laugh. "Congratulations, dude."

Jay swallows hard, his eyes still forward, his face still unreadable. "Baby," he says like he's testing the word on his tongue. He pauses, and Claire looks at me, her face full of fear. We all know Jay's past and everything that he's been through. Not that the two of them haven't talked about kids, but it wouldn't be surprising if the idea of having them before he feels ready, is terrifying to him.

"It's okay if you're not excited," Claire says, slowly sitting up. I look at Ronan thinking maybe we should give them some space, when Jay speaks again.

"That is... " We all brace ourselves for what may come next. "Incredible," he says, and I can feel the tension fly from the room. "Fucking incredible." He grunts as he turns his legs off of the bed, then carefully hobbles over to Claire. "I love you," he says.

"I love you too... Dad." She giggles.

"Wow." He rotates toward Ronan, grimacing from the movement. "You hear that? I'm gonna be a dad."

"Hell yeah you are, brother." Ro walks over and properly hugs him. "And a kickass one too," he says in his ear. I watch their embrace, and see Claire watching too, realizing for them, this moment means more than she or I could ever imagine.

"Guess that explains why I felt like garbage the whole weekend," Claire says.

"Oh my God," I say, remembering her ridiculous hangover and constant exhaustion. "So, you're not old! Just knocked up!"

Claire smacks my arm, and as if on cue, a yawn escapes her lips. "Maybe a little old," she says.

"Or concussed," Ro chimes in, and we all laugh despite it not actually being that funny.

"In all seriousness, guys, you think you could let her get some rest?" Jay asks.

"Yeah, man," Ro says, clapping Jay on his good shoulder. "We'll hang out there awhile. Just let us know if you need anything."

"Coffee. Please."

"You got it."

I give Claire one more hug, this time leaving my body weight off of her. "You're going to be the best mom ever."

"And you, the best aunt." She squeezes me as much as her body allows, and when I pull back, her face drops momentarily.

"What's wrong?" I ask.

"Nothing. I just... I guess we're not getting married this weekend." She turns her face to Jay whose eyes dart to mine.

"Well, do you want to?" I ask.

"Of course," she says instantly.

"Claire... " Jay warns.

"You don't want to?"

"Sure I do. But you need to heal. We can't be driving all over and be around all of those people."

"I don't care about that," she says looking down at her belly. "I just want our little family to be... official."

If looks came with captions, Jay's would say: **And that was the moment he was mended completely**. He puts his forehead to hers. "Then we'll make it happen."

I look at Ronan who shakes his head and shrugs his shoulders as if he doesn't know what to think. "No. *We'll* make it happen," I say, then kiss Claire on the cheek. "You two don't worry about anything but taking care of our baby."

Jay snickers, and I put my arms out for him to join us. "Bring it in J-Daddy."

Everyone laughs, and Jay side hugs me with his good arm like he used to. "Dare I say I miss your Hulk arms around me?"

"Actually," he says. "I kind of do too."

I'm texting Mrs. Dawson about my wedding ideas when Ronan comes back into the waiting room after delivering Jay's coffee. They've already taken Claire to get scanned, and Jay is getting his fix while he sits with his newest surprise. I left that part out when I texted Mrs. Dawson, figuring Claire can tell everyone about the baby when she's ready. As far as the wedding goes, her mom has agreed to call their friends and family and tell them that we have to cancel our plans.

Ro sits down next to me and exhales loudly. The whole day has been such a whirlwind of emotions that I almost forgot that I'm mad at him. Between the ups and downs, the missed calls, the accident, the baby, and now the wedding, I just can't seem to keep up with how I'm feeling—Or how I'm supposed to.

On one hand, it was nice of Ronan to be here today, for his friends and for me. On the other, our breakup didn't just disappear, and I still don't like how everything went down with the Maggie incident.

"How's it going?" he asks, leaning over the arm of the chair. After talking with Claire's mom, I have a pretty good idea of what we should do, but now I just have to make it happen.

"It's alright," I say, and I know I sound short, but between the stuff with us and now this, I just can't seem to muster much more.

"Chloe, listen... " He shifts in his seat so one leg is now propped on the chair, turning his body so he's facing me. I keep my gaze on my phone until I feel his hand on my chin. He tilts it up, forcing my eyes to find his.

"Chlo, come on. You gotta talk to me."

"About what?"

He drops his hand and throws it in his lap. "What's going on?"

"What do you mean?"

"You know what I mean."

"Do I?"

He pauses, his face stern, his lips pursed. "Why are you being so hot and cold with me?"

"Me?" Now he has my attention. I turn my body so it's mirroring his. "You think *I'm* being hot and cold with *you?*"

"That's what I said."

I stare at him, adrenaline suddenly running through my veins. My pulse quickens, and I can hear myself puffing air through my nose—a bull under the stress of attack. "How's Maggie, Ro?"

He instantly pulls back, tilting his head and narrowing his eyes "What are you talking about?"

Him playing dumb only deepens my anger. I cross my arms over my chest and tilt my head sideways. "I saw your text last night. After the... Pine Village. I know you're talking to her."

His eyes double in size, and he runs his hand down his mouth as he stands up from the chair. "You have no idea what I'm doing." He turns to leave, only to spin right back around. "Is that why you got all weird last night? Why you ignored my calls? Why you're acting strange now?"

"Well, now I'm worried about my pregnant best friend's wedding that was supposed to happen in—"

"You know what I'm saying," he interrupts. "Is that why you went cold? You think I'm talking to Maggie?"

"No," I shoot back.

"Yes, it is."

"It's not."

"Chloe."

"Well, aren't you?"

The volume of our voices has slowly increased, to the point where I practically yell my question. I look around, now hyper-aware that there are several other people sitting close to us. One old man wakes from his sleep in his chair, while a couple whispers to themselves. Their young son with his hand wrapped in a towel, makes no effort to pretend he's not listening.

Ronan scowls at me, then nods toward the nearby hallway where he just got Jay's coffee, already walking away. I roll my eyes, reluctantly following him towards the vending machine that dispenses coffee like sludge and lattes that are more powder than milk. He stops abruptly at the end of the hall, and I bump into him as he spins around. Our chests all but touch as he glowers above me.

"Not that I need to explain myself, but I am *not* talking to Maggie."

The admission alone makes my heart skip a beat, but it doesn't hurt that Ronan's so close to me that I can feel his breath on my skin. My body visibly tenses, a reminder that Ro has this grip on me. Plus, now I'm embarrassed that I may possibly be wrong.

Because I refuse to back down, I gather myself, a difficult task for my racing mind. "I saw the text."

"When?"

"Last night at the fire."

He closes his eyes and exhales, stepping from me. He pivots so he's facing the wall, and my body relaxes, the facade that I'm fine breaking just briefly. Ro spins around, and I snap back into place, squaring my shoulders like I'm ready for battle.

"You saw *a* text," he says. "But it's not what you think." I wait for him to continue, my heart hanging on every word. "Yes, Maggie texted me. But it's not because we're talking. It's be—"

"Yo!" A familiar voice cuts him off from behind me, but I can't seem to take my eyes off of him. "She's back."

Ronan looks past me to where I know that Jay stands, but despite knowing I should, I can't turn around. Ronan huffs out a breath. He hangs his head, and though I'm desperate for him to continue, I know that he won't.

22

Before

"I know they won't care that it's perfect, but I do." I adjust the flower arch for the fourth time, fiddling with the hanging ivy that's not quite even on both sides.

Mrs. Dawson squeezes my calf as she stands below me, holding the ladder to make sure I don't fall. "Claire is lucky to have you," she says. "They both are."

The two of us are hosting Claire and Jay's wedding shower in their house, just weeks before their big day. Much like the ceremony itself, neither of them wanted anything extravagant. My original vote was for a winter wonderland theme in a barn nearby that you can rent out for parties. They have snow machines, do carriage rides with horses, and I could have even had an ice sculpture made in the shape of Jay's linebacker body. All of that however, seemed a little too close to lavish for them.

So, when I sat down with Mrs. Dawson, we decided a familiar place, comfortable to them, was the perfect setting to celebrate in. Then, when Claire said I could take the reins on the decorations and plans for the day, I sort of fell in love with the idea of turning their living room into the party of their dreams.

We decorated with bushels of flowers on every flat surface and gold framed pictures of the couple from all different times throughout their relationship. There's a candy bar to satisfy my girl's sweet tooth and cigars for the guys to enjoy on the porch. I made favors with homemade soaps from Bella's Boutique and Mason jar centerpieces that *someone* suggested. Now, if I could just get these greens to sit right on this arbor, I would be ready for the bride and groom to get here.

Ronan, who I volun*told* to cater the event, is walking around to each of the few folding tables, covered in white tablecloths and lace runners, setting down baskets of warm, homemade rolls. It's a treat watching him serve food that I know is delicious in something other than jeans and a t-shirt, and I can't seem to keep him out of my sight. Gawking at him, I almost lose my footing, stumbling just briefly, bracing myself on the handle. The movement catches his attention, and he leaps from where he is to the step ladder I'm on. He appears right below me, placing a stabilizing hand on my thigh. Claire's mom smiles and steps aside gracefully.

"You better be watching my girl, Mrs. D. She'll fall from this thing right on top of you, and Claire's two best ladies will be out of commission."

Mrs. Dawson giggles like she always does around Ronan and Jay, then makes knowing eyes at me. "Well, Chloe Belle," she says, placing her hand flirtatiously onto Ro's shoulder. "Looks like we have ourselves our very own knight in shining armor."

I step down from the ladder, and when I safely have two feet on the ground, I roll my eyes toward my boyfriend. He gets way too much joy out of being one of Mrs. Dawson's three favorite men. "Oh, yeah. My hero," I say, and he winks at me as he walks back to the table.

Mrs. Dawson snickers, then talks close to my ear. "That boy is just crazy for you," she says coyly. I fold up the ladder for the last time, finally satisfied with the way the damn flowers are set.

"That's what I've been told," I say, my eyes easily finding him in the kitchen like he's my North Star. "I think I might be kind of wild about him too."

Mrs. Dawson, who I have known for many years and has never been anything but polite and angelic, literally cackles in my face. I gape at her, stunned, not quite sure how such a devilish howl just came from such a reverent woman. She gathers herself, clearing her throat and pushing her bangs from her face.

"I'm sorry," she says, as she continues to snicker. "It's just so funny how you pretend you aren't completely, immensely, devastatingly, head over heels, for-the-rest-of-your-life-kind-of-in-love with that boy."

My mouth hangs open as she continues. "Chloe, dear, I have known you for a long time. I knew you before Ronan, and I know you now during Ronan, and I'm just telling you, there is no you *after* Ronan Caruso. Regardless of how you feel about marriage, and yes Claire has told me, the two of you are forever. You mark my words."

I nearly drop the ladder from my hands, my fingers going slack. Ro and I have been together for over a year now. I know how good we are and how much we truly love each other, but hearing it from someone else with no stake in the game, means so much more than Mrs. Dawson could ever know.

I look at her, tears hiding behind my eyes. She smiles at me and then her face lights up as she looks towards the door. "They're here," she squeals, squeezing the life from my arm, and that's when I see Claire and Jay have arrived.

The next several hours are spent taking pictures, eating food, and playing shower games, much to Jay's dismay. We play vow mad libs, where each guest fills in blanks for traditional vows with words with no context, and then the Newlywed Game, challenging the bride and groom.

The vow game was fun, but highly inappropriate for Claire's side of the family, when Jay's mechanic friends started using curse words and body parts as their verbs and nouns. The Newlywed Game was quite eye opening as well. Not only did Jay admit that his favorite karaoke song is *Ring of Fire* by Johnny Cash, but Claire admitted that he's ridiculously good at singing it. We also found out that if Claire was an animal, she'd be a walrus, which I'm still unpacking, and if Jay could pick any actor to play him in a movie, it would be Charlie Hunnam. That answer was actually kind of spot on, but for some reason, Jay would ask him to keep the long hair and unique, British accent.

Afterwards, Claire and Jay opened their presents, wine glasses here, an air fryer there, and three different toasters because of course, the two of them didn't register for anything. Claire is too nice to feel like she's *asking* for gifts, and Jay couldn't tell you what a registry is if his life—or better yet, his car—depended on it. Regardless, it was nice fawning over two of the most selfless people I know. Jay pretended he hated the whole thing, but I caught snapshots of him with his face full of pride and the way he so eagerly took it all in. And Claire cried more than once, the good kind of tears, where you just feel so content and in love with your life.

Now, just the four of us sit at a table. Everyone else has since gone home, the decorations taken down and the food put away. The flower bouquets went with each guest as a gift, which doubled as an easy way to clean this place up. We packed up the frames and leftover favors for the wedding and saved the candy and the cigars to have after the ceremony.

"Guys, I just have to thank you again," Claire says, taking a sip from the signature cocktail I made. "I know I've already said it, but this was just perfect."

Jay drapes his arm behind the back of her chair and adds in, "For real. Thank you, guys. And Ro, the food was awesome. That salsa you made with the little toast things... so fucking good." Claire and I look at each other, confused because we know the menu that Ronan prepared.

Ro stares blankly at Jay. "Bro, that's bruschetta," he says, and I let out a snort. "But now that you mention it... " He rocks his head back and forth and sticks his bottom lip out. "Italian salsa's not a bad way to describe it."

Now all three of us laugh, and Jay just shrugs his shoulders, completely unfazed by how goofy he sounds. "Call it whatever you want. I just need more of it."

Ro points behind him. "The leftovers are already in your fridge."

Jay pounds him from across the table as Claire chimes in. "You really did crush the food, Ro."

"Yeah, you did," I say, leaning in to kiss him on the cheek. Ro lifts his chin upward just once, too humble to make any more of a gesture.

"And Chloe," Claire adds. "The decorations, the set up, that beautiful archway—so stunning."

"It was nothing," I say, turning my head to one side, my neck still definitely kinked from adjusting those florals.

"It was everything," she says. I extend my hand to meet hers. "We're so fortunate, you guys. To have each other. Yes, we're friends, but it almost feels like we're family, you know?" We all nod in agreement as our eyes wander the table.

I look around at the people that have become so close to me this past year, and I know how Claire feels. This little foursome of ours feels like so much more than just a couple of friends or two couples that *are* friends. Jay and Ronan are practically blood already, and after a couple more weeks, Claire and Jay will be related through marriage. But I feel just as close to them all.

First, my gaze flicks to Claire, who is the best friend I've ever had. It doesn't matter that I haven't known her the whole span of my life. This girl came to me when everything changed. When I was just finishing college and decided to move to a little town a couple of hours from the only other home I'd ever known. I was leaving behind my sisters, my parents, the place I grew up, and a house that was changed, that I just couldn't go back to.

I was leaving a school I had been at for the last four years and people I had grown accustomed to seeing. Venturing into the world of adulthood, with my messenger bag and black, pencil skirt and taking on a dream of running a classroom—only to be sidelined instead, with the roles of copy lady and filing girl. A classroom assistant is an important job, but it's not the one I had set out to fill. Without Claire by my side, I don't think I would have made it past Jefferson. I probably would have packed my bags and headed home, leaving the aspirations I had then and the life I have now, back here in Maple Grove.

Then there's Jay. He and Ronan both came into my life at the same time, and it already feels like I've known them forever. Jay came from basically nothing, and he spent his entire life dealing with things that no one should have to, let alone a small boy. He's hardened to the world, less now than he was, but he's still a little rough around the edges. But Jay is also strong, and I'm not just talking about the size of his biceps. He has endured some of the worst things in life, and he's still there for everyone he knows. He's a steady force, resilient and protective, and completely soft once you really grow close. Most of all though, Jay loves my best friend with every inch of his heart. And for that, I'm forever grateful for him.

Finally, I turn to Ro. He's sitting almost sideways on his chair, one arm slung over the back of it and one resting on the table, a beer in his hand. The apron that was once tied around his waist has since been removed. Now he just wears his dark, navy chinos and light, sky blue button up. The color of his shirt makes his eyes look unreal, almost transcendent when he brings them to me.

It's funny because I used to look at him and just see... Ronan—Jay's sort of quiet, sort of alluring, sort of best friend, sort of brother. Then, somewhere along the line, he became more. He transformed into a prospect, an interest, a subject that consumed all of my thoughts. Now—he's everything. Ro is my other half, my soulmate, my future. He's the person I want to spend all my days loving. I want to make a home with him, a family, and a life we will spend with each other forever.

"I'd do anything for any of you," Claire continues, dragging me back to the moment.

"So would I," I say to no one in particular.

"Me too," Jay adds.

Ronan clears his throat. "Not a thing I wouldn't do."

"Then it's settled," Claire says. "This is it. The four of us no matter what. No dying, no leaving. Don't even move too far away."

Ro crinkles his brow. "This feels oddly cultish." Jay busts out laughing.

"Call it what you want," I say. "But I agree. The four of us—RoChloJaire forever!" Jay's face scrunches up and Ro lifts an eyebrow. "What? It's a working title."

"Whatever, I'm in. You couldn't get rid of me if you tried," Jay says, but it's mostly for Claire.

"Me either," Ro adds, and when my head rolls to him, it's me that he's talking to.

The group of us spend the rest of the night reliving memories and making a playlist for the dinner after the wedding. Jay and Ronan argue about whether or not John Mayer or Tom Petty did the best *Free Fallin'* version, while Claire just repeatedly tries to sneak P!nk songs onto the list. I give my two cents—no *Chicken Dance* or *Cha Cha Slide*—but mostly, I just take in these three people that I love more than anything.

These are my porch friends. The ones that I'll sit with when we're older, drinking our coffee, the sunrise in front of us. At first it will be to watch our kids run around in the yard and then to share worries about what our teenagers are up to. Eventually, we'll be old and gray, and so much will have changed—but not us. We'll talk about the good old days when we were young and first met, or our children were born, or our jobs were the worst, or when we sat at the table and picked out songs for a wedding. We'll laugh, we'll cry, and we'll probably bicker like hell, but we'll have each other. And that's all that we'll need.

23
Now

Claire and Jay spend the next three days at the Dawson's recovering. Of course they won't be fully healed for a couple of months, but Claire's mom and dad insisted that they stay with them for at least the first week so they can wait on them hand and foot. Mr. Dawson has switched all his office days so that he's working from home, and Mrs. Dawson has her entire church group praying over them constantly.

For the most part, Ronan has been in Grand Oaks working on the new restaurant, so I've been dropping by to help, talk, and just be there if they need me. Jay mostly just growls every time someone tries to do something for him, but Claire seems to at least like my company for when the *"chick flicks"* are on, as her fiancé has named them. Ro has called them both every day since the accident, but there hasn't been any interaction in person—with them or with me.

Ever since he told me that he and Maggie weren't together like I thought, I've been trying to decide how I feel. On one hand, this might mean that what happened between us was genuine, and that he and I may still have a chance. But on the other hand, whether or not he's with Maggie might not change what happened between us at all. It also doesn't change that he seems to be hiding things from me.

He texted me the day after Claire and Jay were discharged from the hospital, but this didn't seem like the type of thing that you discuss over the phone. Not only that, but I have been constantly moving, trying to take care of them and prepare for the wedding they don't know anything about. I've barely had a chance to eat, let alone worry about my relationship—or lack thereof—and if I'm honest, the distractions have actually been kind of nice. I'm desperate to finish the conversation with Ro and find out exactly what's going on, but I'm also scared I might not like what he has to say. For now, I'm burying myself in the work for this wedding, which brings me to where I am now—the frosty backyard of the future bride and groom.

The original ceremony was going to be held at a venue not too far from Maple Grove, with a simple dinner to follow. Because of their injuries though, the drive was too far, there was too much to do, and despite it being small already, there were still too many people they'd have to entertain.

This is why Mrs. Dawson and I decided that doing it here, in their backyard, would be the perfect compromise between keeping the plans from before and canceling all together. However, because it's the middle of January, I wasn't quite sure we could make it work outdoors. It's freezing in Maple Grove, and the last thing Claire and Jay's healing bodies need is to be frosty and stiff in the frigid air. And from my current experience, their privacy fence is no match for these strong, winter winds.

Luckily, Mrs. Dawson, who is pretty much the queen bee of her small, but supposedly fierce, church community, says that they have plenty of year-round events that they hold outside. The solution—rent a heated tent that is made specifically for this type of thing and that I had absolutely no idea existed. A crew will set it up outside, and we'll add a handful of chairs up front for a ceremony and two long tables organized in the back for a brief meal after "I do."

We will decorate the tent with greens and gardenias, accented with pine cones and berries to tie in the season. The only attendants will be the Dawsons, Jackson—Jay's older brother—Ronan, the three other Carusos, and me. The people will be fewer, the setting simpler than what they would have had otherwise, but if it all works out, it should mean just as much—if not more now with the most recent news.

The fact that my best friends are going to be parents in less than nine months is completely unbelievable. Claire and I once stalked Jay at his work, and now the two of them are going to be responsible for an entire human being. In some ways, I'm terrified for them—less money, less sleep, less time for themselves—but in some ways, I'm kind of... jealous. Here I am, in this weird limbo with Ronan, and they are building the future of their dreams.

I'm fighting with a tape measure that is definitely hostile, trying to verify the size of the yard, when my phone goes off from my bag by the gate. I, not so nicely, toss the tool onto the ground, then stomp on it for good measure on my way over to see who it is. I fumble with the zipper of my purse, another hunk of metal that seems pissed off at me today, before I'm eventually able to slide my phone from its pocket. If my insides could run both warm and cold, that's what happens when I see Ronan's name at the top of the message.

RONAN: I think we should talk before Saturday.

Okay, so apparently the distractions are over. In fairness, he's probably right. The whole purpose of this hiding-our-breakup thing was to spare Jay and Claire's wedding any unnecessary drama. We survived the weekend at the cabin, and in a twist of events—thanks to the accident—we were able to survive this week too. But everything has already changed so much for them. All I want is for their day to be perfect. The last thing they need on top of everything else, is to deal with our issues on their big day. I tap out a simple answer, my fingers practically frozen.

ME: Okay.

I attempt to type more, but my hands are so numb that it's all I can manage. I hit send and bounce in place, waiting for his response.

RONAN: Really? Is this what we're doing now? One word answers?

I throw my head back and groan. I work out the start of my next response, then try to explain my previous text. I'm halfway through the world "freezing" when my phone autocorrects it to "frenzy." I try again, but all of the letters come out wrong, and it ends up looking more like I'm hammered than slowly turning to ice. I surrender to the typos and delete all of the words but the first one.

ME: Sorry.

I blow on my hands while I wait for a reply and curse myself for not sneaking Claire's house key out of her purse. The back gate was open, and that's all that I needed, but it didn't occur to me that we live in the arctic.

RONAN: You know what? Fine. You let me know when you want to talk. I'm back in Maple Grove for the night. Going to Enzo's later if you want to meet there.

"Oh, for God's sake!" I throw my hands in the air, and my phone almost goes flying. This is pointless.

I toss it in my purse and pull my bag over my shoulder. I'm done here anyway. I have the numbers I need, and that tape measure can rot in this yard for all I care. Things are already rocky enough as it is with Ronan. I can't risk him being pissed because he thinks I'm being short with him. Instead of calling and getting into it now like I know that we would, or worse—getting hypothermia standing outside—I settle on going over to his apartment. At least then we can talk in person... and I can use the heat in his place to thaw out my body.

The short drive from Jay and Claire's to Ronan's apartment did nothing to defrost my fingers. By the time I get to his complex, I think they may somehow be even colder than before. It doesn't help that Ro lives on the first floor of his building, so the air from outside constantly cools down his hallway no matter how high the heat is set.

I shiver my way to his door, rubbing my hands together in prayer, which may be more fitting than I realize depending on how this conversation pans out.

When I get to his place, I reach for the knob on instinct before realizing, I may no longer be welcome to just walk in unannounced.

Before we broke up, I was always here, or he was at my place. Never once did we feel the need to ask for permission to come through the door. We both have keys to each other's apartments too. In fact, his still sits on my keyring, the extra eight grams of weight now more like an anchor. It's the reason we never moved in together. Between both of our places, and the room behind Enzo's, we saw it as a bonus to technically have three places to hang out, all within a five minute drive. Plus, with our opposite schedules—I'm up early to get into school, he's up late closing down the restaurant—it was almost more convenient to have our own respective places to sleep if we needed. But I would never pull that key out now. Partly because I wouldn't physically be able to hold it, but mostly because it feels wrong. It doesn't belong to me anymore.

I drop my hand from the knob, the strangeness of it almost chilling me further, then raise my fist to the door. I tap twice gently, afraid that the hard wood against my icy knuckles may actually split them in two. When there's no immediate answer, I brace myself to bang with more force. I wince as I knock harder, and this time, I'm rewarded with the sound of footsteps on the other side of the threshold.

Ronan opens the door hesitantly like he's not sure who would be here, probably because he isn't. I give a small wave once it's opened enough for him to see that it's me. His eyes grow wide, like I'm a grizzly bear rapping on the door asking for permission to attack him, rather than his barely over five-foot-tall ex-girlfriend. I wonder about his reaction, but I write it off as the weirdness that still lingers between us.

He quickly steps past the door and into the hallway as I stumble backwards in an attempt to move out of his way. Swiftly pulling the door closed behind him, he says, "What are you doing here?"

I scan him, noticing he's already dressed in an Enzo's t-shirt and his favorite dark jeans. He's wearing a backwards hat, no shoes, and his keys are dangling from his front pocket as if he was getting ready to leave or was just getting in. "Well, hello, Ronan. I'm fine, thank you for asking. How are you?" The fact that his response was so harsh when he was so annoyed with me for my one word answers, is laughable. And he has no excuse. From the gust of heat I felt when he all but slammed the door shut, his apartment is the perfect temperature for when it's subzero outside.

"I'm sorry," he says stiffly. "Hi Chloe... " His teeth find his bottom lip as he continues. "What are you doing here?"

"You wanted to talk."

"And you clearly didn't."

I puff out a breath, my knee jiggling from the fact that my body temperature is still way too few degrees. "My hands were too cold to text actual answers. I was in Claire's yard, and it's freezing outside and... wait, why are we out in the hallway?"

Ronan's throat moves up and down, and it's the first time that I notice his hand is still on the knob like he's ensuring that only *he* has access to it. He looks at his feet, his argyle socks moving up and down as he wiggles his toes. When he doesn't answer, I ask again. "Ronan, why are we in the hallway?"

"It's a nice hallway."

"Why?"

"Well, for one, the carpeting is—"

"Why can't we go inside, Ro?" I start getting antsy, the fact that he's being so mysterious spawning a weird feeling in the pit of my stomach.

He puffs out his cheeks, blowing breath through his lips. "Chloe, I... "

My body starts trembling, but suddenly, I'm not cold anymore. In fact, I'm not warm either. I feel nothing at all. It's like an out-of-body experience where I see myself looking at him intensely, holding firm to my question, but my insides are mush, my mind in the clouds.

Does he have a girl in there? Is *she* in there?

Neither of us speak for what feels like an eternity. You would think that pause would give me time to formulate an actual sentence, but all that I respond with is, "Oh."

My eyes blaze through the aforementioned carpet as I wait for him to speak, or for this hallway to open up and swallow me whole, whichever comes first. "Sorry, I—"

"Woah," he says, reading me like he's always been able to. "I don't know where your head just went, but if you think—"

"I don't think anything," I say, speaking too quickly to be telling the truth.

"You do," he says, tilting my chin back to him. "And it's nothing like that. It's just... "

"Just what?" My voice comes out as a cross between hopeful and desperate, and the way he looks at me like the answer is painful, makes me all too afraid that it actually is. He hesitates again, and I feel anxiety creeping up through my chest. "Tell me, Ronan!" I yell, like my worry pushed the words out. With that, he throws the door open.

I push past him, his body rocking dramatically from my blow before swinging back into place. He closes the door behind us as I take in the sight that's in front of me. I scan the once familiar space, confused and thrown off by what's in my view. Or lack thereof.

"Did you get robbed?" I ask, only partially kidding but surprised at the relief I feel at the thought that a thief, rather than Maggie, may have been in his place.

"I did not get robbed," Ronan answers, but as I look around the apartment, once decorated with a charcoal gray sectional, wooden coffee table, and land-scapes of mountains and lakes on the wall, I'm left unconvinced.

The floors are missing his soft, neutral throw rugs, and the light almond paint has been covered over in white. There's virtually no furniture, minus one padded folding chair and a metal tray table. A book sits on the table next to a red Solo cup, and his shoes lie on the floor near the legs.

"Where's all your stuff?" I ask, spinning to face him. He lifts his hat and runs his hand through his hair before settling it back down, forward this time.

"It's not here," he says, and I nearly give myself whiplash from the way that I throw my head around dramatically.

"No shit, Ronan. I'm freezing, not blind." He runs the side of his tongue along his teeth, and his first two fingers sweep over each other like their twigs sparking fire. I feel my body returning to a less hypothermic state as he sits his hands on the top of his head, exhaling loudly. "Will you just tell me what's going on?" I snap, the thawing process relaxing me enough to say what I need.

"I'm leaving," he says.

That quickly, the ice returns to my body. Or at least to the once-beating heart in the middle of my chest.

24

Before

I throw my hand to my heart, sitting up in my bed. Ronan stands above me, a tray in his hand. He just woke me up, the sound of his sweet, low voice calling me out of my sleep, but it feels like I'm still dreaming by the vision in front of me.

From this angle, I can see that the wooden tray that he's holding is filled with steaming hot coffee, a little baby orange juice, and what smells like the world's best chocolate chip pancakes. He's in just his boxers, which is a sight in itself, but he's wearing a smile that's new to me. He looks happy but almost borderline giddy. Like it's Christmas Eve, and he's nine instead of nearly thirty.

"What's all of this?" I ask, folding my legs in a pretzel. I strain my neck upwards to try to get a better look.

"I wanted to surprise you," he says, taking a seat by my knee. He swings the tray over my lap, and the sweet smell of chocolate and butter fills my senses even more than before. With it laid out in front of me, I can see the full tray and its contents. There's the pancakes, coffee, and tiny cup full of juice, but there's also crispy fried bacon, utensils and a single red rose.

"Aw, babe," I draw out. "This is so sweet. You didn't have to do all of this."

He leans in and looks at me intensely for longer than usual. "I just want this Christmas to be your best one yet."

"Well, I love that," I say, lifting the flower to my nose. "But you know it's not until tomorrow."

Ronan sits back again and reaches for the tray. "Oh, well in that case, I'll just take this—."

"No!" I tighten my grip on the surface, shooting a fake evil eye in his direction. "Don't you dare." He laughs, his voice still shaky from sleep, then retreats back to his spot, stealing a piece of my bacon along the way. I follow his hand as he brings the slice to his mouth, then take in the rest of him—his tight, black, spandex boxers hugging his thighs, his lean chest exposed, the way his hair's still disheveled in the best possible way. He licks his lips as he chews, and suddenly, I'm hungry for more than just breakfast.

"Seriously though," I say, clearing the want from my throat. "You didn't have to do all of this. Christmas will be perfect just because it's with you."

Ronan rubs his hand over the back of his neck. "I hope so," he says. I hear in his tone that he's somewhat distant, his eyes almost cloudy. I can't tell if it's because he's still tired or what, but it almost seems like something else is going on.

"Hey, you okay?" I ask, pulling his elbow to me. He places one hand on the outside of my waist, slouching over me as he shoots me a smile.

"Yeah, for sure," he says. He kisses my forehead, his scent hitting me like a gust of wind. It's a combination of his woodsy cologne, minty toothpaste, and the smoke from the bacon, and it mixes together in a smell that's erotic. *I'm awake now.* "I just wish I didn't have to go to work today." He sits back and brings his hand to the outside of my thigh, rubbing small circles on it with the tip of his thumb.

"Me too," I groan, hyper-aware of his touch on my leg. "I guess you have to?"

He lets out a sigh. "I wish I didn't, but Mikey's already at Nico's going over some things with the contractors before they get started on the booths." He slides his palm up my thigh casually, but the way the top-half of his hand slides under my sleep shorts, brings every nerve to life. "But tomorrow, I'm all yours." He kisses me once, a tease of his lips, before pulling away.

I take a bite of my pancakes trying to distract my mouth from the lack of his, and either the sugar shoots right through my veins, or it's Ronan who has caused my blood to start pumping. Despite the fact that these may truly be the best pancakes I've ever had, I stand up abruptly, setting the tray on my dresser.

"No good?" Ro asks, as he looks at me puzzled. He shifts into bed and sits back on the pillows, his face a mixture of concern and confusion. Nothing Ronan has ever made me has been anything but great. Add on the fact that I basically eat everything, and he's probably wondering where he went wrong.

"Oh, they're perfect," I say, placing one knee on the foot of the bed. "I'm just in the mood for... something else." I raise my leg so I'm now kneeling in front of him, his face full of shock. I swear I can see the wheels turn in his head as his mind registers where this is going.

He sits up straighter and runs a hand down his face. His legs are stretched out in front of him, his entire being like art on display. I crawl over to him as he blows out a slow, shaky breath.

"How much time do you have?" I ask, bringing my lips to his ear. I trace the side of his neck with the tip of my tongue, and a gravelly sound escapes from his throat.

"All fucking day," he says. His voice is breathy, and I laugh into his shoulder at the sudden change in response.

I straddle his lap, suspended over him, and rake my hands through his hair. I tug at it gently, and he pulls my weight down onto his lap, tightening the grip of his hands on my thighs. I feel him grow harder between my legs, and I rock my hips, creating friction against him. Ronan moans into my mouth, and I hum into his, a passionate melody of lust and desire.

Ro slides his hands up the sides of my shirt, the tips of his fingers like live wires to the nerves of my skin. He reaches the flesh where a bra strap would be if I slept with one on like a girl with a death wish. The sigh he expels becomes my new favorite sound, up until he utters his next three words.

"Arms up, Chloe."

I obey his command, lifting my hands past my ears, and he glides the hem of my shirt up and over my head. His eyes float over me as if he's afraid if he keeps them glued in one place, he'll miss the full picture. They settle in the spot right over my heart, and I bring one hand to my neck, suddenly way too aware of his fiery gaze on my exposed upper half. Ronan has seen me countless times. My body feels almost as much his as it's mine. But his look now, feels incessant. It's as if he's looking, not at me but through me and into my soul.

Ronan zeros in on my forearm obstruction and skims the length of it from my elbow to wrist. He dips his fingers beneath my palm, breaking the seam that binds it flush to my throat. He flicks my hand off so it drifts back to my side and replaces my gentle hold with his. Inhaling a steadying breath, he skims his thumb past my lips.

I still under his touch, the feeling somehow different—more intense—than it's ever been before. The way Ronan is looking at me tells me he's more than wound up. He's committed, devoted, bound to this moment, and it's almost like it feels like it's something new.

Ro kisses me hard and reaches behind me, wrapping both arms around the small of my back. I settle into his embrace right as he rocks us both sideways, spinning me so that I'm now under him. I gasp at the movement, bringing my hands around to the top of his neck. I squirm underneath him, still too many barriers between us to feel what I want. Ronan stares into my eyes as if he's reading my thoughts. His chest heaves just like mine, so that they touch on our inhales.

"Chloe," he breathes, his forehead falling to mine. The muscles between his shoulder blades flex from the weight that he bears on his arms, and I massage them with the force of my fingers. He groans as he dives in for a kiss, his tongue sweeping me gently. His movement is slow, but it's urgent—needy but heated. "I love you so fucking much," he says with a rough tenderness, an expression on his face I can't quite place.

I feel his confession pulse between my thighs, like even my body can tell this is more than we're used to. "I love you too."

Ro pulls back from me, searching my eyes once again, and I find myself feeling like I need to convince him. I brush my hands along his cheeks, holding his beautiful face in my palms. "So much," I say, my voice soft but unwavering.

His eyelids fall closed as he turns his lips in. "Forever?" he asks. His voice splinters, and his eyes remain shut. For a second, a low panic burns in my belly. His need for reassurance makes me think something's wrong, but the second I echo his thought, he comes back to life.

"Forever."

He growls into me, burrowing his mouth in my neck, then dips his knee between my thighs, driving them apart. He moves his parted lips to the soft spot below my ear, and I open the length of my throat up to him as he drags his mouth to the middle of my chest. He trails kisses down the front of me, speaking in phrases in between them—a pattern of his mouth and words. "I want you. Today. And tomorrow. And always."

"Mmm," I hum at the end of his sentence. He hovers above the band of my shorts and my hips wave underneath him, craving his touch.

"Tell me you want that." His warm breath teases the sensitive skin below my belly button, and I arch in response.

"I want that," I pant.

"Tell me again."

I squirm beneath him. "Ronan," I say.

"Tell me."

"I want that. I do."

At those last two words, he tears my shorts to my knees and then carefully guides them down past my ankles. I'm instantly breathless as he bucks his hips back just enough to slide his boxers to the floor. The sight of him so alive for me is enough in itself to push me close to the edge. He inches back over, taking my body in fully but at the same time, showing his off to me. He dips down to taste me, but as much as I want that, I want all of him more.

"Come here," I say eagerly, scraping my hands in his hair. He kisses me greedily right on my center, and I whimper when he leaves, despite tugging him toward me.

Ronan skates up my body, the length of him taunting the spot where I need him most.

"Ro."

"Chloe."

"Please," I beg.

He nudges my cheek with his nose. "I love you," he whispers.

"You said that," I tease. He rewards me with a fishhook smile, then pushes into me hard. Suddenly, not a single thing seems funny.

Our movements fall into sync, a familiar rhythm, like two bodies designed to fit just like this. Somehow though, it still feels different. Ronan and I have sex all the time. Sometimes it's eager and rushed, other times it's rich and unhurried, but this takes the term *"making love"* to new heights.

Ronan rocks into me, our mouths still connected, and I wrap my legs around him. I'm pulling him so he's closer, deeper, when he rolls us both, sitting up simultaneously. I gasp as he fills me even more than before, the weight of my body settling into his lap. I still, now above him, as he claws his fingertips down the length of my spine. I throw my hair to one shoulder, and Ronan gathers it so it's clutched in his fist.

I bring my legs to my sides and push to my knees, a delicious torture of losing him briefly before sinking back down. Ronan wraps one hand around the curve of my ear and brings me to him so our breaths intertwine.

"You're perfect." He groans as I continue to move, all the while, crashing my lips into his.

He pants through our kiss, and I mimic his breathing, both of our pleasure now building together. It feels so good, so right like it always does, but there's a lingering need still between us—*more, more, more, more.* More touching, more wanting, more him, more me. Harder, faster, closer. Closer. Closer. I need to somehow be more on him, him more under me. We need our hearts to be physically twisted into one so there is no way to see where he ends and I begin.

Out of nowhere, Ronan flips back around, the two of us still tethered together. Sweat slicks our skin as I climb to my peak, and right as I'm about to free fall past the ledge, Ronan freezes.

My eyes shoot to his, my body quivering beneath him, desperate for motion. "What's wrong?" I gasp, shifting my hips to create some sort of friction.

Ronan searches my face with the same focus that he had before this began. "Nothing," he says, as he pushes in deeper. I cry out from the pressure in the best possible way. *More.* "I just want to take this all in."

"Think you'll forget?" I ask with a wit to my tone.

Ronan shakes his head, his breath still ragged. "I know I'll remember. Just tomorrow, everything could be different."

My once writhing body stills completely, as I think about his past. *Is that where his head went?*

"Bad different?" I ask. Ronan curls his bottom lip in, then runs his teeth down its middle.

"I don't think so," he says, and then he pulls out completely before slamming back into me. I whimper and arch into him. He answers with a groan as our bodies, once again, teeter the edge.

"So much better," he says, and I don't know if he means tomorrow or now that we're moving again, but either way, I agree.

"Best Christmas ever."

25

Now

I stand in this bare apartment as Ronan's voice echoes off of the empty, white walls. He said he's leaving, but I can't seem to wrap my head around the meaning of those words. "Leaving where? This building?"

Ronan brings his hands to his hips and exhales heavily. "I'm moving, Chloe. To Grand Oaks. *I'm* running Nico's."

All of the feeling that I just got back in my limbs, suddenly drains to my feet. "But I thought," I start saying, but I can't seem to find the rest of my sentence.

"That Mikey was doing it?" Ronan finishes for me. I nod slowly. "He was. I mean, that was the plan. Until we... " he spins his hat so it's backwards, filling idle time with his hands. "Well, until I didn't really need to stay anymore. He'll be here in Maple Grove and handle Enzo's, and I'll go there, at least for a while."

I swallow the saliva that's now flooded the space beneath my tongue. I want to protest. Tell him he's making a mistake. Tell him that he can't leave because we need him here. *I* need him here. But I'm frozen. Stunned by his confession and paralyzed by my regret.

The second that three word sentence left his mouth—*"I'm moving, Chloe,"*—I knew how I felt about everything that happened. Four weeks, one trip to the cabin, an accident, a wedding, a mixup, a memory—none of that had as big of an effect on me as those words. Suddenly, I know exactly what I want, what I *need,* and it's him. "You," I whisper so softly he doesn't even notice. *A good thing—it's you.*

"That's why she texted me, by the way." I shake my head from my realization, my eyes flying to him in confusion. "Maggie," he continues. "That's what she does, real estate. Her mom owns an agency, and that's where she's working. She's been figuring out how to get Mikey's name off of the place that he rented and get mine on instead."

The memory of Maggie's text flashes through my mind. That's why she wanted him to call. Sure, I could do without the smiley face she tacked on at the end, but at least it answers that looming question. He's not seeing Maggie. He's using her professionally, because of the fact that he's *moving*. But what about the rest of it? The hair, the backpack, and his clean-shaven face. I attributed all of that to her, but if that's not the reason, then...

"What's with the hair?" I ask, and he's just as shocked as I am that it's the first thing I say.

"What hair?" he asks as if there's so many options.

"If you didn't grow out your hair and shave your face for her then... why?"

Ro shoves his hands in his pockets, shrugging shyly. "Maybe I needed a change too." His gaze moves to my collarbone where the ends of my recently chopped hair sit frizzed from the weather. His eyes rake over the width of my chest before flicking back to mine.

"And the backpack?" I say, my voice quiet and husky. His face turns from soft to confused. "The backpack, Ro. Mr. I-Wear-Design-er-Jeans-to-Throw-Pizzas," I say, waving at his current attire. "If it's not because you just didn't give a shit, then how come everything you brought on our trip could fit into a shoebox?" He looks at me like he's almost surprised. Either that I paid attention or that, *oh God...* that I thought he would still care about impressing me in the first place. "Unless you didn't care," I add.

"I did," he says quickly. "Care." I blow out a slow breath. "But all of my stuff was already packed when I realized that I didn't leave clothes out for our weekend. I had to scrounge through my stuff and by then, half of it was already in Grand Oaks, and what was left didn't work or was wrinkled." He pauses his ramble, and my lips part as I think back to his black, buttoned shirt with the crease down the front. "That's why I was in Grand Oaks all week. I just finished getting all of my stuff over there and had to unpack it so I could finally wear more than the same three shirts."

I nod, processing all of this, finding it hard to find actual words. So, Ronan wasn't seeing Maggie, and he did care all along. But he left. He left then and apparently, now he's leaving again.

"You just left," I say, my endless loop of thoughts continuing to spurt out in short questions and phrases. He waits for me to go on, so I do. "At the cabin. I know things were weird the night before—well, at least at the end—but now you know why. I saw the text from Maggie, so of course I was off, but you just left out of nowhere the next morning. Without saying goodbye."

Ronan's jaw grows tight as he walks to the kitchen island that once held recipes, bottle openers, and a little plate for his coins. Now it sits empty like the rest of his place. I follow him as he leans against the counter. It seems like this is a conversation we should sit for, but unless I sit on his lap, both of us will not fit on that chair. And doing that, mixed with the tension in here, might take all of this talking down a much different path.

"I had to get to the leasing office to sign papers. They're only open for a few hours on Sundays, so I had to leave pretty early to get there." *The phone call*, I think. That's what he was talking to Maggie about when he was late getting ready.

"Besides," he continues. He rests his forehead in his hand and rubs his eyebrows with his first two fingers. "You have no idea how hard it is to say goodbye to you, Chloe." My whole body seizes. His words echo in my chest that now sits vacant—my heart in my stomach, my lungs now deflated. He stands back up, his face flushed with sadness.

"At the cabin?"

"In general," he says, growing agitated.

"Like when?" I push.

"All the time!" He slams his palm on the counter. Ro wraps his thumb around the edge of the granite and squeezes it like it's holding him up. He hangs his head between his arms, an image of defeat. "The cabin, the breakup—shit, I had no idea how I was going to do it when I left here for good. And we're not even together anymore. That's the thing!" He snaps back up and pushes from the counter. "But I still can't do it. I can't walk away from you without feeling like my heart is ripping out of my chest, Chlo. I can't." He grips the fabric of his sweatshirt that lays right between his ribs, and I bound over to him, placing my hand over his.

"Then don't do it," I say, and for once in the last torturous month, I finally speak what I know in my heart to be true. The feelings I have been trying to bury.

"Leave?" he asks, his voice breathless and desperate. He sandwiches my hand between his.

"Walk away from me. Ever."

His eyelids fall closed as he sucks in a breath. When he releases it, they crawl open, and the look that he gives me is undeniably earnest. "I can't do this again, Chlo. The back and forth."

"There's no back and forth. Or at least no back. Let's move forward, Ronan. We can get past this. I'm sorry for everything."

His body stills for what feels like forever. Then, he drops his hold on me and cradles my cheeks with his hands. "You know... I get it now," he whispers. "Why you said no."

"I didn't say no," I rush to correct him.

His face relaxes, the hints of a delicate smile form at his mouth. "Just let me finish." He pauses, then stands up straighter, pulling his hands down and taking mine in between us.

"I've thought about this a lot the last month. Hell, it's all I've thought about. And I do. I get why you didn't say yes." I swallow hard, and he squeezes my hands in response. "I know that you're scared." A sigh of relief escapes me now that there's finally some spoken understanding between us. "And I know that your past makes you think that you have no control, but those are the same reasons why I felt like I *had* to ask you."

He turns his lips in, then puffs out a quick breath before speaking again. "My parents died, Chloe. They died and that sucks, but you know what was the one thing that *almost* made it okay for me? The one, tiny, fucked up thing I held on to? They went together. With the love of their life that they weren't too afraid to fully let in. I know you're worried that marriage would cut our relationship short, but *life* is short, Chlo, and that terrifies me. Look at Jay and Claire's accident. Things could have ended so much differently, and that could happen to any of us. I don't want to spend a single second of what time we have, pretending that I don't want to be your husband. That I don't want you to be my wife. I'm sorry that I didn't tell you this sooner and that you felt caught off guard and bombarded, but I truly thought that with the way that we are... " He clears his throat. "With the way that we were... that if anything could show you some bullshit curse isn't real, it was us."

A tear falls down my cheek, and he moves his top hand to brush it away. "I knew you were scared," he repeats, "but I also know that you're stubborn as hell, and I thought that if I just took the leap, that maybe you'd take it with me."

I swallow the second half of a laugh that escapes from my throat, his beautiful, perfect face now blurred by my tears. "I want to, Ronan. I want to take that leap. I know that now." I close what small gap lies between us, my body now pushed flat against his.

"You do?"

"Yes," I say confidently. "I'll leap, jump, hurdle... God, I'll gallop if you want me to."

"Well, I didn't until now," he says through a chuckle.

"I was scared, and okay, I'm a little bit stubborn."

"You're a mule."

"But I'm *your* mule," I say, touching his cheek. "These last couple of weeks have been the worst of my life. I let the idea of that stupid curse get the best of me, and it tore us apart in a whole different way than I was afraid that it would. But I see all of that now." I press a kiss to his lips, and he leans into my touch. "*You* are what's good to me, Ronan. The best thing. The only thing."

He brings his hands to my cheeks, holding my face just inches from his. "And you're fucking flawless to me."

"Then ask me again," I say, closing my eyes and reveling in the feel of his touch, the smell of his skin, the sound of his words.

He brings his mouth to my forehead and inhales a breath. On the exhale he says, "I'm not gonna do that."

My legs go weak, and Ro holds onto my shoulders. He brings his eyes so they're level with mine.

"What?" I say, my voice and my heart both breaking together.

"As in not right now." His words don't heal me. Not like they should.

"Why?" I scour his face for answers. I know he's been patient. I know that I hurt him. I know that I don't get to make these rules, but I'm ready now. I've realized my mistake, and I won't freeze this time. I won't even hesitate. He asks and I'm his. So what is he saying?

"Because, Chlo, this is all so sudden. The cabin threw us right back together, and there was the photo booth, which meant everything to me. But then Jay and Claire had their accident and got news of the baby. Now you're in the middle of replanning an entire wedding for three days from to—."

"I don't care!" I say, cutting him off. "I want this! I want *you*. None of that matters as much as you do."

He brushes my hair behind my ear, his fingertips dragging down to my chin. He holds my gaze up at him, his face so sincere it just makes me more certain. "It does," Ronan says. "And that's okay. I'm not going anywhere." Despite everything else, I instantly relax, the tension in my shoulders finally settling. "But the next time that I ask you, and I *will* ask you, it will be on a random day, in the middle of our boring lives, when everything else has faded away, and even after it all, you're still just as sure."

"I love you so much," I say, the weight of each day we've been apart leaving my body. So much has happened, and there's still so much to work through, but when he wraps himself around me, it's like all of that vanishes. Here, surrounded by emptiness—no decor, no furniture, no color on the walls—in this little pocket between Ronan's two arms, I feel full.

Against my will, Ro breaks our embrace, dropping his lips to my forehead. He turns so his cheek is pressed to my skin. "I love you too, you little sasshole."

26
Now

I fiddle with the clip pinned above my ear, made of delicate pearls and shimmering crystals, that keeps falling down and getting caught in my hair. The whimsical wires form intricate snowflakes, and although it's absolutely stunning, it's also a huge pain in my ass. Leaving the pin to sink as it may, I scan the rest of myself in the full-length mirror.

Unlike the clip, my dress sits on my body like I was born to wear it. The chiffon, v-neck maid of honor dress that Claire and I picked out in the fall, is a perfect fit. The soft, flutter sleeves frame my narrow shoulders flawlessly, and the boning in the bodice provides ample support but also shows off my curves. I sway to catch a glimpse of the keyhole back, and the a-line skirt moves effortlessly with me. We picked the dark mauve "rosewood" color because at the time, it matched the decor of the venue. Now, it ties in perfectly with the berries Mrs. Dawson and I used to accent the flowers that we hung from the tent.

Claire still has no idea what's in store for the wedding. She's been staying with her parents so she hasn't seen the hustle and bustle it's taken to turn her backyard into the ceremony site of her dreams. All that I told her was that she was to get ready as if the original plan was still on, and I personally guided her in the front door so that she couldn't see the set up waiting outside.

I pull a lip gloss out of my clutch before checking in on Claire. "You okay in there?" I call to her, still just a little afraid to leave her alone. She's healing up nicely, and her concussion is well under control, but this has shown me how fragile we all are.

"Yep! I just finished shaving my legs. I can't believe in a couple of months that will be so much harder to do."

I laugh on the other side of the bathroom door. "Oh my God, can you imagine? You'll look like Mikey in a matter of weeks."

Claire pokes her head out, her hair and makeup already finished. She's beautiful even with the gash that still shows by her eye. "Yikes. That guy's hairy as hell!" I nod in response and she shrugs her shoulders. "Nice legs though."

"Right? I've seen him in shorts."

She retreats back into the bathroom. "I just need like ten more minutes!"

I check the time on my phone. "Alright, I'm going to meet Ronan and Jay downstairs really quickly. Then I'll be back."

"Okay!"

I walk towards the hall before pausing at the door. "Oh, and Claire!"

"Yeah?"

"No peeking!"

"Less than nine months of freedom, and you ruin it all."

I roll my eyes to myself and pull the door shut. I head toward the stairs, careful not to trip on the hem of my dress in my chunky, nude heels. I hear a murmur of voices spilling out from the kitchen and then my favorite sound in the world—Ronan's animated chuckle of a laugh. It's been a whirlwind three days, two of which he was at Nico's, but that first night was enough to hold me over.

The two of us spent the night together at my furnished apartment. We stayed up late, with our bodies and thoughts intertwined, making up for the too many weeks that we wasted apart. We filled each other in on how we spent all of our time—him throwing himself into work and me twisting my body like a pretzel trying to master every position in my *Revenge Yoga* book. None of them worked, but the details of how I got my leg over my head for one of the poses, did seem to have a transformative effect on a sex-deprived Ronan.

Like muscle memory, we fell back into bed together, like the weeks we had just discussed in length, never happened at all. We were all rough hands and soft lips—a delicious recipe of touching and kissing.

The recollection of that night, mixed with the two Ronanless days that followed, make it suddenly harder to walk in these shoes. Add in the sweet echo of his laughter that floats up the stairs, and I have never been more weak in the knees. Or more ready to see him.

As I round the corner at the bottom of the steps, I brace myself to see his face, a feeling not at all foreign to me. I always expect Ronan's bright eyes and lazy smile to take my breath away. I'm just glad that it's back to being because I'm in awe of him and not because his presence suffocates me because he's no longer mine. I look into the kitchen, and of course, because we're like two opposite poles, our gazes immediately find each other. To be fair, the only other person at the table is Jay, but when he looks at Ro as I walk into the room, Ronan has his eyes only on me.

He jumps from his seat, the jacket of his steel blue suit still tossed around the back of his chair. His bright, white dress shirt is only half tucked in, which is an interesting look, but where my eyes go first is to his razor fresh fade. He comes over to me, no pretending this time, and takes my hands into his. "I missed you," he says.

"I missed you too," I say back, not a stutter to be heard. "And I like the new hair. Old hair? Whatever hair it is, it suits you."

He brings his hand to the side of his head and sweeps the low sides, then pats the longer part on top that's gelled into place. "I figured I didn't need the change anymore."

The corners of my mouth curve into place as I mimic his gesture and brush the hair by his ear. "I love it," I say. "But if you like it long, that's good with me too."

"You just like to pull it in bed," he whispers, his lips grazing high on my neck.

"Well, yeah. Who says you get to have all the fun?" He either laughs through a growl or growls through a laugh, then kisses my cheek before standing up straight.

"Have I mentioned you look incredible yet?" He takes my right hand and lifts my arm over my head, giving me room to twirl underneath it.

"Damn, Chloe," Jay says from his seat. "You look good."

"Stunning," Ro corrects, without turning from me, and I blush, I'm sure, a shade close to my dress.

"You clean up nicely yourself there, Blue Jay," I say, playing off the coloring of his suit. Jay touches his temple with his finger on the hand that's not in a sling, then points it at me as if to tell me I'm clever.

"A man of such few words," I say to Ronan.

"A man who's driving me nuts," he whispers to me. "If this guy asks if it's 'time yet' one more fucking time, I'm gonna tear his good shoulder so he's got a matching set."

"Little antsy?"

"Ya think?"

I peer over at Jay who is chewing the inside of his cheek like the nicotine gum he finally quit in the summer. I check the time to see we only have about twenty minutes left until the ceremony starts and about five until I'm supposed to be back up with Claire. "I have an idea." I walk to the table and place my hand on his back. "Want to go see where you're about to marry our girl?" Jay gapes at me like a toddler on Christmas, and I tilt my head towards the backyard to tell him to follow. Until this point, everything has also been a surprise to the groom, but considering in about fifteen minutes I need him at the altar anyway, I might as well toss the poor kid a bone.

Ronan, who also has no idea what he's in store for outside, only knows that the wedding is here. He has no idea how it all came together. He wanted to help, but with the restaurant and us not really talking until about three days ago, I gave him jobs he could do from afar. He handled the food, getting his uncle to clock back in just for the day—This way, he and Mikey could just enjoy the whole thing and not have to worry about catering after. I also put him in charge of the song that Claire will walk down the aisle to. The dinner playlist was picked, but this one was left out. Claire's easy to please, but music is like a second language for Jay. I knew if anyone could pick a song he would like, it'd be Ro.

We step through the backdoor and from the outside, the tent looks like a white roof with blurred, plastic windows and tubing that connects it to the portable heaters. But when you walk through the main entrance, a flap in the walling that's rolled up and lifted, you get the full picture of what we created.

I lead the boys through the opening, and even I am overwhelmed with how gorgeous it is. I did all of the grunt work, with the help of the Dawsons and some of Mrs. D's church friends, but this morning when I did my final once over before getting Claire, all of these finishing touches weren't done. The fragrance from the flowers hadn't yet filled the room, and the twinkling lights strung from the rafters of the roof hadn't yet been turned on. There were no instrumentals playing lightly in the background, and I was in sweats with my hair pulled on top of my head, rather than all done up to fit into the scenery.

I study the archway up front, happy to see that this time, the ivy is hanging just right. I continue my scan of the place, making my way past the chairs draped in tulle. Behind them are two long tables on either side of the walkway, dressed in creamy white cloths and gardenias for miles. The tea lights are lit, the pine cones sprinkled throughout the trail of greens that lead from one end of the table to the other, and the best part—it is a balmy seventy degrees.

I feel an arm brush past me as Jay walks up the aisle to the altar where he and Claire will promise their lives to each other in a matter of minutes. "Chloe," he says, his voice somewhat thick. "Claire is going to love this. Shit, *I* love this." He shoots a finger at Ro. "Don't you dare say a word."

Ro offers a chuckle and steps up behind me, lacing his fingers in mine. "I wouldn't dare," he says to Jay, then he whispers to me. "So, not at all into weddings, huh?" He squeezes my hand and I turn to him. Our eyes are perfectly level thanks to my heels.

"I think I'm starting to be." His lips crash into mine, neither of us caring that he now wears as much lip gloss as I do.

"Alright you two," Jay interrupts. "Can you go get my girl? Let's fucking do this."

I look down at my phone and jump at the time. I'm already late to getting back up to Claire, and the last thing I need is for her to come looking for me. I drop Ro's hand and nudge him towards Jay. "You two get ready. Jay, just wait there. Ronan, tuck in your damn shirt and tell everyone who's huddled at Enzo's to make their way here. You have the song cued up on the laptop hooked to the speaker?"

Ro huffs out a laugh. "It's ready. Go get the bride."

I nod just once, then sprint back inside. When I get back to Claire's room, I open the door. I'm already huffing and puffing from my trek up the stairs, but I lose any other air that was left in my lungs when I see her.

Claire spins around, her dress hugging her perfectly because she's not showing yet, minus one gap on either side of her hips where the pearl buttons have yet to be closed. "Will you help me?" she says.

Tears form in my eyes, and I wave them away before stepping up to her, both of us finding each other in the mirror's reflection. "God, Claire. You are... " I say to her, cinching her waist. "Such a MILF." We both laugh through the blur in our eyes.

"That is exactly what I was going for," she says, reaching back to squeeze my wrist.

"Still feel good about this?" I ask, and I notice I don't get that hum of anxiety that I typically do when I think about marriage.

"I feel great," she says without missing a beat. "And Chlo?"

"Yeah?"

"It's okay if you think so also. You know, that maybe this would feel great to you too." I glance at her reflection hesitantly, waiting for her to fill in the silence. "I just mean that you don't have to punish yourself for your family's marital track record." She turns to me so we're facing each other. "Take it from me, it's never too late to decide that you just... change your mind. Jobs, passions, beliefs—all of those things belong to you, and only you get to decide what you think about them. You don't want to spend the rest of your life feeling like you're missing out on something just because you're afraid to change course."

I swallow a lump that's grown in my throat and think of my mom's words from almost a decade ago.

"Change is scary, girls, but so is living a life unfulfilled."

My next thought is Ronan. How those few weeks without him were some of the worst, most unsatisfying, weeks of my life, and how coming back to him in the middle of his bare kitchen, I felt like I was whole again. Like I was full. I sit in reflection until something else comes to mind.

"Wait," I say, clearing my head. "Why are you saying all of this now?" Claire gives me a knowing look and takes my hands in hers. "You knew, didn't you?"

"We had an idea."

"How?"

"Chlo, how many times have we gone through this? You guys are family. We know when something is off with you two." I close my eyes, shaking my head with a smile. "That and Jay stole Ro's phone that night after Posto Felice." My mouth hangs open. *That's why he gave me that look at the fire.*

"But if you knew—"

"Oh, I didn't. Not until the drive home from the cabin. Then with the accident and the baby... Well, I just figured you'd tell me when you were ready."

"I didn't want to ruin any of this for you," I say softly. She steps close to me, bringing our hands that are still clasped together, up between our chests.

"You, Chloe Carlson, are my best friend in the world. My sister. You don't ever have to worry about being honest with me." This time tears really do fall, and we both try to stop it before our makeup is ruined.

"Well, that's good," I say, grabbing a tissue from the dresser and dabbing my eyes. "Because honestly, that little niece or nephew of mine is going to be so goddamn spoiled, and I don't care at all what you or Jay have to say about it." Claire smiles at me and hugs me tightly. "I'm going to be the best aunt ever, I promise."

"I know," she says. "Best godmother too."

27

Now

Claire and I spent another couple of minutes upstairs touching up our makeup and getting ourselves together. The talk we had was full of love, and the fact that she basically knew about Ronan shocked me less than it should have. I could have sat there all day and gone through everything she missed, but we will have plenty of time for all of that later. For now, we have a wedding to get to.

I walk down the steps, Claire trailing behind me, and lead her to the kitchen. She reaches for her jacket, her eyes wandering for what I assume is her purse, when I place my hand on her arm. "Stop," I say gently. "You don't need any of that." She looks at me puzzled, and I pull her towards the back entrance. The faint sound of a piano floats under the door, and Claire's eyes grow wide, her jaw dropping slightly.

"Wait," she says. "Is my wedding... "

"Happening right here in your back yard?" I nod, a small smile on my face. I'm hesitant to be too excited until I know that Claire is happy with what her mom and I decided to do for her. Her face drops for just an instant, and my stomach goes with it until I realize it's only because she's overwhelmed with emotion."Stop!" I bark, smirking at her. "We literally just fixed your face." She flashes her hands in front of her glistening eyes.

"Okay, okay," she says. "It's these damn hormones, I swear. And the fact that this is the sweetest thing, Chloe, seriously. I'm not sure today would have even happened if it hadn't been for you. This is exactly what I wanted—to get married to Jay in the home that we're building together—and I didn't even realize it until right now."

I pull her in for a quick hug. "I was hoping you'd say that."

"Gah," she groans, shaking her emotions away. "I promise I won't be a wreck the entire day."

"Just most of it."

"Exactly. Now let's do this."

I open the door and walk to the entrance of the tent that now has the plastic door rolled down. Mr. Dawson stands at the bottom of the steps that lead from the house, and his face almost glows when he sees his daughter step outside. I give him a quick hug and leave them to have their moment together with the photographer Claire hired a while back. I approach the tent entrance and lift the flap just a few inches. I find Mikey standing right at the wall on the inside like I asked him to.

"You ready to cue us in?" I ask. We've practiced this only a half-dozen times, so I'm hoping when it's time for us to walk in, he remembers to stick his thumb through the sheet like we went over.

"I got this, amica. Don't worry." I'm a tiny bit worried, but I smile at him anyway, then wave Claire and her dad over to join me.

"When the next song plays, I'll walk in and meet the boys at the altar. They're already there. Then the song after that, it's your turn, okay?"

Claire looks at Mr. Dawson, a daughter's need for her dad's reassurance never quite gone. He kisses her cheek with encouragement, and Claire looks at me. "Okay," she says breathlessly, and she lowers the bouquet that the photographer gave her so it grazes her belly. A gesture, I'm sure, to her future baby, readying both of them for this next great adventure.

I turn back to the tent and see Mikey's tan thumb poke through the side of the sheet. I reach for the flap, but before I make contact, it lifts on its own. I peek my head through the slit and see that it, indeed, didn't just fly through the air.

"Hey, you," Ronan says, holding open the plastic. He reaches his hand out towards me. I gape at him as my heart skips a beat. "I thought you could use some company on your walk up there." He turns back to Jay who tilts his chin up to us, both hands clasped together in front of him, not a sling to be seen. *Typical Jay.*

"I'd love some," I say, linking my arm through his. Ronan has always known what I needed, sometimes even before I did. He knew it when he got on one knee, and he knew it now, as I braced myself to make this walk on my own. "I love you," I whisper before we descend down the aisle.

"Forever," he answers, leading me on.

When we get to the front, Ronan softly plants a kiss on my temple, and then we separate to our designated spots on either side of the arch. Ro stands behind Jay, right next to Jackson, and I place myself just a step behind where Claire will be. I feel the lack of his arm on mine the second we pull apart, missing him even though he's just a few feet away. Unlike before though, where missing him was an emptiness that almost swallowed me whole, now it's the good kind of void. The kind that's just holding his place for when he comes back.

Our melody fades as I wait to hear what Ronan has picked for the song that will usher Claire in. I'm staring at Mikey, waiting to see him give the go-ahead once the new song begins, when I hear nothing but the ting of guitar strings being plucked.

My eyes shoot to my laptop, its screen now pulled down, and then trail to the source of the glorious sound. My gaze lands on Ro who is looking at me, playing the song I've heard a dozen times before. The same song we played by the fire the night at the cabin where everything changed—or at least I thought it did. The song we used to listen to in the car. The one he was playing the morning we had our first kiss. The same song that I have listened to countless times in the last few weeks, only this time, it's not tainted with pain. Instead, it's full of promises. Almost like I'm hearing it for the very first time.

Ronan winks at me, then turns to where Mikey is standing as my best friend steps inside. Claire takes in the venue. She scans the chairs where the Carusos and her mom are sitting, with two empty seats for her dad and Mikey. Then her eyes land on Jay. He rakes his hand down his face and blows out a breath, his stoic demeanor beautifully broken in the best possible way.

Mr. Dawson leads Claire down the aisle, then shakes Jay's hand when he gets to the end. "Take care of our girl," he whispers to him.

Jay's jaw grows tight as he pushes through his emotion. "You know that I will."

Claire hands me her flowers. "Amazing," she mouths, and I'm not sure if she means the song, the venue, or Jay and her dad, but she's right either way.

Everything, all of it—amazing for sure.

The rest of the ceremony was perfect. The officiant was great. Jay fumbled his way through tears for his vows, and Claire announced to the rest of our little group that they weren't just witnessing the marriage of two people but rather the start of a family. I cried, Mikey wept, and even Ro and Jackson both shed a tear.

Dinner was delicious. Nico hit it out of the park, and I convinced Ronan that the gnocchi he made had to stay on the menu. The ten of us sat around the two tables—the parents at one, the six of us at the other—eating, drinking and laughing until we had tears in our eyes. It wasn't a giant wedding. It wasn't even the wedding Claire and Jay planned in the first place, but it was centered around two people more in love with each other than anything else, surrounded by everyone that's special to them. It was everything a wedding is supposed to be.

Now, the group of us are sitting around, eating wedding cake and Nico's cannolis, our preplanned playlist playing in the background. Ronan stands from his seat and walks to the speaker, turning it down just slightly.

"Hey, that was my jam!" Mikey says, sitting up in his chair.

Ronan rolls his eyes. "I highly doubt *Lady Marmalade* is your jam but okay. This will only take a minute." Mikey slouches back down, and the rest of us bring our attention to Ro. He grabs his beer off the table and stands between the bride and the groom.

"I know we aren't doing the typical reception," he starts. "But I still wanted to give a little toast if that's okay." He puts his hand on Jay's good shoulder, the other put promptly back in the sling thanks to Claire. Jay puts his hand, palm up as his answer, and Ro slaps his into it before pulling away.

"I've known Jay for a long time now."

"Too fucking long," Jay jokes, and then winces under Mrs. D's playfully disappointing look.

"Way too long," Ro continues. "And in that time, I've seen it all. The good, the bad, the downright ugly, and nothing has ever affected him like Claire has." Claire reaches for Ro's hand and gives it a squeeze before smiling at me.

"When he met her, everything changed—including his fashion sense, thank God." The group of us laughs as Jay purses his lips. "He was happy for once, more at peace. His confidence went up and his walls fell down. He even sends emojis sometimes in texts now, which is kind of weird."

Jay quickly looks at Claire's mom who is dabbing her eyes, blocked by a tissue, and then flips Ro off before he continues. "I'm just saying, you have always been one of the best people I know, but somehow, she made you even better. You're my brother, you know that, and I just want to thank you, Claire, for sticking by him. For sticking by all of us. It's nice to add a sister into the family." Claire lets out a gasp and hides her face in her hands, tears falling now even more than before.

"Oh, and for giving me my future niece or nephew. That kid is going to be the most loved one here. To all three of you," Ro says, holding up his beer. We cheers him back, and then before I can question it, I'm standing as well.

"Yay," Claire squeals as she sniffles through tears.

"As you all know, this stuff makes me nervous." Comments erupt from everyone. The Carusos giggle, the Dawsons snicker, and Mikey and Jackson both raise their brows. Claire and Jay roll their eyes at each other, and Ronan lets out a snort that you could hear across town.

"Okay, so not really, but in all seriousness, I just can't believe we're here. I haven't known Claire quite as long as Ronan's known Jay, but it feels like we've already made a lifetime of memories. There have been days of work, nights of movies, sleepovers, birthdays, and I'm sorry Jay, but believe it or not, there were boys before you." Jay growls in his seat, and Claire leans in to kiss him. "But watching the two of them grow has been my favorite thing yet." I frame the rim of my glass with my finger and sneak a glance at Ro before I continue. I get lost in his eyes for a second, only retreating when his wink breaks my stare.

"Some of you don't know this, but I never pictured this for myself. The beautiful wedding," I say, my arms open wide. "The life-long marriage." I gesture to both sets of parents that have now been together for over half of their lives. "But the second I watched Claire with Jay, I saw it for her. This is what she's dreamed of—the life she's always wanted—and it's been inspiring to watch them get here. Life changing," I add. "For both them and me." Claire smiles at me, and then blows me a kiss, a silent message of our talk from before.

"So Jay," I say, raising my glass. "I apologize for you having to deal with the two of us, but we're a package deal, your girl and me." Jay holds out his fist, and I meet it with mine. "To all three of us!" We all cheers together in a jumble of laughter.

After everyone's gone home, and even the bride and groom have gone in for the night, Ronan and I are still stacking chairs in the tent.

"I liked your speech," I say as I lift the last of the chairs onto the pile. Ronan takes it from me, setting it down into place.

"It wasn't as good as yours."

"Well, no, I never said that," I joke. He dives over to me and bearhugs my arms. I wiggle and squirm under his hold, but really, it's my favorite place to be. He loosens his grasp, his hands sliding down to my wrists.

"Did you mean what you said about feeling inspired to change when it comes to all this?" He looks around the now meaningless tent. The altar's been stripped, the chairs are all stacked, and the flowers lay in a pile by the door. But I know what he means.

"Well, it might not have been *just* the two of them who inspired me," I say, linking our fingers together.

Ronan raises his brow and tips his head down as if to say, "Me?" I respond with a kiss, and he breathes into my mouth.

216

"So what about the curse?" He asks once our lips break apart.

"Well, I've been thinking. It's the 'Carlson Curse,' so if I'm no longer a Carlson... "

"Didn't work for your sisters," he challenges.

"They didn't change their last names," I fling back.

He tilts his head thoughtfully. "That could work." He brings his hands to my hips, and I put my arms around his neck.

"You just can't wait too long to ask me again."

"And what if I do?"

I chew on my lip. "Well, I might change my mind." Ronan looks at me blankly. "Too soon?"

He pulls me in closer. "You always did get cold feet."

He drops his forehead to mine, and I search for even a drop of anxiety about the topic at hand, but there's nothing. No nerves, no worries, no doubts in my mind. Just love for this man and hope for the future.

Epilogue
8 Months Later

I place the wine and sparkling cider on the counter next to the "Italian salsa" that Ro made for today. I did extensive research on the subject, and technically Claire can drink real alcohol again, but I know she's taking this new motherhood thing as cautiously as she can. Plus, it makes today even easier for me. There's ice in the cooler, meats and cheeses on the island, and my dinner party playlist on in the background.

"All set?" Ro asks, adding beers to the cooler.

"Ready to go." Ro closes the lid, and I clap in excitement, the anticipation of seeing my best friend and my new, baby niece almost too much to handle.

Norah was born just over a month ago, and although I've seen her many times since, it's never enough. Claire went into labor two weeks before I moved into Ronan's apartment. She was at home in bed, editing her new book, when the cramping began. She called *me*, like I was supposed to know what to do, and at first I thought maybe she should wait it out.

"People are in labor for like days, aren't they? I don't think you need to rush to the hospital."

I stayed on the phone with her for over an hour. Then, because the contractions seemed to be coming closer together, and because I'm a little afraid of her husband, I told her I thought it was time to call Jay. Luckily, he was just across town at Monroe's, because our Norah girl came just a few hours later. Claire always was an overachiever.

Ro's phone vibrates from his pocket. "They're here. Jay just said the baby is sleeping, so we better not be playing music 'too fucking loudly.' " He makes air quotes around those last three words, and I roll my eyes. Jay is the most protective dad I have ever seen, and the girl can't even hold her head up yet.

I move to the living room and turn down the music. Almost instantly, the silence is filled with a loud wailing sound as the knob on the door starts to turn.

"Well she *was* sleeping!" Jay yells over the crying, the car seat swinging from the crook of his arm.

"She just loves the car," Claire says.

Ro throws up his hands. "So how dare you stop it?"

I take the car seat from Jay and set it on the floor by the couch. Norah is still screaming as I unfasten the clips. "I think she just wants her Aunt Chloe. I pull her from her seat, and she does that adorable newborn scrunch that fresh babies do. I bring her to my chest and bounce her around, breathing in her glorious smell. "God, I wish I could bottle that scent."

I sway her back and forth, and after a few more motions, her sobs settle into more of a whimper. "See," I say to the rest of the group. "She might love the car, but she loves me the most."

"Not as much as my boobs," Claire says matter-of-factly.

"Her and Jay both," Ronan says.

Our friends nod in agreement as they all move to the kitchen. By the time I follow behind them, Norah is back asleep, her little chapped lips plumped to perfection as her head rests up on my chest.

"So, how's it been going?" I ask, my voice soft.

"Good," Claire says, popping cheese into her mouth. "She's sort of, occasionally, sleeping at night."

"And she eats like a champ," Jay adds. He's practically elbow deep in the damn bruschetta, and he wonders where she gets it from.

Ronan holds his fist out to Jay who meets it with his. "Momma Ruso would be proud."

"Damn straight," Jay replies. "How's the new place?"

The four of us have seen each other plenty of times since Norah's been born, but Ro and I always went to their house. Newborns are easy in the sense that they sleep most of the day, and they can't run around, but man, they need a lot of stuff. With Claire still healing and Jay running on even less sleep than normal, we always thought it'd be a lot to ask them to come over to our place—Especially when they've already seen it plenty when it was just Ronan's. This week though, when I asked if we could bring dinner over, Claire suggested that they come here. I think as much as they love being home with their girl, they may be going just a little stir crazy from barely leaving their house.

"Well, it's not new to me," Ronan says, "but the lack of closet space sure is."

"I was wondering how that was going to go," Claire says. "I'm not sure what's bigger, Ronan's shoe collection or the pile of graphic t-shirts that Chloe has in her drawers."

"We're making it work," I say with a pretend attitude. "And we won't be here forever. We're hoping by this time next year we can be in a house. We just want to wait until something comes up in Maple Grove."

"Yeah, you guys can't leave," Claire says in a panic.

I loop my finger under Norah's tiny hand. "We wouldn't dream of it," I say to the top of her head.

"Oh! I almost forgot." Claire wiggle walks back to her purse by the door, no doubt still recovering from her sprint of a labor. Ro pulls two beers from the cooler then pours a white wine for me and a cider for Claire. He hands me my cup and gives Claire hers as she hands him a picture. "Newborn photo," she says, and I practically throw my glass on the island trying to see it.

"No," I say, looking over Ro's shoulder. Norah is laying with her hands over her head, her eyes closed, and her mouth open mid-yawn. I can feel my heart flutter as Ronan brushes his thumb over her squished, little face.

"That's my girl," he says. He looks back at me. "Besides you, babe."

"No, I totally get it. That's my girl too," I say. Then, I look at Claire.

"It's fine. She's cuter than all of us honestly." And as if in response, the baby starts stirring.

"Here, I'll take her," Jay says, reaching for Norah. I hand her to him and smirk like I always do. She's only a month old, so of course she's small, but in Jay's massive arms, she's an actual peanut. I take the picture from Ronan and walk to the fridge. Grabbing a magnet, I stick it up next to a ripped photo strip and our new save the date.

Ronan and I got engaged three months ago at the start of the summer. I thought about him asking me again every day after Claire and Jay's wedding, but honestly, we were caught up with so many things.

First, there was the matter of sorting out Nico's. With us back together, Ronan wanted to stay, but all of the paperwork for the place in Grand Oaks was already written up under his name. There was a lot of back and forth—and Maggie wasn't happy, which was a little bonus for me—but eventually, it all fell into place. Nico's opened on Valentine's Day, where much to their dismay, I convinced Ronan and Mikey to sell heart shaped pizzas to kick off their first day. The town ate it up like I knew that they would.

After that there was Claire's baby shower, Easter, and the usual end of the school year stress. Then, the next thing I knew it was summer.

Ronan had just gotten home from ten hours at Enzo's. They were swamped, and he was training new servers all at the same time. He walked through his door after a gruesome day, and I was there waiting for him.

"You're here," he said in relief as we moved towards each other.

"Always," I said. "You had a long day." I moved in to hug him, and he melted into me. Breathing in his usual scent—Cashmere Woods meets pizza shop—I ran my hands over the tense parts of his shoulders, and he moaned as he nestled into my neck.

"I should shower," he groaned. "Or at least change." He kissed me once hard.

"You do that," I said. He walked to his room, and I made my way to the couch to scroll through movies.

Five minutes later, I was trying to decide if I wanted The Waterboy or Happy Gilmore, when he came and stood over me.

"Hey," I said. "I was thinking Adam Sandler, but I don't know if I want—"

"Chloe?"

"Yeah?" I tried to look past him to see the TV, but he was standing in front of me blocking the view.

"Can we just wait for a second?"

"Okay, but if you're going to try to convince me that it should be Mr. Deeds, we may have problems." I set down the remote and focused on him as he shook his head and laughed. He had changed into sweatpants and his favorite hoodie with the strings that

are missing. His eyes hung heavy, but the rest of his face looked more energized than it should have after such a along day. "What's wrong?"

"Nothing," he said as he dropped to one knee.

I sprang from my seat in the opposite direction, my hands flying up to cover my mouth.

"Chloe..."

"Yes."

"No, you can't—"

"Yes."

"Will you just—"

"Yes!"

He reached for my hand and took a deep breath. "Can I please get this out?"

"Yes," I whispered. He parted his lips then curved them up in a smile before starting again.

"Chloe, I have loved you since the moment I laid eyes on you in Center Springs mall almost three years ago. I've tried this before and, well, it didn't work out, but in some ways I think that might have been for the best. We have been through so much since that day—grown so much, together. I know you have worried about marriage in the past. I know you think you're cursed to end up like the rest of your family. But I believe in us, and I know that I love you so fucking much that I wouldn't even let fate come between us."

He reached into his sock and pulled out the same ring from before. A simple, yet gorgeous, gold band with a large, emerald cut ruby. "So, Chloe Carlson," he said, holding it up to me. "This time, I'm not asking. I'm daring you to marry me. And damnit, I'm daring destiny to try to tear us apart."

I stared into his eyes, awestruck at both him and the ring, my gaze fluttering between the sea of red and ocean of blue.

"This is when you say y—"

"Yes!" I said, cutting him off this time. I threw my arms around his neck and kissed him like I knew he was mine forever. Because he was.

"Remind me again why we have to wait until two days after Christmas to get you guys married," Claire says, eying the announcement and bringing me back to the moment.

"Timing," Ro says, taking a pull of his beer.

"Yeah, I'll already have off for those two weeks at Christmas, and the few days after the holiday are typically slow at the restaurant."

"Plus, I'm hoping we can sneak off for a few days over New Years," Ro adds. "Little *pre*-honeymoon."

I clear my throat adding, "Right, but if not, we'll still plan something bigger for over the summer."

"All-inclusive," Ro and Jay say together, the two of them nodding over free food and beer like teenagers, rather than full-grown men.

"Okay fine," Claire says. "You just better hope that Norah's walking by then because this flower girl has duties to tend to." Claire leans over Jay and kisses her daughter's cheek before stroking the same spot with her finger. I watch her eyes well with pride and can't help but want the bond that the two of them have. Claire has always had a heart of gold, but now that she's a mom, she's an even better version of herself.

"Are your sisters excited?" she asks.

"For what?" I shoot back.

"The wedding, silly."

I huff out a laugh and refocus my attention. "Yeah they are. Mom and Dad too. I think everyone just knows that this one will be different." Ronan drapes his arm around my shoulders and trails the tip of his nose from my jaw to my ear.

When I told my family about the engagement, not one of them even thought to mention the stupid curse. I don't know if somewhere along the line it had all been forgotten, or if they really do think that Ronan and I are the exception to the rule.

Either way, they were all thrilled. Cara and Casey immediately started bickering about bridesmaids dresses, and Mom and Dad began forming a timeline for all the events. We celebrated and drank too much champagne because I guess that's what my family does when people get engaged. They're all looking forward to it, but for now, they also all have their own things going on.

Dad's still busy working, but he and Ronan go golfing together like twice a month. Apparently they're both really improving, but I'm not quite sure that means all that much.

Mom has a new "friend" that she met through her book club. He's Canadian and says things like "eh" and "hoser." He's very nice, but Mom is in complete denial that he's interested in more than just her thoughts on Danielle Steele.

Casey is also dating again, but she stopped doing the whole online thing. Instead, she has made some serious progress on her work-life balance and has been going out and meeting new people.

Cara though, is the busiest of them all. After hearing Ronan's story, and our dreams to both have our own children and adopt one day, she was inspired to look into the process. Now, she is the foster mom to my eight-year-old foster-nephew Skylar. He's the sweetest little boy, and Cara finally found the love of her life.

"Well, good. So are we." Claire says. Norah starts fussing, and Claire looks at the time. "I should probably feed her before we eat dinner. Jay can you change her real quick?" Jay nods and shifts into dad mode, finding the diaper bag and heaving it over his shoulder.

"Jamison Errington on diaper duty," Ro says. "Never gets old."

"Just you wait, man. I'm telling you. The diapers are shitty, pun absolutely intended, but the rest of it… Best feeling ever." I watch as Ronan claps his hand on Jay's shoulder, smiling without hesitation. Butterflies awaken deep in my belly as I think of him being happy just from the idea of being a dad.

"We'll get dinner set up," Ro says as he opens the cabinet to reach for the plates.

Jay and Claire both escape to our bedroom, and I head to the fridge to pull out the salad. Reaching for the handle, I pause momentarily, my eyes going to our save the date photo. Like Ronan with the picture of sweet, baby Norah, I brush my finger across both of our names. It's crazy to think that for so long, I didn't think I wanted this. Didn't think I could have it. But now, thinking of

Ronan and our plans for the future, there's not a doubt in my mind this is where I belong.

Ro comes up behind me, wrapping his arms around my waist and reaches in front of me to touch the date on the card. "I'm ready," he says.

I think about the pregnancy tests burning a hole in my purse, and I move my hands to my belly without causing attention. I picked them up on my way home from work but haven't gotten a chance to put them to use. It doesn't matter though. I have no worries about what the results will be. Babies, weddings, bring everything on. My future no longer scares me at all.

I look at our announcement and then at the picture of our niece right beside it. "I've been ready," I say.

And I am.

For all of it.

The End

Book Playlist

Songs From The Story

1. Semi-Charmed Life – Third Eye Blind

2. All the Small Things – Blink-182

3. Wonderwall – Oasis

4. Thinking Out Loud – Ed Sheeran

5. A Sky Full of Stars – Coldplay

6. Sorry – Justin Bieber

7. Ring of Fire – Johnny Cash

8. Free Fallin' – John Mayer

9. Free Fallin' – Tom Petty

10. Chicken Dance – Werner Thomas

11. Cha Cha Slide – DJ Casper

12. Lady Marmalade – Lil' Kim, Mya, Christina Aguilera & P!nk

Vibe Playlist
Can You Name The Scene?

1. Just My Type – Kyle Hume

2. Pop Out – charlieonafriday ft. Bankrol Hayden

3. I Love You, I'm Sorry – Gracie Abrams

4. If You Love Her – Forest Blakk

5. The Only Exception – Paramore

6. Strangers Again – Matt Hansen

7. Traitor – Olivia Rodrigo

8. Sun to Me – Zach Bryan

9. That's So True – Gracie Abrams

10. Back To December – Taylor Swift

11. Good Things – Kaylee Bell

12. 28 – Zach Bryan

Acknowledgements

Thank you to everyone who took a chance on *Beautifully Broken*.
Daring Destiny would not exist without you.
When I first pushed my debut novel out of the nest, I wasn't sure what to expect.
I wrote it with the intention of binding one copy for myself just to say I did, but thanks to all of you... it flew!
It is because of you that Chloe and Ronan finally got their moment.
To my family, I cannot thank you enough for your steadfast support. From celebrating victories to wiping tears, you have been there through it all. Your reactions to my writing have made the highs higher and the lows well worth it.
I hope I am making you proud.
To Stefanie, thank you for being my sounding board. You have picked names, chosen outfits, even created or deleted scenes. I'm not sure where I would be—in my writing or in life—without you. Your friendship means the world to me.
Look at us fulfilling our dreams!
To my author friends, this community we share is everything. I never thought that writing a book would lead me to my people, but here we are. Thank you for loving my characters as your own, answering my stupid questions, and showing support in all of the ways that you constantly do.
Lastly, to my readers... I can't even believe I have readers!
The fact that some of you have fallen in love with Jay, Claire, Ronan, and Chloe the way that I have fallen in love with certain fictional characters blows my mind! Thank you for taking time out of your lives to read my books. Who would have thought that the words inside my head would ever leave my tiny little corner of the world?
But they have. And they do everyday, thanks to you.